THE EXACT IMAGE
OF MOTHER

The
Exact
Image of
Mother

by

PATTY FRIEDMANN

VIKING

VIKING
Published by the Penguin Group
Viking Penguin, a division of Penguin Books USA Inc.,
375 Hudson Street, New York, New York 10014, U.S.A.
Penguin Books Ltd, 27 Wrights Lane,
London W8 5TZ, England
Penguin Books Australia Ltd, Ringwood,
Victoria, Australia
Penguin Books Canada Ltd, 2801 John Street,
Markham, Ontario, Canada L3R 1B4
Penguin Books (N.Z.) Ltd, 182–190 Wairau Road,
Auckland 10, New Zealand

Penguin Books Ltd, Registered Offices:
Harmondsworth, Middlesex, England

First published in 1991 by Viking Penguin,
a division of Penguin Books USA Inc.

10 9 8 7 6 5 4 3 2 1

Grateful acknowledgment is made for permission to reprint the text from Jules
Feiffer's cartoon. © 1974 Jules Feiffer.

The first chapter of this book first appeared in *Xavier Review*
as "Passing at Le Havre."

LIBRARY OF CONGRESS CATALOGING IN PUBLICATION DATA
Friedmann, Patty.
    The exact image of mother / Patty Friedmann.
        p.   cm.
    ISBN 0-670-83491-2
    I. Title.
    PS3556.R538E9   1991
    813'.54—dc20   90-50512

Printed in the United States of America
Set in Granjon
Designed by Ann Gold

FOR BOB,
WHO MADE AN
HONEST WOMAN OF ME

I hated the way I turned out . . .

So everything my mother did with me I have tried to do the opposite with my Jennifer.

Mother was possessive. I encouraged independence.

Mother was manipulative. I have been direct.

Mother was secretive. I have been open.

Mother was evasive. I have been decisive.

Now my work is done. Jennifer is grown.

The exact image of Mother.

Jules Feiffer cartoon, 1974

THE EXACT IMAGE
OF MOTHER

CHAPTER 1

I should have suspected something when my father reduced the Holocaust to a simple, Hardyesque little romance. "Your mother and I, we probably saw each other at Le Havre," he said. "We probably even bumped into each other. Just brushed past, you know." That was about all he told of those years, and I imagined that scene until it crammed enough into itself to make sense. He was sharp and trim, a superlative sort who was getting out when maybe others didn't quite merit it as much; why else? I saw him in my mind's eye with one small valise that carried a silver esrog box, two gold coins, and a change of underwear. The box and the coins were all he had from the time before he came over. I put the evidence together. With my mother, Letty, it was easier. There are many photographs of her from that time. Black-and-white photographs, but I can imagine Letty in color. Her Persian lamb coat, her reddish-gold curls, unkempt, a puff of a rich girl, just wafting behind her own mother, with absolutely no sense of history. I picture my grandmother with a cigarette dangling from her mouth. For no particular reason, except it seems like a damned cavalier thing to do, and I know my grandmother smoked from the time she was fifteen.

When my grandmother—I called her Marmee—took me to Europe in 1961, I didn't see Le Havre, probably for a reason no one ever thought of hard enough to bring to the surface. The *Liberté* dropped Marmee and me off at Southampton. It didn't dock, just deposited us on a smaller boat that ferried us in. We made it across Europe by other means, a plane to Amsterdam, a train to Paris, a car with a driver to take us into the Swiss Alps. So the one time I went to

Europe I never saw Le Havre. But I saw bits of Marmee's 1939 trip with Letty. Like the opera house in Paris. Rich with history, the opera house was full of Marmee's own story, too. She took me to a spot under the grand staircase. "Here's where I read Letty the cable from your grandfather," she said. " 'Get out of Europe immediately,' it said. She and I just laughed. They were doing *Faust* that night, too." For years after that I wondered how, in 1939, or in any other year for that matter, they managed to get a telegram delivered to my grandmother at the opera. Finally, I asked Letty. "Oh, it came to the hotel. She just chucked it into her purse and waited until intermission to open it." They didn't take it seriously, Letty agreed; they had to see the rest of the opera, of course, and they still had a lot of shopping to do.

Marmee probably got a number of bargains those last few days in Europe, as the center was about to fail to hold. She was still a terrific shopper in 1961, when she took me. A platinum watch, as thin as an eggshell for my grandfather; fine linen suits, covered in embroidery, for me, suits that made me look like an unrefrigerated prune after a few hours of squirming around in some vehicle, looking out of the window to get Marmee's money's worth; queer copper lustre pieces and a real Rouault for herself. I kept waiting for a global drama to unfold, something that would take me back home and away from the civilizing influences of my grandmother. She watched my food, she had my hair and nails trimmed in every capital, she made me read the guides and pamphlets until all the fresh excitement was wrung out of a place before I got there. But nothing happened in the world to take me back; Hemingway committed suicide when we were in Montreux, but I could see that that struck no particular fear in Marmee. She just kept shopping and touring, and we took a plane back to the States from Athens. We never made it back full circle to the European ports of entry along the Atlantic.

After a month home the polish had worn off of me. The linen suits were all on hangers, yes, but at the back of my closet, never cleaned or ironed. The ends of my hair were uneven, and my fingernails were grown out shapeless. What happened to the girl who came off the plane? my father asked. I couldn't read his tone, I couldn't tell at all if he was mocking what I now saw as pretension, or if he was just a little sorry, having had illusions all along that I was going to be a rich puff of a girl, as Letty had been, trailing along the quais, maybe fanning away some of the cigarette smoke drifting behind her mother. She was sixteen, and he liked to believe he had seen her.

No, it all wore off, even the learning. After a while I no longer knew in what century Louis XIV lived, what decade *Faust* was written in, what year the Archduke Ferdinand was shot in. But I did know the day my mother and my father were at the docks in Le Havre, each waiting to take one of the two remaining ships out of Europe. I knew the date before I got on the boat with Marmee, and I came back knowing the date.

I hated it, I told Letty. I'm just not the sort she wants me to be. I want to be simple, not to broadcast anything when I'm out. She didn't do anything permanent to you, for God's sake, Letty said. And then she laughed. A private joke with herself. "What's so funny?" I asked her.

"When my grandmother tried *her* style of culture on me," she said, "she left long-term effects." I looked at her quizzically. That would have been my great-grandmother, who died when I was four. I remembered her, I thought, though she came up often enough in conversations and photographs that maybe she was just another of my fantasy constructions. She wore deep purple all the time, incipient schizophrenia, a sure sign, was the way Letty interpreted it for as long as the subject came up. And it still comes up, every time deep purple is big in fashion. Though probably it wasn't when my great-grandmother wore it. A rich lady, no doubt, because Marmee lived well on inherited money; my great-grandmother was not too aware of her wealth. "She took me to the stockyards when I visited her in Chicago," Letty said. "And she bought me chocolate candy after the tour. Right at the stockyards she bought it. I swear it tasted like the stench of the place, and I couldn't eat chocolate for years after that."

Marmee and I bought a lot of chocolate in Europe. In Scheveningen I got hot chocolate every morning with my breakfast. Creamy and sweet. And cheeses and thin, pale ham, dry toast triangles and real butter. After a while I got used to the richness of the food. I even expected it. But the trip wasn't long enough for me to get arrogant, to go on expecting exquisite treatment because we had a lot of money to spend. Marmee barked at the serving people, the waiters, the hotel clerks, the drivers. Her time was very valuable, and they simply were not supposed to waste it.

It was still very hot most of the time that September when I was eleven. I had gotten to the point where my trip with Marmee two months before was a lavish bad dream. She was back to being my grandmother in familiar contexts, abusing only those people whose names I knew, Letty, her city house-keeper Murray, my grandfather. They all loved her, of course, and I imagined I would develop adult mechanisms to be insensitive to that kind of self-centeredness—one day. So I didn't mind the notion of being with her, without the buffer of my parents, and I was fairly pleased when, just after school had started, she offered to take me along on one of their weekends at Pass Christian.

You have to ask your father, Letty said when I told her of the call from Marmee. It was a funny kind of permission to have to ask for; I really didn't understand it. I could see the value of mulling over whether I could sleep over at a friend's house when the friend had a mother newly divorced and a little wacky with it. I could understand needing per-mission to bicycle to the pharmacy: I had to cross two fast lanes right past a river-following curve in the avenue. Grand-parents didn't seem to represent hazards. They had raised Letty to responsibility, intact.

I let her ask my father. That was her request: I'll talk it over with him after he's had dinner and a chance to relax a little. That would make it after ten, after I was asleep. He was a manager at Marino's supermarket. We live on your grandmother's money, Letty made sure to tell me whenever an expenditure seemed to exceed what was reasonable to expect from a family headed by the manager of a supermarket. My father always worked until eight on weeknights, though in those days the store closed at six-thirty.

For a while I believed he had been saved that day in Le Havre. It was a perfect little tale, the way he told it; it never took him more than ten minutes to run through it all. "Nobody believed anything could go so wrong, you know. My mother was a superstitious old Jewess, that type. Maybe she would have been smart if she had been born now, but then she was just flighty and foolish. That was the word in the street. No one believed what was happening. But I was working for the American government there. They were actually succeeding in getting Jews out of the camps, and they could use me. Use me well. I was twenty-three, a bit of a bohemian, wild enough to take those sorts of risks. They said get out. I took my mother's word for days, but they got more and more emphatic, and one day I believed them. My mother wouldn't come. So I had to tell her good-bye." At that point I always began to cry. Matter-of-fact, he said it just matter-of-fact, but it was like any familiar story when you know the ending. "I got the last train to the border. The SS came on board, and you know, for some reason I had had the good sense to bury those gold coins in a bar of soap. A bar of soap! They would have killed me for less. But I got out, the last train to Paris. The last of two ships left at Le Havre. Your mother and I, we probably even bumped into each other. Just brushed past."

But he really wasn't saved, not when all it came to was keeping the shelves stocked for the rich ladies of uptown, and keeping the poor cashiers, who often lived right around the corner from the rich ladies, content and pleased enough with his democratic ways not to quit.

"They're trying to turn my daughter into someone I don't like." I could hear him through the wall. Usually I was asleep by ten, but I'd been straining to stay awake to know his decision. I could leave school at noon on Friday for such an excursion; I'd been allowed to do it once before. I didn't want to wait until morning, having to creep into the kitchen and try to read Letty's expression before finding out.

"Darby foils them," Letty said with a tinkly, conspiratorial sort of laugh.

"You don't know how she'll turn out. Darby could go either way. I don't like these dizzy, spoiled women here."

"My mother's oppressive. Anyone with any sense rebels. I did. You've managed to live with me." There was almost a seductive tone in her voice, though then seduction to me had nothing to do with anything but getting one's way.

"Well. I'm certainly not going to forbid her to go. I let her go to Europe, I'll let her go across the lake. Making it off-limits would only make it appealing. I know better."

It got quiet, and though I thought I would sleep well, I seemed just to coast on the cusp of sleep the rest of the night. It occurred to me that maybe I wanted to make a decision about going with my grandparents, but I couldn't quite weigh the good against the bad. The good was the last sun of the summer; even if there was no one else on the beach, I could run at the waves. There were smells of the beach that I remembered from when I was too small to walk, and those smells gave me a most terrific sense of well-being. And staying at a place housing my grandmother was totally indulgent. She had an old Cajun woman who lived in the house to tend it during weekdays, when Marmee was back in the city, harassing Murray, and on weekends the woman cooked and cleaned and even made the beds. I just couldn't figure out the bad parts, the abstractions that might not even amount to anything. I finally fell asleep when I knew that letting my father decide was the wisest course.

My grandfather had a white Lincoln, a sleek car with sharp, angular tail fins. I thought it was the most elegant car on the road that year. But even at eleven I knew that the way he drove was sometimes not quite right. I didn't put it together until years afterwards that his drinking was connected with it. When we drove across the lake he maneuvered adequately. It was the middle of the day. He had put in four good hours at his law office; my grandfather was a lazy sort of maritime attorney who whiled away his days when he felt like it, sure in the knowledge that he did not need to work, much less succeed. But on Sunday evening, when we came back, he was wobbly at the wheel, yet strikingly self-assured. Marmee seemed not to notice. She just stewed over last week's *New York Times* crossword, watching the roadway only occasionally, when carsick from the concentration, needing to get grounded back in space. The car was full of smoke from her cigarettes.

I was riding in the backseat. For me that was unusual, because up until the time we went to Europe I always had ridden stretched across the rear-window shelf. Before I turned eleven and became a world traveler, I never stopped much to think that I was quite a visible spectacle, scrunched up there in plain sight of any cars following us. I just enjoyed doing what I knew was a bad thing, something my father never let me do. I always had managed to slink down from out of there when we approached our house. Even when I was very small and didn't know streets. But now I was just urbane as hell, arrogant in my own way, and full of those first rushes of self-consciousness that come as a girl's body starts to change. So I was riding on the backseat, more comfortable than I'd ever been in one of their cars, to tell the truth. The sun began to set, and I was full of rich food and puffed with Gulf-water salt and burned from hot sun on overcast days. I fell asleep, and as the car danced down the highway I worked my way around in my sleep until I was stretched happily across the seat, my head bumping up against my small overnight case, every muscle loose and trusting.

Something happened to jolt me out of sleep, and by the time I was clear enough to sit up and open my eyes, we were parked alongside the highway. It was dark out, and the cars kept zipping by us. Traffic was heavy heading in our direction, though few cars were going the opposite way, from the city to the beach. There was a small filling station maybe a hundred yards ahead of us, and there were two rusty advertisements planted just past the car. My grandfather was at the wheel, but Marmee had gotten out. I lay back down, to see what would happen, and I saw her come back and tell him to get out. I waited for what seemed like hours, not feeling abandoned because there seemed to be a lot of activity around the car. When I saw a flashing red light, I peered out and saw a police car. Frightened, I lay back down again. Then I heard a siren, but I didn't get up. It came toward us, it stopped, time passed, and it started up again, tearing away from us.

Whatever happened, we certainly weren't detained long. I stayed supine on the backseat, not letting on that I had been awake for anything. For quite a while, they said nothing to each other, each just looking straight forward. It was nighttime now, and Marmee had nothing to amuse herself, but still she didn't talk to my grandfather. "He's going to live, for Chrissake," my grandfather finally said. "They told you he's going to be all right."

"I just feel funny, that's all," Marmee said.

"It was his goddamn fault. Even the police told you he was drunk. Just walking along, as drunk as he could be. It was his fault."

"You think we should have done something?"

"Like what?"

"Well, he wasn't exactly a half-dead dog on the side of the road."

"Naw, he was a drunk, half-dead dog on the side of the road," my grandfather said, and they both laughed.

Of course, these were the only grandparents I ever knew, and maybe they weren't half-bad, but I had little point of real comparison. "I'm a lucky woman, I've never had to contend with in-law troubles," Letty used to say, and when she said it in front of my father he always looked at her queerly. But his look didn't deter her from coming out with it again. All I knew of my other grandparents was a single black-and-white photograph my father kept in that silver esrog box, right on top of the English drop-leaf desk, seventeenth century, in the living room. I had heard Marmee say it was tacky, inappropriate there. "For a Jewish woman, you sure are anti-Semitic," Letty had said back. Fiddling around the desk, I found the photograph when I was very small, though I was almost grown before I knew what it actually meant. It was a double grave, two stones. And on the one with my grandmother's name it said, at the bottom, 16-3-1943 NACH THERESIENSTADT. My parents were married in the summer of 1941, and once I called Letty on that fact. You had a mother-in-law for almost two years, I told her. Well, hardly, she said, the poor woman was trapped over there. She showed me a bundle of letters, all in German, and all I could interpret was the postmarks. They started in January of 1940, and they stopped in August of 1942. Letty didn't know a word of German, but I guessed she remembered the letters coming; some of the later ones had a New Orleans address. "Trapped," she said, brandishing the bundle at me, then shrugging a little sadly and shoving them into a desk drawer. It was the drawer next to the one they kept their tax papers in, and it was otherwise empty.

"What the hell happened to you?" my father said as I walked up the front path. My grandparents were in the car in the driveway, the motor idling, knowing better than to get out. But my father was deliberately loud, his accent thick and funny with the idiom of twenty years' accumulation not quite rolling off his tongue. He signaled to my grandfather to come in, and my grandfather stepped out of the car with that sort of swagger a man has when he's just bought off a policeman or two. That wasn't enough. He signaled again, and I could see the fretful annoyance in her movements as Marmee reached over and cut off the lights and the ignition.

"It was a bad accident, but we're all right," my grandfather said before my father could say another word, before Marmee could even get halfway up the walk.

"A man, badly injured." Marmee was dramatic, breathless.

"So why didn't you call? We were worried sick." So many *W*s in his sentence, each one an immigrant's *V*. My poor father.

"From the side of the goddamn highway?"

"You didn't go to a hospital, a police station, something?"

"You know how those things go," my grandfather said, remembering to be pleased with himself and forgetting to be circumspect with everyone else.

"You paid your way out, you bastard," my father screamed. We were still not in the house. I was still not shooed away.

"It can be done," Marmee said sweetly.

"And twenty years ago? Where was all the money then? When I needed you? It could have been done. I saw the American government setting it up in Stuttgart every goddamn day. You could have gotten my mother out!" I recoiled: the Holocaust had been nothing more than a romantic passing at Le Havre, and quietly told tales of saying good-bye to the grandmother I'd never met. My father had kept his pain awfully well concealed, at least to an eleven-year-old.

He was frantic, and I could see the vein at his temple swelled to the point of bursting. "You could have done it," he said softly.

I went up to my room. Marmee had made me promise at the beach that I would shampoo my hair and shape my nails when I got home. I had salt in my hair, my clothes were acrid with sweat and Gulf water. I didn't undress, I just fell into bed as plain as I could be, and when the porch light went out I fell asleep.

CHAPTER 2

*B*ecause I believe that every visit to Metairie Cemetery is followed by a calamity, I rarely go out there and don't feel guilty about it. My grandfather, with his millions, has a fine mausoleum on a stone avenue of rich people. My father is in what he often called the low-rent district, a small field of green near the duck pond, with bronze markers in the trucked-in dirt and thick St. Augustine. Altogether a more normal place, an anywhere place, good for a man who was born on one continent, lived out a big block of years on another, and died on a third. My father and grandfather aren't far apart, maybe a hundred yards, typical New Orleans, where the rich can turn around and find the poor hanging out wash in the adjoining backyard. I sometimes wonder if they were in a race to see which one could get out there first. Technically, of course, my grandfather won, and he won fair and square. He worked at it for over fifty years; my father only took a few minutes.

Marmee once told me that my grandfather had killed an entire bottle of crème de menthe the day Letty was born, the last of his Prohibition stash of good stuff. I'd seen crème de menthe doled out in half-ounce glasses after dinner when my parents had company. "Some schnapps?" my father said, mocking the wealthy. I'd tasted it. That was why my grandfather had none of his original teeth, I assumed. I was twenty-seven when I learned that he had very little of his original liver left, either. When that organ was almost entirely gone, the poisons went straight to my grandfather's head and out his mouth, vilifying Murray and his night sitter, Ora Lee, and, finally, Marmee. Murray was old with her years of work-

ing for them, a dried-up yellow woman with the face of a
Chinaman who'd smoked too much opium. One of her fore-
bears must have been a black gandy dancer from New Orleans
who met up with some Chinese in Promontory Point, bringing back the genes for looks but not for brains. All my grandfather's sensuality came ripping out for Ora Lee, but not for
Murray. "Your mama's nothing but a black piece of nigger
trash," said the man who'd sent money to the NAACP back
in 1955 because Marmee had told him to. Ora Lee took the
abuse: "You take me down to Basin Street, fuck me a little
bit of dark meat," he told her. It was Ora Lee's profession,
taking the night shift when helplessness first set in, watching
the old people lose the good parts of their minds, the bad
parts of their bodies. She got the death shift; death usually
came early in the morning. She didn't show up for the funeral,
just went on to the next rich old Jew. She passed from uptown
house to uptown house, two-year stints, never out of a job
for long; no one lasted long enough to question her com-
petency.

Murray recited my grandfather's day's vitriol to me when
I visited, but, come to think of it, Murray was the only one
who ever gave me such reports. Marmee heard the night
screaming; she told me that. They filled him with Thorazine
and moved his cot to the uptown-river corner of the house,
as far from Marmee as possible without building an addition.
He became yellower by far than Murray, incoherent and
unknowing. We came to see him the day before he died,
more out of superstition than anything else.

At the funeral what I noticed most was his ears. Huge
with age, elephant ears; they were more at eye level than any
other part, I guess. I didn't cry. My grandfather sent his dues
to the synagogue, and that was it. The rabbi gave a generic
sort of eulogy, handy for rich men who have given five dollars
or more to anything besides the United Way. It took my
grandfather such a long time to die that I didn't feel sorry
for him. He hadn't noticed, so why should I?

My father could have postponed their trip that year until

after the will had been read, digested, ranted about, and forgotten, but he didn't. Mr. Marino probably would have let them change their plans. Delta Airlines and Norwegian Cruise Lines would have, too. But my father was one who thrived on Hardyesque coincidence, if only because it took away any responsibility for feeling bad at cataclysmic times. Someone being paid by the word was scripting his life since he left Stuttgart. He had taken me to see *The Pawnbroker* once when I was a lot younger, and he had left his umbrella behind the back-row seat. The movie had left him close to hysteria. He couldn't go back in to retrieve the umbrella, and he wouldn't let me go back in, either. Finally he had bought a new umbrella. I had been in high school at the time; I knew nothing. I asked him what the film was about. "It's about borrowed time, Darby," he had said. "I can't figure out if you're on borrowed time, too, or not. It's a good question." He could have postponed their trip until after the will had been read, digested, ranted about, and forgotten, but he didn't.

Letty and my father brought their suitcases right into William's office. She had on a fine knit suit and he was wearing a coat and tie, but there was something steerage about their going downtown with their luggage, walking up Carondelet, as if they were on their way to Traveler's Aid, no matter that Letty's bags all matched. The flight to Miami was at 3:59, and they were going to take a taxi. Marmee could have driven them, but they wanted to live through the first leg of their trip. Lately Marmee had become a terrible driver. She stopped where there were no stop signs at intersections, she braked for phantom animals where only leaves were skittering, and she ran red lights. I would have driven them, but my car, a Karmann Ghia, was a two seater, and only an adventurous small person could fit on the low bench in the back.

I wasn't at all surprised by William's offices. He was a generally mediocre sort of man, so I expected him to be a mediocre sort of attorney. With the office to go with it. The waiting room was like my orthodontist's, hung with paintings of French Quarter patios with dull banana trees, brass-and-copper sculptures of feather-leaves, a mirror that could have come from Woolworth's. "Do your patients give you these things?" I once had asked the orthodontist, wondering whether I was supposed to come through at Christmas. "I leave decorating to my wife," he had said, not understanding and miffed, scraping my gum so hard I thought he'd hit bone. William didn't have a wife. His wife left him when he'd been out of Tulane Law School four years and showed no promise of ever affording a house in Lake Vista. My grandparents were probably his solitary clients, and only because William was Marmee's nephew.

"I'm telling you right now that you're not going to like what you hear," Marmee told my father. The suitcases took up all the floor space in the waiting room.

"You know what's in it; why're you here?" my father said.

"It's not over 'til it's over," Marmee said. "He could have drawn up a new one that I don't know about. Though I think he'd have told me."

My father looked at his watch, and instinctively I looked at mine. Two o'clock. They would have to get a cab within the hour if Letty wasn't going to be all agitated. "It's cutting it close," she'd said at the house the night before. "So we miss the flight, so we get a later one. We don't leave Miami until morning," my father had said. "I don't want to," she'd said.

"What do you mean, we won't like it?" Letty said to Marmee.

"I didn't say you wouldn't like it; I said *he* wouldn't like it." She never called my father by name. "I should keep my big mouth shut."

"It's too hot to be running after ambulances this time of the afternoon," my father said when William ushered us in at two-twenty. William gave him a smirk, and I knew right then that the will had something to say that my father wasn't going to like.

It was dated October 29, 1961. Whatever my grandfather had told Marmee still held. William read the will aloud. "How much per hour do you get for this?" my father joked, when William took a deep breath between subclauses. "Darby, you ought to consider law school. You can already read," he said. I giggled.

I was bored, and by the time William came to the part about my mother, I wasn't even listening. "That's not legal!" Letty yelled.

"Calm down," William said. "One more paragraph, and you'll understand." He read on. "And I expect that out of respect for her mother and me, Leticia will abide by my wishes."

"Doesn't matter," my father said and walked out of the room. Letty followed, and I ran behind. They saw me in the waiting room, just as they were divvying up the suitcases between them for a fast exit.

" 'Bye," I said softly.

Letty kissed me, and I tiptoed up to kiss my father. "Can you lend me ten dollars?" I said. "Just until you get back." He reached into his wallet. It was chockful of twenties as if he were a wealthy man, not someone who had gone to the Whitney Bank and withdrawn five years' worth of savings for this trip. And not someone who just had been cut out of a rich man's will. He handed me two twenties. "Keep the change," he said.

I was in the waiting room five minutes after they left, and no one came in. The door opened, and Marmee peeked out. "She didn't say good-bye," she said.

"Neither did you," I said, smiling.

"I don't understand what this is all about," Marmee said testily.

"You *told* them they weren't going to like it," I said.

"Now why would I say such a thing?"

"Well, they *didn't* like it," I said.

William walked out. No one else was in the waiting room, though I didn't judge him for that, the way I judged my

orthodontist. "You have a way home, Cecile?" he asked
Marmee.

"I'm in the Pere Marquette Building," she said. I was
immediately annoyed; I'd packed up my stuff in my trunk
so I could go straight to her house with her from downtown.
If I'd known she was bringing a car herself, I could have
gone back home on the way instead. I said nothing. I didn't
quibble with Marmee that year especially, with her fury at
having disliked my grandfather almost since their wedding,
and then at having to nurture him through gritted teeth. She
had no notion that he had any value to her whatsoever. The
first time she went over to Pass Christian after he died, she
asked Murray what the E stood for on the gas gauge. Murray
hadn't known, either, but she'd had the sense to phone Letty
and ask before Marmee backed out of the driveway.

I asked William to tell me what this was all about. He
handed me a photocopy of the will. It was self-explanatory,
he said. I asked him what the illegal part was, and he gave
me a look of disgust, as if I were criticizing his legal integrity.
"Hey, 1961. You were just a kid in 1961. What're you so
bristly about?" I said.

"I was older then than you are now."

"Oh."

"Your grandfather said Letty'd respect his wishes. He
wanted Cecile to stay in that house and have use of the income
from all that capital."

"Well, sure."

"Not in Louisiana, at least not in 1977; maybe next year,
but that'll be too late," he said, giving me a sweet, conde-
scending little pat on the shoulder. "Get your Marmee home
okay, all right?"

"I'll get her to the Pere Marquette Building."

I was parked in the Pere Marquette Building. But as it
turned out, Marmee wasn't. She rifled through her alligator
bag with the gold watch embedded in the side, an open
invitation to a Canal Street mugging, I thought. There was
no ticket. We got to the parking garage, and she sat down

on one of the plump vinyl chairs. She made a little trough with her skirt and dumped the contents of her purse in her lap. No ticket. No one remembered her coming in; there was no silver-gray '74 Cadillac in the garage. Marmee stayed in her chair, fiddling with the bits of paper. I phoned Murray at the house. "Tell her I called United Cab myself," Murray said. "She got to remember she went down in a cab, all the fussing she did when that man showed up here fifteen minutes late. Bet she didn't tip that cabbie squat. Her car sitting in the driveway, big as life." I stuffed Marmee and her bits of Kleenex and fuzzy Life Savers into the front seat of my car, tipped the attendant a dollar, and pulled out.

Marmee was lucid again. "Your father married Letty for her money," she said. We were still in downtown traffic, not even to Poydras Street. Maybe she could turn it on and off at will.

"No, he didn't." It wasn't only the evidence, that he worked at Marino's like anyone else with an eighth-grade education. It was what Letty said, in her moments of introspection, when she was using me the way a mother shouldn't, as a trapped audience, hearing things she should have learned to talk about over lunch with women her own age. He wanted a family, not just his own children, but to be the child in a family, too, Letty had told me. But his mother was still alive, for Chrissakes, I had reminded her. That doesn't matter, Letty had said. Letty was strong on looking for reasons why she had a husband. She knew that as a shy, overfed rich girl raised by bored housekeepers she'd been doughy and moon faced with frizzes of uncombed hair that didn't flatter her when everyone else was sleek and exuberant.

"If he married her for money, he sure is stupid," I said to Marmee. "If not for getting into it, then for staying in it this long."

"He thought today was the big payoff. He booked that trip as soon as your grandfather got his first touch of jaundice."

"He saved for this trip since I finished college," I said hotly.

"Well, he never should've hollered at your grandfather. Not after all we'd done for you. I spent ten thousand dollars on that trip to Europe for you; that was more than your father made in a year, surely."

I pulled the car over. We were on Earhart Boulevard, right past the point where the train tracks cross the street and rip the axle out of any car going over ten miles an hour. No one was ever going to fix Earhart Boulevard; that stretch ran between the Amtrak tracks and the Calliope project. We were about the only white people who took that back way uptown. The high school Booker T. was across the street. I figured it was not somewhere Marmee wanted to linger, though Marmee probably had no notion whatsoever who lived in the Calliope and who went to Booker T. In that neighborhood, people only came out after dark, like tree roaches. The project could have been a run-down seminary, for all Marmee cared.

"Please don't do this," I said, putting the car into neutral and turning off the ignition. It was a more loaded act than Marmee knew. My car was temperamental, and twice in the past month I'd had to have someone push it until I could pop it into second to start it.

"You might as well know the facts," Marmee said, not caring where we were.

"Now?"

"Your mother's in trust for twenty years, though it doesn't matter. I have usufruct of the entire estate. I can't break the capital—that's Letty's, on paper—but all the income comes to me. Nothing to Letty until she's out of trust."

"In twenty years Letty'll be as old as you are now."

"And your father will be eighty."

"I get it. He won't be eighty; he'll be dead."

"William's the executor of the trust. He can be most generous; he'll sell stock when she proves to him she really needs the cash."

"Why, 's he get a fee whenever he sends her money?"

"Executors get an annual sum. Don't be cynical, Darby."

"Shit," I said, folding my arms across my chest. In a Karmann Ghia, there wasn't room for grand gestures. I was feeling claustrophobic. I'd be able to smell Marmee's breath if I faced her. Murray put garlic in everything. Murray put too much salt in everything, too, and I'd once asked her if she realized that she had the power to kill my grandmother.

"Fast or slow?" she'd said, and I'd laughed.

The car didn't start. I turned the ignition key, and there was one swift little click. Marmee sat facing straight ahead, as if she were on a train that was temporarily delayed. I tried again. Dead.

"You're going to have to jump start it for me," I told her.

"Okay."

Marmee had learned to drive before automatic transmission, of course, but she had conveniently forgotten such things as returnable bottles and iceboxes and gearshifts as soon as she could get away without them. I gave her a quick lesson in clutching. She forgot everything as soon as I told her. I got out and began pushing. We got up to a nice roll. "Okay, pop it out and turn it over," I screamed. No cars were passing. I pushed harder. The car coughed and rolled to a standstill. We tried again. I was wearing heels and panty hose. I slipped and ripped my knee. I kicked off the shoes and threw them in the passenger window. I wanted Marmee to push instead, but I knew I'd have to push her all the way to the Shell station rather than ask. She popped it out, but forgot to turn the key. Two boys came running over from the direction of Booker T. "I'll pay you to give me a push," I said, reaching through the passenger window for my purse.

"Nah," they said, "no problem."

"Get out," I told Marmee. She stood on the side of the boulevard, her face registering terror. "Now get in," I said, as soon as I was in the driver's seat.

"No!" she screamed.

The sun was still hot at that point in the afternoon; there

was a limit to how long the two boys were going to stand there and watch, no matter how foolish we looked. I ignored Marmee. They gave me a push, and I got it started a half block down. I looked in my rearview mirror. They were waving triumphantly, and Marmee was still standing where I'd left her, waiting to be killed. I U-turned and pulled up alongside her. She plopped in with more agility than she'd had in twenty years.

"You take so many chances," she said when we were safely onto Fontainebleau Drive.

"You used to be on the board of the Urban League," I said.

"That was different."

"You're telling me."

I didn't want to camp at Marmee's while my parents were out of town. Letty wanted me to do it for Marmee's sake, because she was alone now and quickly was losing her trustworthiness. Some things Marmee was going to be able to skate through life never having learned; she could pay for them. To have her grass cut and her meals fixed and her lingerie hand washed and her quarterly tax forms prepared. But at some point, she had to depend on her own sense; responsibility for the simpler stuff wasn't for hire, not even if she were seventeenth-century French royalty. She had to know her own history and her own cast of characters and whether she was constipated or not. Losing that, she wouldn't be a person anymore. And Letty had a feeling that those bits of sense were dropping off one fragment at a time. I'd agreed to stay there, a spy for Letty, pretending that at age twenty-seven I couldn't take care of myself while my parents were away.

The phone awakened me Thursday morning. Marmee had a sky-blue Princess phone on the table next to her bed, but she didn't answer. I was sleeping in my grandfather's old room. Not the one he died in, far from Marmee, screaming up to the final month in what was once Letty's room, but the room he'd been exiled to before I was born. They shared a connecting bathroom, and nothing else. I'd never asked why. My grandfather was repulsive. His genitals hung out of his swim trunks at Pass Christian; they were so large, they seemed diseased. Not that I had anything to compare them to; it was just that no other man on the beach looked like that. "Bet Cecile ran the four-minute mile on her wedding night," my father whispered to Letty once on the beach when he didn't think I could hear. I hadn't thought about my grandfather's genitals at the funeral, only his ears. If gravity could pull at those poor, outsized ears, it had its effects else-where as well. The mortician must have had quite a fright.

I picked up the phone in Marmee's room. Marmee was on her back, snoring. She rolled to her side, irritably, facing away from me.

I could hear static. Then Letty. "Darby?"

"Can you hear me?" I shouted.

"Sit down," she said. I looked around. There was nowhere to sit except Marmee's bed. So I stood.

"Your daddy died."

She told me the facts, the details, more than I wanted to hear. I felt nothing. I had no urge to cry, no thoughts about my father. She was telling me a story, a grim and hideous story. He hadn't died, he had killed himself. There was a difference, though Letty never saw it that way. He died. He got up in the middle of the night on the ship, silently emptied a large Winn-Dixie vegetable bag that Letty had dropped her nail polishes into at the last second, sat on the tiny floor in the sink compartment of their stateroom, and slipped the bag over his head. Letty heard a bump in the night, she said, but the lights were off and they were in a strange place, and she'd gone back to sleep.

"I'm doing okay," she said, though I hadn't asked. "There's a beach here, and I can sit on the beach and think. I'm fine. Taking care of everything." As if she'd lost her traveler's checks. I felt nothing. She kept up her monologue, telling me to call Mr. Sontheimer, who surely knew how to call the authorities in Caracas; surely my father wasn't the first Jewish person in New Orleans that Mr. Sontheimer had had to bring back in a wooden box from some elaborate vacation, making his profit only on the limousines and the chapel. She told me flight numbers. The first thing I said was, "I don't have a pencil." I made my voice sound sad, because I thought I should.

He died yesterday. Father died yesterday. Or was it today? Mother died yesterday. Or was it Father? *New York* competition: Change one word in a famous quote to alter its meaning. I had no idea what time it was in Venezuela. Did he leave a note? Yes. What did it say? None of your business. Nothing about me? Only kind things about you. But they only make sense in context, and I'm not telling you the context. Was he sad? He was happy. So happy. The people on the ship loved him. I'm very popular, he said before we went to bed last night. I have a Polaroid photograph from last night. In the buffet line. How does he look? So happy, I told you, so happy. What's on his plate? Letty sighed. A *lot*. Half a pound of ham for starts, she said and laughed.

CHAPTER 3

*I*t all started when Letty decided she wanted a nude photograph of herself for Eddie Marino. That was also when it ended, my patience with Letty's widowhood. It was as if someone had given her some sanction, a bill of entitlement on the ship, allowing her to be as badly behaved as she wanted, only to lapse into selfish bouts of anger at my father for having left her, if someone called her down.

I managed to remain at her house for ten days after the funeral. I would remember that after Honor was born, my limit with Letty. She got off the plane ordering people around worse than Marmee ever had. Indignation that she wasn't deplaned first. "I've just lost my husband," she said to the unsuspecting ticket agent at the gate. "They should have let me off first. My daughter's lost her father." "Makes sense," I said to him, smiling lamely.

We went shopping the next day. What I planned to wear to the funeral wasn't good enough now. I had a black skirt with tiny red and pink flowers on it. The black had gone a bit to brown with washings, but it was a discreet sort of skirt, fine with a black turtleneck washed to fading in equal measure. Just this once, Letty said ambiguously, and I went out with her to Lakeside to find a black crepe dress, suitable for cocktail parties on later occasions, she pointed out. We came home to find a note in the mailbox from the rabbi, who had dropped by unannounced, expecting us to be there. "Could be worse," I said. "He could've bumped into us at the Estée Lauder counter at Godchaux's." Letty smelled terrible, with the heady, chalky spritz of perfume she'd absentmindedly taken while dropping fifty dollars on makeup.

Letty also had a new dress. Black, too, but cut so her

23

droopy little breasts could be pushed up hard into the dé-
colletage. "You'd think you were about to be a wealthy
widow," I said, wondering if now Letty was going to have
to get a job.

"William is going to take me out of trust," she said, as
if I knew what that meant.

Eddie Marino liked Letty's dress. He came back behind
the curtain off the chapel to pay his respects and he stayed,
claiming the seat next to Letty on the brown brocade sofa. I
sat on the other side of her for a few minutes, then saw he
wasn't leaving and edged off, taking one of the wooden chairs
across the room. Waiting for the service. The rabbi hadn't
found Letty, hadn't bothered after the note. I'd phoned him
the afternoon before. "My father had a sense that he was
living on borrowed time," I'd told him. "You could jump on
this for a nice sermon on what history did to people like him,
but don't. It wouldn't be fair. You could jump on it for a
sermon on what New Orleans does to people like him, and
I'd prefer it, but I know you won't." The rabbi hadn't known
what I was talking about. My father never went to the synagogue, gave the requisite amount each year so that he could
recite the Kaddish for his mother once in the fall, and that
was it. The rabbi had access to the ledgers; that was where
his own fate lay. My father was straight dues, no more, no
less. "He got out of Nazi Germany September 1, 1939, goddammit. You don't need to know any more, do you? He
works—he worked—at fucking Marino's. But I'm in grad
school, and he's paying for it. So he did something right."

"You must be terribly upset," the rabbi had said, and I'd
let it go at that. He gave a much better eulogy than the one
he gave for my grandfather, and to me that was all that
counted.

Eddie Marino's wife killed herself, too, but slowly. That
was pretty much the way people died in New Orleans, fast
or slow, but on purpose. It was too hot to do anything *but*
wait for it to be over with. "What was the weather like the
day he killed himself?" I asked Letty. "Actually quite cool,"

she said. "I thought so," I said. Eddie's wife, Nat, had smoked her way right into pancreatic cancer, puffing right along when she couldn't eat anymore. They'd given her three months; she'd managed to go in two weeks.

I didn't like Eddie Marino. He made poor jokes. He cornered Mr. Sontheimer at the funeral and said, "Just make your costs on this one, eh?" "Where'd you get the Winn-Dixie bag he used?" I heard him ask Letty when I was still living in her house. I moved out ten days after the funeral, though that sort of question never would have been funny. Letty giggled.

"Winn-Dixie's open until nine," she said. He was part of that network of businessmen who swapped the latest scatological jokes over the phone lines all day. Poo-poo, anal-stage-of-development stories. He banged Letty fast; Nat never must have gotten up the nerve to tell him different, Letty said. Though she complained about it enough to other women, even to Letty, who was really only the wife of an employee.

"I don't want to hear it," I said. I had no money to speak of, only a pet shop job and a tuition stipend that was offset by having to drive to Baton Rouge twice a week for classes, and an allowance my father had given me regularly. I moved out. The rent on the shotgun house off Tchoupitoulas Street was a hundred twenty-five dollars a month. I had a mattress that I tied to the roof of my car and a desk I brought over in Marmee's trunk, and that was enough. I didn't have to listen to Letty giggling on the phone. I didn't have to listen to her fretting when he didn't call for three days, busy selling six-packs of Coke and hogshead cheese and strawberries. I only had to listen to the trucks on Tchoupitoulas, filled to capacity and shaking the houses so badly that I was glad I didn't own one. Particularly mine. You could drop a marble on one side of the room, and it'd roll to the other side as fast as if you shot it.

In the six years after I moved out of Letty's, my father was the only one who did any real changing, rotting in a cheap

wooden coffin from Venezuela. I got my degree and it got
me a library job that paid no more than the pet shop, Letty
froze emotionally in her petulant-child state, loving to feel
that way, as who wouldn't, and Eddie Marino made no commitments. Eddie had learned, in fact, how to pork a grand
collection of overpainted women, now that he was a premium,
a single man over sixty. It made Letty crazy. She probably
could have had him then, if she'd wanted him, but something
in her was self-protective. He forgot her birthday, and she
called and screamed at him. At the store, the day of the
double-coupon sale. "It's not much to ask, to remember a
birthday," she said. I stood over in the corner of her kitchen
eating vanilla wafers. She bought cookies only so I'd go
through a whole box when I was there. Half the time she
got them at Winn-Dixie, thinking, I supposed, that Eddie
was keeping track of her shopping patterns and would be
worried if she didn't come into Marino's twice a week.

"I made your birthday a goddamn national holiday!"
Letty screamed at him on the phone the morning of her own
birthday, expecting the payoff for having bought him a cake
from Gambino's and having written him a poem with an
AABB rhyme scheme, two pages long. Eddie came over that
night, knowing he was going to get laid unselfishly. The next
morning, Letty phoned me. "He left a hundred-dollar bill on
my dresser; he thinks I'm some kind of whore."

"You wanted a birthday present," I said, tired.

"I'm going to call him. Right now. What time is it? Seven-
thirty. He's at the store, counting his money. I wonder if
they'll answer. I'll call you back."

"Don't call me back. I have to take a shower."

"Okay."

I had shampoo in my hair when the phone rang. It wasn't
supposed to be Letty, so I thought it might be Charlotte. I
wrapped my soapy head in a towel and got out, trailing water
from the bathroom to the next room. Puddling on hardwood
floors. I was glad they weren't mine. "He said go buy myself
something nice," Letty said triumphantly. "I've had my eye

on these earrings at Hausmann's. What do you think? Though maybe I should get my ears pierced first. I don't know. They're very heavy. Can you wear heavy earrings with pierced ears?"

"Most people do," I said.

"That's what I'll do," she said and hung up. I only had two towels in the bathroom. I dumped the one full of soap in the hamper, and when I got out I dried my body with the remaining towel, then wrapped that towel, all damp, around my head. It didn't matter. Usually I let my hair dry as the day went on anyway. It was healthier like that.

I had a morning's worth of catalogue cards stacked at the edge of my desk when Charlotte told me the call was for me. She gave me a look of conspiratorial empathy, and I knew it was Letty. Letty was about the only person who phoned me anyway, unless I was being reminded of a dentist's appointment. Except for Murray, who'd call and blather and then say "I better stuff these mirlitons if Miss Cecile's going to have them for dinner" and hang up. With her I could catalogue and listen. To Letty I had to pay enough attention to answer, even if only in monosyllables.

I reached across my desk to Charlotte's, pulling the receiver to myself. The spiral cord danced about six inches above the desk surface and neatly swept the stack of catalogue cards onto the floor. "Shit!" I said. My hand covered the receiver: with Charlotte, I got a better reaction cutting off what I said from any other listeners.

"Hello," I said, no question in my voice.

"I've made a decision."

"Oh?"

"I was thinking." Letty didn't have a job, Letty didn't have a cause, so Letty did a lot of thinking. "With this money, I could get a wonderful present for Eddie."

"He wants you to get something for yourself," I said. I reached for the spilled stack. The cord was stretched as taut as it would go. My hand flicked the top of the pile, scattering it worse. I sat up.

"I want your help."

"Sure," I said.

"I want to get a nude photograph of myself taken."

I grinned from ear to ear. I snapped my fingers until Charlotte looked up, then I punched the air. It was my signal that she was going to hear a quite wonderful story in a matter of minutes.

"For Eddie?"

"Isn't that what I told you? What do you think? That I want it for myself?"

"You could put it on your refrigerator." Letty was painfully thin, not with sadness or sickness, rather with enforced starvation because now she was a rich woman. "What's Eddie going to do with it?"

"What do you think? He'll put it in his bedroom. To look at."

"You don't think his other girlfriends will find it a little too cozy with you in there?" Charlotte stopped working. She was saving up my halves of the conversation.

"You're not funny, Darby," Letty said.

"This *is* funny."

"No, it's not. Are you going to help me or not?"

"I'm not taking the picture." Charlotte's eyes were crinkled with amusement now. She wasn't going to need much debriefing.

"I don't want you to. This is art. And I have money earmarked for it."

"I could use a hundred dollars," I said. My house off Tchoupitoulas Street still only had four pieces of real furniture in it. I threw Marmee's old scraps of crewel over wood crates from Martin's and set lamps on them, I bought a set of lawn furniture for eating on; it rusted indoors. I hung my clothes on a dress rack from K mart. When I got a full-time job Letty cut off my allowance. I'd been better off, the welfare mentality, getting the two hundred a month and all the benefits of being poor. Letty had grudgingly paid my medical bills. I'd thought that without the dependency on her money,

I'd make her go away, not being owed anything. It hadn't worked. She paid nothing, but acted as if thirty-three years had accumulated a debt she'd never tire of calling in. Still I stayed at St. Francis. I figured that as long as I was there, surrounded by Catholic sisters, earning very little money, Letty would be embarrassed by me, the way she was embarrassed by my father. To me Letty's discomfiture was a perquisite of the job.

"Find me a photographer," she said. I worked in a library. Letty could get me to answer anything. Or so she thought. I wasn't in reference, knowing where everything was. I was in cataloguing, sending new stories and facts into the right slots, then forgetting about where they were.

"Why can't you do it?" I asked.

"You're younger," she said and hung up.

Early that same evening, I saw this photographer I'd been lusting after in the R&R Foodstore. Sometimes I lapsed into my own form of spirituality, believing that all my life's co-incidences were really very romantic, destined to happen be-cause they were so right. I'd seen him often enough to have fantasized about him at night. He had eyes too green for him ever to have had delusions that people wouldn't notice him, and model's bones, the planes of his face all sharp and good for the other side of the camera. It was the straightness of his nose that I liked most. I saw men in eugenic terms when I thought about it; his nose was a rhinoplasty dream, too good to be the product of scraping off bulby flesh and chips of bone. He wore pleated pants, not trying to show off any-thing, but I could see the muscles of his back through his shirt.

It would be in the grocery, of course. I lay in the bed one night, scanning the aisles in my mind. The corner by the bread. Mostly white bread, because that was the demand. Too open. Wait, a space next to the Hubig's pie rack. Right in there. He'd be standing, not saying anything. All dressed, except his pants were unzipped. And an enormous cock stood out. There among the honey fruit Hubig's pies. I slipped my finger into my underpants. He was tall, but this wasn't real. I hiked up my skirt. He said nothing, waiting. I slid his cock inside me. I slipped my finger inside me. We stood like that, it was so good. He kissed me, his tongue in my mouth. No matter that it didn't work anatomically, this wasn't real, ignore it. I moved back and forth, my finger slid in and out. So wet. I could picture that cock. I looked down, I could see just the base of the shaft, moving in and out, remembering what it looked like. Maybe there were footsteps, coming up the detergent aisle. Not real, they could approach, give us anxiety, a need for speed. He was moving faster now, so fast. *Nnnn.* He shuddered, the footsteps were closer now. *Nnnn.* Faster for me, too. So intense it hurt. *Nnnn.* Another one, gentler.

His name was Parker. Lucille had given me his name and told me that he was a photographer; Lucille the black yenta. I watched him as he paid, only for basics, Clorox and toothpaste and cooking oil. I bought my real food there, cans of Blue Runner red beans and corned-beef hash. Lucille had seen me watching him. Later I'd find that she had suspicions that she kept to herself, probably not wanting to see them. "He does photography over there," she had said the first time, pointing to a warehouse across Tchoupitoulas. Another time, I had been right behind him again. She had taken his check, had put it in the cash register drawer. When I had come up, had handed her a ten-dollar bill, she had opened the drawer, not saying a word, and had flashed his check out so I could see it. Parker Rutledge. Four dollars and seventy-one cents. "His mother should've known better," I'd whispered to Lucille.

"What you mean?"

"You're not supposed to give a person a first name that ends in the same letter as the last one begins with. It gets all screwed up. Like you don't know where the first name ends and the second one begins. He has to hesitate in between, so people'll know which name is which."

"Bad enough the woman called him *Parker,* you ask me,"

Lucille had said and smiled. Lucille had a gold tooth in the front of her mouth, a gold tooth with an *L* carved in the middle, so only an *L* worth of tooth showed. Her dentist needed penmanship lessons; the *L* formed about a ninety-five-degree angle.

I had looked him up in the phone book. First in the Yellow Pages, to see whether Lucille was right. Parker Rutledge, by name, on Tchoupitoulas Street, listed under Commercial, not Aerial, not Portrait. I had looked in the White Pages. Same phone number, same address. He lived in the warehouse, though I'd thought he might, buying cooking oil right in the neighborhood.

When I saw him in R&R that evening, I thought about trying to speak to him. I threw good stuff into my basket, conscious that I might beat him to checkout. I could get a carton of Lucille's greasy fried rice when I got up there, a respectable dinner if all you did was look at it. "Are you a photographer?" I thought I might say as I stood in front of the canned vegetables, a shelf I usually ignored. That was dreadful. I considered maneuvering until we faced each other. "Hi, I'm Darby Cooper." Too perky. I hated my name. He went to checkout, but I only had a can of corn and a box of Ritz crackers in my basket. As he left, I watched him through Lucille's plate-glass window, which hadn't been smashed in over a year now. I put the crackers and corn back. I could go to the Winn-Dixie later, if I had to have something. Probably I'd go to Burger King and come back tomorrow.

I saw him cross the street, and I watched the broad gateway that led to his parking lot. It was one-way-in, same-way-out. I'd seen him at night, a passenger in some man's car, driving in when all the workers from Import China had gone home to Chalmette. They'd pulled in and made a complete three-sixty, headlights searching for someone's white teeth to shine in the shadows. I understood how it worked. If he went through the gateway, he was in for a while. He went through, I counted to ten, and I bolted around the corner.

I dialed as soon as I got my breath, before I could think

of what to say. Do you do nude photography? I asked. Not thinking; he'd picked up on the first ring. He laughed: No, generally, I wear my clothes. Quick. He must have heard this question before. I considered hanging up. Oops, I said.

"Is this serious?"

"Well, yes and no. Yes, I mean it. No, it's ridiculous."

"You want boudoir photographs?"

"You mean all draped and whorish like in *Pretty Baby*?"

He laughed again. "That's one way to put it."

"I don't know. It's not for me." He was quiet. That was a new one. "It's for my mother." No answer. Where were we going with this? It wasn't too late to hang up. There were two columns of commercial photographers in the Yellow Pages. And maybe I was supposed to be calling portrait photographers instead. But I thought they were little bald Jewish men who gold-stamped their names in the corner of their pictures. Letty wouldn't want to get undressed in front of one of them. Except maybe if it was a friend of Eddie's, one who'd be so titillated by the newness of seeing a woman whose Cooper's ligaments still held that he would tell Eddie, giving him something to think about.

My mother's the *subject*, I told him.

He began to laugh. "This ought to be good," he said.

"Why?" My feelings were hurt. For all he knew, my mother was forty and quite beautiful, skin untouched by sun, flesh where it was supposed to be, from a casual way of living out her life. He was picturing me on the phone, I knew it, the way I pictured boring people I called and didn't know: the car-insurance agent who told me I had a two-hundred-dollar deductible and forced me to put Con-Tact paper where my passenger window used to be, the Sewerage and Water Board clerk who didn't believe that I couldn't run up a thirty-dollar water bill, the cataloguer at Jefferson Parish Public who was always a step ahead of me. They were all desiccated and ugly, I knew it. Parker was picturing me as someone old and tired enough to have a mother who should never take her clothes off except alone in a dark room. Which was true.

He said he would do it. That he'd done boudoir photography when he was in graduate school and everyone was ready to lay their unwashed, naked bodies on an old Indian cloth and help him see shadows and tones. He was older than I thought.

Appointments? Fees? I was tempted to ask him if he charged by the pound; Letty was down to ninety-eight. She'd get change. He told me a sitting and two eight-by-tens would be seventy-five dollars. "A sitting?" I said. "A *reclining*; is that better?" he said, and I laughed.

I told him I'd call back. He asked me to leave my name, maybe out of good promotional sense, maybe out of curiosity. "You can see why I can't," I said before I hung up.

"In your neighborhood? I'll get a disease," Letty said.

"The neighborhood's good enough for me." Sometimes I hoped Letty would worry enough to call and say, Here's a promise of five hundred a month; go get yourself an apartment at 1750 St. Charles. Which looked and functioned like a prison, though everyone who lived there was rich. And unimaginative as hell.

"You don't have to take your clothes off," she said.

"What do you think I do at night?"

"You know what I'm talking about." Letty was a great proponent of mind reading. She never bothered to read other people's minds, but she expected everyone else to read hers.

I told her that Parker Rutledge was gorgeous, and that meant something to her. I wasn't sure what. She wasn't the type to enjoy taking her clothes off in front of a younger man; she was two years behind on her Pap smear, indestructible. I wanted to think that she was relieved that at thirty-three I hadn't given up on myself. But given a choice, Letty would take a second husband for herself over a first husband for me. I didn't ask her what made her go along with the idea of Parker; that would have been like asking a little kid why he took the carrot instead of the Fudgsicle. Make him think.

She wouldn't go over there alone. I offered to watch her

cross Tchoupitoulas Street from my front porch, ready to run out and save her from the black people she imagined were sitting on their front porches waiting for a lady in too much jewelry to pass by. I suggested she drive there. There were few rules in Parker's parking lot, aside from those of common courtesy, of not blocking someone who was flush up against a brick wall. No one would do anything if she pulled her car alongside the entranceway steps, slid across the seat, and swung her legs right out onto the second step. "The people who work for Import China must all make minimum wage," I told her. "People on minimum wage don't commit crimes."

I walked her to the entranceway. There was only a five-by-five covered space, enough to give a little protection while waiting for a very slow and noisy elevator. "You'll be here when I get back?" she said. I told her it could take an hour. "So?"

I sat on the steps. All I had with me was my door key. A tractor-trailer truck pulled into the lot. I watched it maneuver among the employees' cars. A skill of inches. There was a single black Audi in the lot among all the ten-year-old Buicks and Chevys and Datsuns with their radio station bumper stickers. I wanted the truck to broadside the Audi. It sat across two spaces at an angle between two other cars. He could do it if he edged in just right. A nice gouge in the rear fender. The trucker would have to pay for it, but the owner would still feel bad after it was repaired. It'd be like a purebred dog that's mated with a mongrel: it isn't good anymore, even if you can't tell by looking.

An hour later, Import China emptied out. Mostly women. Six Hispanic girls piled into a rust red Ford Grenada; its left rear fender was crushed. They giggled as they stuffed in, thigh to thigh and glad to be out before there was no day left at all. A tall white girl, so pasty and fat, headed for the Tchoupitoulas bus. Fat as she was, I could tell she was pregnant. She wore no ring. I thought she was about nineteen. The driver of the Grenada beeped at her, I thought to get her bulk out of the way, a cruel act, but she waved as if she did that ritual with them every day. I knew what they did in there: they packed and unpacked stuff that was going to show up in garage sales in about two years. Little figurines of pale peasant girls tending ducks, lamps of clowns holding balloons, wind chimes of birds that clacked against one another. Lucille had about one of everything behind the counter, gifts from the girls who were grateful for an extra smear of mayonnaise on their drippy roast-beef po-boys. They probably stole them.

I waited still another half an hour. It was going to be dark soon. RUTLEDGE PHOTOGRAPHY 3 was etched on a small brass plaque next to the elevator. When I pushed the button, I heard a groan of reluctant machinery a floor or two up. It took forever to come. The parking lot was empty except for the Audi out in the middle and a new blue Toyota with a WWOZ bumper sticker set so close to the building the driver couldn't have gotten out. Now that I'd decided that I was going up out of nervousness, everything made me nervous, gave me a reason to go up and be indignant, if I had to. The elevator door closed, but when I pushed three nothing happened. I pushed two; like trying the root beer button when the Coke didn't come, finding out if the machine worked at all, though risking the possibility that I was going to get something I had no use for. The elevator rose slowly, the door opening onto a semidark loft, stretching back as far as I could see. A woman in her early twenties was waiting for the elevator; no one else was there. It must have been her blue Toyota, new because she did something a little fancier than stuff ceramic Garfield figurines into cardboard boxes. I told her I was trying to get to three, and she got on, took me down to one, keyed a switch, and sent me up to three. The door opened on three, and a wrought-iron gate blocked my exit. I put my finger on the Door Open button and kept it there. Another loft, this one different, with a paper sail hanging down from about ten feet, halfway to the ceiling, coming down and curving to cover the floor. Parker was standing in the center of the paper, his camera on a tripod, not noticing that the elevator had come. I couldn't see what rested in the great paper backdrop. I called Hey; I didn't want to call him by name. The strobe went off, and I heard Letty complaining that she wasn't ready. I called Hey again, and he stood up.

"What?" he said irritably, and I liked him more.

I asked him to open the gate, and he shambled over, a man who had had about enough. "This is *really* taking too long," I heard Letty trill out behind him. I considered leaving.

"You live near here," he said, fishing for his keys. He had a ring of more than a dozen. Getting into and out of a warehouse intact was complicated, I supposed.

"That's my mother," I whispered.

He let me out of the elevator. I knew how big this space was from the outside, though those dimensions are deceiving, I know. My house looked wretched from the curb, but I couldn't fill it. Parker had half a city block, and he blew everything up to size. Photographs big enough to cover my living-room wall corner to corner to corner to corner. Wooden worktables so big they must have been pulleyed up through one of the twenty-foot windows. A living nook of surprising intimacy, scaled down under an imaginary eight-foot ceiling, so far back to the uptown-lake corner that it was private from where I stood. I'd thought about this place, expected the mean smell of cat shit and musky partitions made from Indian cloth. I smelled lemon oil. The color photographs had only splashes of orange in them.

"I'm Parker Rutledge. But then you know that." He was deciding how to act. It could go either way, depending on whether he smelled my fantasies on me.

"Darby," I said. "Cooper."

Letty appeared right then. She was covering all the dark places in front with a fine swath of antique lace. Or trying to. Those brown nipples, so dark for never having nursed me, that dark thatch that I thought had begun to gray before she started sleeping with Eddie. I could see her limbs, froggy, scrawny sticks, mottled from too much sun, veins ropy and struggling in lost patterns. How was she going to go back without making me sick? "I thought you *knew* each other," she said. "How could you do this to me, Darby? A total stranger?"

"Get your picture taken, Letty. I'm going home." I stepped back into the elevator. It was a kind of sadness that goes beyond needing to cry. It had to do with losing something I had no claim to anyway. Or that's what Letty would have said if I'd asked.

CHAPTER 4

When I was in first grade, there was a picture of a snake in the science book. It was on page twenty-one; I knew that by Christmas. That meant that for all the hundred thirty more pages of lessons about seasons and planets and seeds, I ran the risk of touching the snake page. It was all I remembered from first grade. Not wanting to touch the snake page. I might turn to it, run my fingers over the pictures of fish eggs and salamanders, but I couldn't bring myself to touch the picture of the snake. A black snake, coiled; "this snake is five feet long" read the caption. Monosyllables, perfect phonics. I've still never put a finger on a photograph of a snake in a book. A primal, protective sense. The same sense that kicked in when Letty asked me to come look at the proofs. I imagined scrawny limbs, trying to be sinuous, blue veins and dyed-red poufs of curls, snakes in a blanket. Medusa Odalisque. Letty would have been unafraid of draping a boa constrictor around her neck; the only reason one wouldn't be in the picture was that she hadn't thought of it. "I think he did a very good job," she said, when I hesitated. "I'm not angry at you anymore."

"I don't want to." I was on the phone at the office. Charlotte had gone over to the administration building basement to buy herself a Diet 7-Up. I wanted to be off before she returned. Not that Charlotte minded my conversations with my mother at all. On the contrary, it seemed to me that she enjoyed watching Letty make me tired of her, as if she were waiting for me to declare myself happily motherless. Charlotte was almost fifty, almost old enough to be my mother. She had no children; Brenda in Circulation told me that in the staff room the first week I came to St. Francis. Sister Roberta fired Brenda three days later for siphoning off library fines to pay gambling debts, so I never got more information. Charlotte was the type who took in everyone else's stories and dispensed wise opinions freely, but refused self-disclosure. I'd tried coming at her on a tangent, showing her an article about how it cost a hundred thousand dollars to raise a child. "Private tuition costs are obscene; I think they're all due to unnecessary plant construction when there isn't sufficient backup capital," she'd said. Less oblique: I'd said I'd begun thinking about getting married and having children. "I haven't," she'd said. She was married. She wore a gold band as simple as the sisters' on her ring finger, and she quoted Arthur as if everyone knew who he was, automatically. I'd looked her up in the phone book. Arthur Altmann—two Ns, not Jewish—on Octavia between St. Charles and Magazine, not Jewish—phone number with no mnemonic meaning, not compulsive. Some stuff I could always get from the phone book.

Charlotte walked in, and I told Letty I had to get off. "I only called you two minutes ago," she said. Letty had a funny, solipsistic view of the world. I envied it, but didn't have the raw nerve to copy it. "Charlotte doesn't know that," I whispered. "Could you be by before five-thirty? Eddie's taking me to dinner at six." She had promised me yesterday that she was going to take me to Wise's Cafeteria tonight. I hated going, watching Letty take a heap of dry lettuce and grill the server on how much mayonnaise was in the carrot salad, then tell me how yummy the fried chicken looked until I had to have it. I had a guaranteed win here. We were supposed to go to Wise's, I told her. "But Eddie called this morning. Sorry," she said. No problem, I told her; I'd go out with a friend of mine from work. Straight from work. It was a lie. Everyone who worked in the library except Charlotte either lived in the convent or was black and older and barely tolerant of my presence. And Charlotte had a closed society with Arthur, as far as I knew.

"You're lying," Charlotte said when I successfully hung up on Letty.

"Of course I'm lying."

"You have to come to our house sometime," she said.

"Seriously?"

"What kind of an answer is that?"

I smiled. "Spontaneous," I said.

She asked me to come to a dinner party a week from Saturday night and to bring a date. That's like going out after work with one of my co-workers, highly improbable, I told her. So come alone, she told me.

I didn't want to come alone. I had fantasies about Charlotte. The first day I saw her, I had a sense that I knew her. She had Catahoula eyes, gray-blue to almost disappearing, crazy fascist eyes. Though she wasn't a fascist as a supervisor. Therein lay her charm, the threat in her born-eyes, so different from her democratic ways. I imagined her as Martha to Arthur's George in *Who's Afraid of Virginia Woolf?*, maybe only because the same sort of craziness came into Elizabeth Taylor's eyes in the movie. I loved the viciousness of George and Martha, sad, sad, sad. I wanted to watch them scream and hurt each other with make-believe children. And I wanted to come in with a sexy, incredulous Nick-sort, watch Charlotte seduce him while I spun in drunken circles in the bathroom. "Okay," I told Charlotte, knowing I was going to lie awake sad and plotting every night in between.

Lucille didn't close until six weeknights. She didn't like to make sandwiches after the lunch hour. "What you think this is, your mama's kitchen?" I'd heard her say to a girl from Import China who'd thought about tucking a ham-and-cheese into her purse before walking down to the Napoleon bus. The girl had left, embarrassed. "I don't *care* if she never come back," Lucille had said, reading my mind.

"This place reminds me exactly of my mama's kitchen," I'd said. Alternating great plenty and total rejection. I didn't need to explain to Lucille; I thought she could see what Letty had done to me without my having to tell her. Lucille stood

behind that counter all day and listened. I knew she wasn't
on the Jewish-princess circuit. For fretting about spending of
mercantile wealth, she would have had to stand up all day
and listen in Marino's. But there were spoiled women everywhere, with their unspoiled children, even on Tchoupitoulas
Street. Lucille knew me well enough. "You come in anytime.
I may not have what you want at any five o'clock, but I can
find you *something*."

As I drove home I thought it would be quite fine to sit
in front of the TV with a roast-beef po-boy. Gravy and
mayonnaise dripping, pickles crunching, French bread a bit
stale by now but soggy soon enough that it didn't matter.
Eating Lucille's roast-beef sandwiches required two dozen
little paper restaurant napkins, one for each bite, when you
ate one with a companion. Alone, I could lean over a paper
plate, periscope my eyes up for the TV, and drip until I was
finished. One paper towel, if I didn't slip up.

"I hear you some kind of saint," Lucille said when I
walked in. No one else was in the store, as far as I could tell.

"Me?"

"It was your mama got her picture done with no clothes
on?" I looked around the store, no heads visible above the
racks. I nodded. "He feel sorry for you. Said you ought to
get out of New Orleans."

"He talked about me?" I whispered.

"What you think I'm telling you?"

"What'd he say?" No one could ever give me the tran-
scripts I wanted of conversations. Especially Letty, who had
a selective memory. She usually picked out the nuggets in a
story that made me feel bad, told only those; added together
into a new story they made a good lie.

"I *told* you what he said."

"Word for word."

"Shit, girl, I don't remember word for word."

"Sure you do." It'd come back syntactically altered, but
I had no doubt that Lucille had it all stored away. Her
inventory wasn't that big; she had plenty of memory cells left

over for conversations that could lead to something that broke the tedium of making sandwiches and stirring red beans and frying rice and selling packs of Now & Laters to the neighborhood kids.

"He come in here and asked me did I know someone name of Cooper. You pay cash, what could I know? You don't need ID to pay cash. I couldn't think of nobody. He told me what you looked like."

"What'd he say I looked like?" This was going to be good. Or terrible.

"You look like what you look like. White girl, cute, *lots* of hair. Live in the neighborhood, come into the shop. Now what white girl's got more hair than you, I want to know?" I had Letty's original reddish-gold curls, and I let them grow past my shoulders. They were healthy and shiny, not sucked dry with chemicals. I had a few white hairs, and I was determined to let them take over until they made Letty look foolish.

"He said I was a girl? Said I was cute?"

"You ain't got babies, you a *girl*. And when you ain't got babies, you be cute, too. Yeah, he said 'cute.' "

The rest didn't matter, but I pulled it out of her anyway. He told her more than I knew, that Letty had wanted the picture taken, that Letty had known that later on she was going to *see* the picture of herself naked, as would Parker, for Chrissakes, but that Letty took a full hour to take her clothes off. That he could tell she treated me like dirt. She wasn't one to say thank you, and I looked like the type who could use a thank you or two. "He told me he been in New Orleans ten years, and he can tell a person who ought to get the hell out from a mile off. Not that *everybody* shouldn't get out, he said, but you got a specially good reason."

Staying in New Orleans was some sort of sickness, an addiction. You learned what the rules were, and you figured correctly that that set of rules wouldn't apply anywhere else. I'd made a few tries, using school as a way of going somewhere different. A summer course in San Antonio, where everyone was either Mexican or transient, and no one spoke to me. A seminar in Philadelphia, where I didn't live long enough to learn the differences among North, South, East, and West. A conference in L.A., where everyone was my instant friend, so I told them my secrets, then never heard from them again. I came back to New Orleans each time, where names meant something. Jewish, I wasn't part of Carnival society, but Cooper was Kuper changed at Ellis Island, distinguishing me from the Eastern European Jews with four-syllable last names who went to the Orthodox synagogues and had houses that reeked of fish and onions. That meant nothing at St. Francis, of course. My eyes were gray and my skin burned after half an hour in the sun, and to them that defined me in all the terms they needed to know.

"My mother made him crazy?"

"Let's just say she got on his nerves in a major way. But you don't mind somebody talking bad about your mama, you got a new friend."

"That's been the basis for some of my best friendships," I said. Charlotte was my only friend those days, if she was a friend at all. A simple life made generalizations easier.

Often I took ridiculous leaps. There were a dozen solid in-between stages from finding out that Parker hated my mother to inviting him to dinner at Charlotte's. I tended to skip those stages, I had a hurry-up-and-wait sort of life. "Would he come to a party with me?" I asked Lucille. I knew what she'd say. Parties were fluid things in this neighborhood. Walk in with some food, some wine, slip into the crowd, leave with somebody for a while, come back and find it still going on. "Sure," she said, and that was all I needed to hear.

I stood there at the counter. I wasn't hungry anymore. "You don't pay no attention," Lucille said. "That boy come in the same time *every* day."

"For cooking oil?"

"You do pay attention."

I smiled at Lucille, and she flashed her gold *L* at me. Twenty minutes, she told me, kill twenty minutes. In here? I asked. Shoot, I kill ten hours in here *every* day. Then what? I asked her.

"You come out and ask him. You want me to ask him? I'm crazy enough, I'd do it. You know that."

"What'd you say?"

"I'd say, 'What you doing Saturday night?' Or whenever. I *assume* you talking about Saturday night. Nobody get bent out of shape over any Friday night."

"A week from Saturday night."

"You want to wait until next week? Not act like you care?"

"I want to get it over with."

"You don't know nothing about having *fun*." I laughed. "You got fifteen minutes now," she said.

"I'm leaving," I said. I pulled a deposit slip out of my checkbook. It was from the Whitney; it had only my name on it. I wrote my phone number on the back. "You do it and call me."

"You want a sandwich?"

"No," I said, and she laughed. I figured Lucille had about three husbands behind her. This sort of stuff was sandbox play to her.

The phone rang at ten o'clock, three hours after I'd given up. I hadn't eaten, I hadn't watched TV, I'd sat on my mattress on the floor and thought about what Parker's bad reaction had been. I answered it wearily, sure it was Letty, who needed to learn that something was happening in my life besides waiting for her deadly stories about Eddie's lifeless dick, which only she could bring to about al dente, and then only for five minutes.

I heard barroom sounds, wailing voices and percussions and people talking soppy nonsense, challenging through the thick protection of alcohol. "You got your date," Lucille hollered. "Now all you got to do is tell him the *de*tails."

"What'd he say?" I hollered back. There was only one other piece of furniture in the room. The neighbors could hear me. I never made a sound, except the TV.

"I got to go. You call him." She hung up fast before I remembered to say thank you.

When Lucille called I was letting myself down to sleep, quiet and disappointed and having nothing to fantasize my way out with. I was cataloguing books in my head, with nothing for segueing into dreams. Now I had a wealth of possibilities. My call. A flowchart of good and bad responses. Encounters in between in the R&R. The Hubig's pie rack. His car, my car? Not the Audi, I hoped. He would be Nick to Charlotte's Martha. We'd reprise *Who's Afraid of Virginia Woolf?* I wanted to be Martha, of course, but I was just as happy to be a spectator. We lived so close; going home would be full of fragments of misunderstanding, tension. I went back to the refuge of the Hubig's pie rack dream, no dialogue to recast, easy to bring on sleep.

CHAPTER 5

T.. he previous time I'd gone to Metairie Cemetery, it was my father's fourth yahrzeit; it was that night that a dog was crushed by a truck at my corner. I'd seen it happen, the head smashed but the body still thinking, legs trying to run. It had taken a long three minutes to become still, with more cars and tractor-trailers passing, some swerving to miss it, others not caring. I'd seen no tags, and I'd gone back into my house and avoided Tchoupitoulas until the dog was a furry gray flat spot in the street. I hadn't been able to be still for days, sweeping my house and talking on the phone, and drinking straight bourbon until I fell asleep at night. I kept replaying the accident in my mind, and I couldn't stand it. I didn't put it together with my visit to the cemetery.

This time my car got a flat. Parked along the drive near the stand of poplars, the only car in the cemetery on a late Saturday afternoon. Letty had a dead battery the only time she went, to check out her real estate. The electricity of the dead, I'd told her. Metairie Cemetery's got a Storyville madam and forty-nine kings of Carnival out there, and the ghost of Jefferson Davis roamed for a while before they shipped his body north. A cemetery full of no-goods. Your father did it, she'd said. He's still angry. Marmee's money paid for that car. He's still angry. You probably needed a new battery, I'd said.

It served me right. I went out there and prayed to him, like sitting on Santa Claus's lap. I asked him to make something happen tonight, to use his powers over Parker. I figured people asked voodoo queen Marie Laveau for intervention all the time, with red-brick Xs on her tomb. I just needed to find the right signal to please my father, I thought. I imagined he'd appreciate some of the roses from my benign-neglect garden and a few kind words. He'd glossed over any greed of mine when he was alive; this shouldn't be any different.

I took out the spare. It was flat. There was a florist shop in the building next door to the mausoleum, a half mile's walk. Parker was picking me up at six-thirty, and it was almost five. You'd be surprised how often this happens, the woman in the shop told me. I was ready to cry. Tell you what, she said, I'll drive you to your spare, drop you at the Exxon station. I don't have any money, I told her. They'll take a credit card. Do I look like someone who'd have a credit card? I said. I had on a translucent Indian-cloth dress with string shoulder ties, no bra, no underpants. She cashed a check for me. Trust me, I said, I wouldn't pass a bad check in a graveyard. She laughed. Most people'd think just the opposite, she said, like they're protected or something.

I drove up to my house at six-thirty, and Parker was walking across Tchoupitoulas Street in my direction. He had on a coat and tie. Shattered nerves and the wet heat and leering filling station attendants had made me sweat, with no clothes to catch the acrid smell, skin sweating against skin, under my arms, under my breasts, between my legs, rivulets. "I'm Darby, and I'm sorry," I said when he walked up. I told him what had happened, edging my smelly body away from him as we walked through the front door of my house. "My father treats me in death about as well as my mother treats me in life," I said, hoping he wouldn't notice my house. There was nowhere for him to sit except the patio chairs in the back room, right outside the bathroom. He could walk through the bedroom and see I'd chosen my clothes before I went out, caring. I swept them up as we passed through. I offered him a glass of iced tea, but he said it wasn't a long walk from his house, he was fine, thank you.

I turned up the shower as high as it would go, which wasn't very high. Parker was only ten feet away, through a door. I stuffed my hair into a shower cap and stepped up

into the footed tub. No time for worrying if my elbows were
smooth, just get the smell off. I began to cry. My face was
dirty; I'd considered not washing it. A few fast swipes, rough,
pulling the skin the way cosmetics experts tell you never to
do. The bathroom was steamy. I couldn't stop perspiring; my
clothes were wet as soon as I put them on. I couldn't open
the door, couldn't let him see me put on makeup. I stood in
the steam; the makeup wouldn't take, just smeared and
streaked. I let my hair go.

"I like the way you look," he said when I walked out. I
told him that I needed a drink. It was so hot, and the alcohol
would make it worse, but I preferred not to care. He said it
sounded like a good idea to him.

Parker was coming because he was kind, though that
didn't reflect badly on me. I had phoned him the day after
Lucille had called, from work, hoping to get an answering
machine. He had picked up on the first ring. Charlotte had
been there, listening. I had been doubly self-conscious. You
sound like you're apologizing for living, she'd said after
I'd hung up. I'd tripped over my words. "It's a . . . a dinner . . ." Party, Charlotte had whispered. "A dinner party. I
was asked to bring a date, and I wanted to make a good
impression . . ." Charlotte had slapped her forehead. Parker
had laughed, as he had been supposed to. I offered to drive,
and he refused. "You're the one with the Karmann Ghia,"
he said. My car was a neighborhood eyesore, but I wasn't
sure if that was what he was implying. I thought maybe he
was interested.

I pulled out a bottle of Jack Daniel's that Murray had
slipped me out of Marmee's liquor cabinet. "The woman don't
get visitors no more, but that William don't know that," she'd
said. I poured some into a Dixie cup until it was three-fourths
full, dropped in two ice cubes, and took a swallow. Parker
asked me if I had any club soda? No. Coke? No. I offered
him Dr Pepper, and he laughed. Water? Tap water. He
shrugged. Four ounces won't kill me, I guess. You don't
know, I said, it could be those final parts per million that

start an oncological disaster in your cells. He put a slug of whiskey in his cup and ran it under the kitchen faucet.

"Here's to carcinogenesis," I said, mashing my cup against his.

"To the mighty Mississippi," he said and took a drink.

It was a seven-ounce Dixie cup. The ice melted fast, and with the numbness in my throat and a growing sense of fatalism for the evening, I emptied the cup quickly. Parker was sipping his slowly, knowing the river water was poison, wanting to be polite. He was studying me, not with a photographer's eye exactly, more with that of a curious neighbor. "I'm not at all like my mother," I announced.

"If your mother had asked me to dinner, I'd have refused."

"Of course. You've seen her without her clothes. Not a pretty sight." I was too full of alcohol to see the implication.

Parker laughed, embarrassed.

The invitation was for six-thirty, and we were an hour late. With Letty that would have been unforgivable. When Letty said six-thirty, that meant that she had timed the food to be ready at six-thirty. Chicken, broiled and dry if it had to wait until quarter to seven. Baked potatoes, cooking in their shells, turning from starch to sugar if I didn't have my key in the lock at six-thirty. Letty ate tomatoes with rice vinegar for dinner, no matter who was eating with her. She bought Mrs. Smith's apple pies and set them in the toaster oven, never turning them, so one side was flaky and light, the other a mass of soggy hot dough. Take it home she told me every time, and I'd go home and dutifully eat tablespoons of half-cooked syrupy pie dough. The next morning, Letty would tell me that she had gotten up at midnight, eaten all the leftover chicken, and thrown up. The competition was fierce between us. I usually even ate breakfast.

The black Audi. I thought that might be yours, I said. He knew to apologize. Those bitches at Import China are so hostile, he said. There's protection going in at an angle. I won't touch that line, I said.

It was only a five-minute drive, and that was how long dusk lasted. From my house, with blue in the sky, to Charlotte's, with the streetlights and porch lights on. Though maybe it was more than five minutes, because I wasn't good at giving directions. Octavia Street, I'll know it when I see it. I'd looked for it once on my way to Ott's, the week I had a goldfish. A fifty-nine-cent goldfish that I spent about ten dollars on, including a little ceramic castle and a box of Gold Fix when it sank to the bottom after I changed the water. Parker expected to be going to Octavia between St. Charles and Freret. That was where New Orleans sorts of dinner parties were more probable. We had to double back. I wasn't paying attention, until we hit Claiborne and hadn't found the house yet. Parker asked me Charlotte's name. Charlotte Altmann. He pulled into the Shell station. A day at gas stations. Two *n*s, I hollered after him, when I figured out what he was doing. The other side of St. Charles, he said when he got back in. That's right, I saw it near Ott's, I said. I giggled. Parker seemed not to mind.

Charlotte's front door was beveled glass, giving a fly's-eye view into the house, with rainbow half-arcs made by the light from a hall chandelier. Charlotte had on a periwinkle blue dress, kaleidoscoped through the glass, when she approached the door, making her eyes crazy as she looked out. She acted startled to see me. This the right night? I asked. It is for me, she said, what about you? The next day she told me that I'd looked quite beautiful; that night I thought I'd done something wrong. Though nothing was mattering much; I was just watching, letting myself try to get into trouble. I wanted stories for replaying when I was lonely. Ambiguous stories, that I could mold and change and use a few dozen times.

A man came up behind Charlotte. I expected Richard Burton, craggy good looks with pocks and flaws and self-destructive tendencies. Arthur was good-looking in a way that made you not have to work at finding it. His hair was very dark, silver at the temples; he'd had a haircut that day, though I couldn't judge whether he always looked as if he'd been to the hair salon. He was a foot taller than Charlotte, an easy mesomorph. Charlotte had a happy matron body and a rubbery sort of face like Felicity Kendall, the English actress; the face was there only to house those eyes. Charlotte and Arthur didn't match. I thought he'd be embarrassed to take her places, that he'd fallen in love with her when the rest of her was as good as her eyes.

"Parker Rutledge. The photographer, right? This may be a lucrative evening for you," Arthur said when we were introduced. He shook my hand distractedly, as if I were Parker's child. I could see this much, that it wasn't a preference for the company of men so much as a preference for sobriety. I was wearing a summer-weight shawl over a halter dress. I let the shawl slide slowly down off my shoulders, and Parker and Charlotte both lunged for it. He let her have it and followed Arthur into the living room. I stayed, watching Charlotte grapple with hanging the shawl on a hanger. Throw it on a doorknob, that's what I do, I said. You want a cup of coffee or something? she asked me.

Charlotte and I came into the living room, and I began watching the conversation. A perfect hierarchy was formed, with Arthur at the top, his vice president, Sid, next, the head of his ad agency, Jimmy, next, the ad agency creative director, Stephen, next, and Parker somewhere hovering around the bottom, with no commitments, but possibilities of assignments. Arthur built shopping centers; Charlotte worked at St. Francis to keep from being crazy and useless.

I knew the creative director, Stephen Norris, though maybe he didn't remember me. He was thrown out of my high school for having an affair with the male English teacher who lived on Chartres Street in the Quarter when we were in tenth grade. A good English teacher, too, who taught us vocabulary and Tennessee Williams when we had no use for either. Stephen was my first encounter, however remote, with homosexuality, aside from slumber party whispers about fairies if you bumped another girl's breast. To me being gay meant Stephen, and Stephen meant being artistic and obnoxious and deservedly in a lot of trouble. Homosexuality was a distant phenomenon, sort of like lupus. You heard about it, you made associations, and then maybe the subject didn't come up again for ten years or so, except in a magazine article.

Stephen was sitting on a brocade settee with Sid, and their knees kept bumping together. Everyone else had a wife. With the wives I watched, protected by liquor from wanting to strain to think of something to say. You'll saturate the markets in five years, Sid said. And that's where *we'll* make the difference, Stephen said, pushing for the creative edge with men who mixed Spanish adobe roofs with English Tudor half-timber facades and liked themselves a lot for it. Stephen had the slightest trouble with the letter *S*. Thtephen, the basketball jocks had called him. It came back to me when he spoke, like seeing someone's handwriting on an envelope after a very long time.

"You're killing the inner cities," I said, thinking about the people I saw boarding the Carrollton bus to Canal, where they could buy tasteless merchandise, marketing analysts' idea of what poor blacks would want. Hot-pink and hot-turquoise stretch polyester, kids' clothes with no-name purple bears and no-name superheroes on the front, faded after one washing, salesladies who remembered your mama. Arthur's shopping centers went after boutiques, hot jeans and cool cottons and salesgirls who worked three hours and went off to study Beckett and Ionesco.

"They deserve to die," said Jimmy. If the client is raping the landscape, then the landscape must have asked for it. Arthur laughed, and I knew that on Tuesday he'd be getting some sort of memo from Jimmy lauding easy auto access in the suburbs.

"Ever think of lining up buses on Canal Street on the third and fifteenth, free rides to Burberry Village?" I said. This was fun. "Two-way, of course."

What's the third and the fifteenth? Stephen said, under-

sycophant, ready to bash me if it made Arthur happy. Check days, welfare, social security, Charlotte said. Hah, that's a good one, Stephen said.

"There may be something in that, you know," Jimmy said. Arthur shook his head no, and all the men realigned themselves in their chairs; I could see it, if no one else could. Even Parker, who never left his studio, as far as I knew, shooting china ducks and naked old women. Parker answered his phone on the first ring; he took what came to him. What maybe was coming to him that night was a chance to shoot Kodachrome 64, full parking lots and little white kids licking strawberry ice-cream cones. He'd be grateful to me, if I could shut up.

Charlotte hadn't offered me a drink, hadn't let Arthur give me a martini, quiet as an oversight. But at the dinner table there were only wineglasses. Charlotte asked if anyone wanted water, but I didn't answer. I was still too lucid, and I didn't want to be.

You don't have any help? Jimmy's wife asked Charlotte as she walked in with the serving platters. With what? Charlotte asked, knowing very well with what. Jimmy's wife had Jackie Kennedy–in–1962 hair and bright red fingernails, and that was about as much as she could be responsible for. I figured she was one of two types: either she changed maids every six months because she found dust on a ceiling fan blade or smelled bologna frying in the kitchen, or she had had the same woman working for her at the same wage for twenty years.

"Charlotte works at St. Francis. How d'you think her associates'd feel if they called up and somebody answered 'Altmann residence'?" I said.

Jimmy's wife looked at me funny, like a kid on the schoolyard who didn't know what to do when someone changed the rules. "Many black people phone me," she said.

I slumped down in my chair a bit. Selling aluminum siding, I wanted to say. I took some wine. Charlotte was a good cook, though it occurred to me that if I ate what was on my plate I'd throw up. I thought I might watch, take stock, figure out who the villains were. The chicken had tomato sauce and parmesan cheese and soft, sweet bits of zucchini, textures to mix and play with. Manners deteriorated toward the top of the hierarchy. Parker left half his meat on the thigh bone where the knife wouldn't go; Arthur crunched the breast cartilage.

Parker's eyes were so green. He sat across from me. Dimmer-switched lights and myopia and wine: green eyes. I thought he was a little frightened. I waited to see whether he'd look in my direction. So worried, probably already having spent some of Jimmy's agency money in his mind. I cut a little cube of chicken, a little arc of zucchini, put them in my mouth, chewed. Parker was watching Stephen, who was sitting next to me, and Parker was trying to think of something to say. "I know you," I told Stephen, jumping in.

"Tenth-grade English," he said.

"Your claim to fame," I said.

"You did a pretty mean Sister Woman yourself." Mr. Garland had thought I was too much like Maggie the cat on the hot tin roof; he wanted me to challenge myself, he'd said. I'd wanted the role of Maggie; I liked any role Elizabeth Taylor ever had.

"Mr. Garland's wishful thinking," I said too sourly. Stephen laughed. Parker was watching. I wasn't looking, but I could sense it. It's that way with green eyes, they seep out of their borders. I figured Parker was guessing whether I was getting myself in more trouble, bringing him down because he was with me. I thought that kind of worrying was very erotic.

With Stephen on my left and Stephen's fork in his left hand, I easily kept his attention, pulling him back to the year he got thrown out of school and made his homosexuality the mead of a thousand midday mah-jongg games. I was wearing sandals. I slipped off the right one and felt around under the table for Parker's leg. I felt panty hose with a prickle of unshaven hair; Jimmy's wife jumped. I waited, knowing now where Parker was. I slipped my foot up under his pants cuff and kept talking to Stephen. I was going to remember this, the fine rib of Parker's sock, the great stiff hairs on his leg. My face was flush, I wanted him to fuck me under the table right then. I thought he might be pale. With those green eyes. He was looking from Stephen to me. I supposed he was worried that I'd make a bad impression on Stephen with my bad behavior, the way he kept looking at him. I might have thought that he suspected Stephen was the one trying to seduce him, except he looked so quietly excited, as if all the blood had drained from his head to his cock. Out of the corner of my eye I could see that Parker was taking a sip of wine. I imagined his tongue in my mouth. Slowly I pulled my foot back. Parker sat up a little straighter, cleared his throat, took a big swallow of wine, didn't look at me. He was looking at Stephen, more worried about Stephen than excited about me, it seemed. I excused myself from the table.

Charlotte had a tiny powder room under the stairs. I slipped in and closed the door quietly. Shades of pink, good pink, rosy and Chinese. Hogarth prints on the wall, antique mirror with spots and flaws over the sink. Then I saw the pig. A nailbrush fashioned from a perfect pink plastic pig. My father had had one exactly like it: I'd always assumed he'd brought it out of Germany with his gold coins and esrog box. His nail *schwein*, he called it. I sat down on the closed toilet and began to cry quietly.

I hadn't locked the door. The crying didn't stop; it became deeper and traveled back across time, picking up the pathetic relics I'd once gone past without paying attention. Maybe I would ask Letty for my father's nailbrush, but I hadn't seen it since he died, and probably Letty had thrown it away. I didn't want to know. I imagined what might have been in a box of things Letty threw away with all the meanness she could muster: the swizzle stick I brought him from my trip to Europe, a ceramic cartoon-style cow he once bought Letty at Woolworth's that she dismissed as not funny, the tie tack shaped like a dollar sign that the clerks at Marino's gave him for his birthday. Gold plate. I cried harder.

When Parker slipped into the bathroom, I didn't try to be pretty. He stood facing me. There wasn't room for anyone else in there. "You want to go home or something?" he said. I want you to fuck me, I wanted to say. There wasn't much light in the bathroom. He looked terrific. I have to leave, I told him, but Stephen likes you, I can see it. What's that supposed to mean? he said. I stepped back. I don't mean *like*, I mean he'll probably want to work with you. I giggled. Oh, he said. I reached up and put my arms loosely around his neck. I began kissing him, and he kissed me back, for a long time, his surprise wearing off quickly. I could feel him getting hard; I could have taken it farther. On the floor, on the open toilet, up against the wall.

I let go and slipped out of the bathroom. He couldn't go back yet; I had time. Everyone was in the dining room. I went out Charlotte's back door, out the gate to her side street, and headed for Tchoupitoulas. I had my house key in my pocket, but no bus fare. In a halter dress, I'd look like a hooker if I stood up straight. I folded my arms across my chest and led with my head, angry at anyone who might approach. When I got home I took the phone off the hook. I'd get the shawl from Charlotte at work on Monday. I'd tell her about the pig, and she'd laugh at me in a way that I liked.

CHAPTER 6

I awakened at four in the morning with immediate clarity. I could drink like a man, for reasons I never understood, except that I had a great deal of practice. I weighed little more than Letty, though I wasn't sinewy and reptilian, but I could put alcohol away with blue-collar gusto, then get up in the middle of the night and balance my checkbook. I kicked out of the bed and put the phone into the cradle. I waited for it to ring, imagining Charlotte trying every half hour, and then I waited most of the day. I read the telephone call story by Dorothy Parker. Parker, née Rothschild: what business did a Jewish girl have going after a man with a name like that? And dumping him, to boot. The story made me feel good, because I wasn't that crazed, making deals with God, let him call me now, I won't ask anything else of You. I was quieter inside my head, figuring that he might be up at eight, that he might not call at noon, lunchtime, that people waited until late on Sunday afternoons, that people were busy on Sunday afternoons. Letty phoned while I was watching "60 Minutes," stopping my heart for three beats, four more rings. Fast calculations, now that I had given up, that it couldn't be Charlotte, who was busy nights; it had to be Parker.

"I think he hated it," she said as soon as I picked up the phone. Letty imagined me in suspended animation, doing nothing between her bulletins, except perhaps obsessing on her behalf, making myself ready with advice she wouldn't take.

"How do you know?" I knew what she was talking about, and I'd quit trying to train her not to presume years ago.

"He didn't invite me in. Just took it, wasn't going to

unwrap it until I made him; he looked at it and put it down, right in the foyer."

"You wrapped it?"

"Wrapped it, framed it, matted it, everything. A nice gray-blue matting to go with his bedroom, very tasteful brass frame. He put it down in the foyer. Facing the *wall*. And didn't invite me in."

"I think he had company, Letty."

"On a Sunday morning?"

"Maybe not." I knew when Letty wanted the truth, which was not often. "It's not your ordinary present, not the kind of thing you can open just any time. He probably liked it when he had a chance to look at it by himself."

"You're right. I should've had it delivered, not made him react in front of me. He has to like it. I didn't even get a chance to tell him it was his hundred dollars."

"Don't tell him it was his hundred dollars."

"Why not?"

"Instinct."

"Well, maybe." Letty knew her limits. She could have reminded me that my instincts were keen for self-damage, that I could easily use those instincts to damage another person, particularly another person whom I liked as little as I liked myself. But Letty wasn't paying attention to me. She knew what she liked to do; she preferred to be mean in ways you couldn't catch her on at all.

I told her I was expecting a call, and she let me go, not asking questions. It wasn't thoughtfulness; it simply didn't matter.

"So you're not dead," Charlotte said when I walked into the office. She didn't look up, though she was never particularly busy first thing. We had a wooden coat tree that we shared, and my shawl was hanging by its label from a hook. It was a wonderful lime green, the only color in a roomful of books in serious tones of brown and burgundy, wooden shelving from the 1940s, the last time they spent money for the library. Probably Sister Roberta's first year, when she was vigorous.

I shook my head.

"We did worry," she said. I shrugged. "We checked on you."

"You couldn't have."

"Parker and Stephen passed your house. The lights at the back were on."

I smiled. By the time I'd reached home Saturday night, I'd wanted some attention, even though I'd left to avoid pain. Like filling the bathtub with hot water, slipping in, slicing one's wrists, crawling out again, sewing oneself up, then going out into the street to find someone who'd be sorry. Sunday the street had been empty.

We'll talk at lunch, Charlotte said. She gave orders, and I took them. We'll walk to College Inn. Charlotte thought a lot about losing weight. We'd done this before, walking half a mile to have meat and potatoes: hamburger and fries, sausage and hash browns, meat loaf and mashed. Charlotte looked like a woman who was happy over a lot of childbirths. I thought about giving her a hug one day, see what it would feel like.

We walked across the drainage ditch that ran past St. Francis into the tony neighborhoods of Metairie. On rainy days it filled up to the top; today it was almost dry, a slow trickle of brown water and Coke cans and fragments of Glad bags. An old man drove his ratty brown Chevy into the ditch my first year on the job, a white man's fast suicide. It seemed impossible that day, to die in the ditch, at least by drowning. We took the downtown side of Carrollton, skirting Gert Town. Clearance Sale at the wig shop: I thought that was hysterically funny. Charlotte walked along, watched me giggle, bring the image back, and giggle again. She was saving up the serious stuff until she had food in front of her. Charlotte was going to get the meat loaf and mashed potatoes, I knew. She had the sort of constitution that could make it through an afternoon full of green peppers and shallots and cheap ground beef and not hiccup or smell bad.

It was that pig in your bathroom, I told her. Ham-and-cheese po-boy, I said to the waitress, then laughed. I'm an

orphan, Charlotte, that little piggy was my sister. I asked for
a beer. Don't bring her a beer, Charlotte said. *Root* beer, then,
I said. Stimulants, depressants, makes no difference to me.
Bring her a glass of milk. That's not kosher, I told the waitress.
What the fuck, bring her a beer, Charlotte said and laughed.
The waitress skibbled off. She was sixty with a hair net, and
she probably only said *fuck* at home. A lot.

"What the hell pig are you talking about?"

"Don't you ever clean your powder room?"

"*That* pig?"

"My daddy had a pig like that. I thought he brought it
from Germany."

"The Plastic Center on Carrollton Avenue, maybe around
1956. Sorry."

I shrugged. "I should have cried when he died," I said.
I didn't want to cry right then, with the waitress taking an
order at the next table, an eye on us, curious. Charlotte looked
at me, waiting for me to say something more. Her eyes were
so pale. "I'm alone a lot, Charlotte," I said.

"I can see why."

"Thanks a lot." I gave her a wry smile. I was getting too
sad to keep much control.

"Parker liked you. Some kind of way, I don't know what,
but he liked you. And if you don't mind my saying so, you
made it particularly *hard*."

"I expected him not to like me." The waitress brought
me a beer and a chilled glass. I poured it in, waited for the
head to go down, and drained half the glass. I was hot; there
was only one block's worth of shade trees between the library
and the College Inn.

"You drink too much."

"Only lately," I said. "I feel lousy. This dog got run over
down the block last year, and I drank for three days straight,
and I noticed I could get comatose until I didn't need to be
out of it anymore. So I take it, like medicine. I hate the taste.
If I could get cough medicine with codeine in it, that'd be as
good. You think I'm an alcoholic."

"No. I'm just watching."

My sandwich came, and it made me very busy. The bread was hard, the ham was fatty, and the cheese slid in the mayonnaise so that it doubled up in places and didn't cover others. I picked and rearranged, took bites and wiped mayonnaise from my chin. Charlotte was busy, too, putting hot sauce on her meat loaf and lemon and sugar in her iced tea, taking meat and potatoes onto her fork in equal amounts, making little sugar maelstroms with her straw. I watched her eat the way she watched me dissolve over time, with fascination, some recreation in seeing change. I liked to stand next to Murray when she cleaned Marmee's stove, methodical, predictable, getting somewhere. She was better than my goldfish had been.

"I lost a baby," Charlotte said quietly.

I didn't know what I was supposed to say to that. It looked like a big deal to Charlotte, saying that, announcing it, really. But I didn't understand. When I was about seven I'd seen a movie on television about a man who had to decide between his wife and the baby she was about to deliver; only one could survive, medical science in the fifties. He chose the baby. I cried, but Letty didn't. It wasn't supposed to be that way, I hollered at Letty. In my mind, babies weren't much more evolved than frogs, easily replaced.

"I'm sorry."

"He was born this time of year. He died at six months. I never get a respite. October weather and April weather, it makes you remember. About the time I get over thinking about his birthday, I start thinking about when he died." Her voice was low but not particularly sad. As if she'd told this often, not out loud, but in her mind. I asked her what happened. I knew from when my father died that people liked to tell the details. I'd liked watching faces for sympathy, horror, even indifference, so that I'd had something to mull over afterwards.

"It was a Saturday. We were both home, Arthur and I, so at least I can't go blaming anyone else. Put him down for a nap, went in the living room and actually talked about how tranquil we were with this business of being parents. Like on some warm TV show, you know, where the baby half the time is a dummy in a blanket; you just lay it down in a bassinet and walk away. We were damn smug, reading magazines. He died in his sleep. I should have nursed him. They say breast-fed babies don't have crib death. Or at least I could have gone in and *checked*. Damn! He'd be ten next week." Charlotte made a figure eight in her mashed potatoes, took a forkful, speared a chunk of meat loaf, then laid her fork down. "So!" She shrugged. "That's that."

"You have my permission to feel bad if you want to."

"Naw, I was just giving you the facts. No big deal. I mean it."

Charlotte was fifty. She'd never told me that, but I'd taken a look at her driver's license once when she told me to take two quarters from her wallet to buy her a Coke. I guessed if the baby had died when she was forty, she hadn't had enough time left to try again. I was almost thirty-four, and I knew in an abstracted way that babies were either coming to me in the next five years or not coming at all. My calendar was nothing more than a time line, birthdays indicating the end of certain possibilities. I was too old to think about medical school or acne or being any sort of prodigy. By forty I'd begin to scratch babies and growing my hair to my knees and marrying for passion off the list of things I might do.

We used the bathroom before we walked back to the library. Two stalls, side by side; I never knew whether to talk loudly to drown out the sounds, or to be quiet and pretend neither of us could hear the other. I said nothing, full of beer, not caring. Charlotte stepped out before I did and washed her hands. She was drying her hands with a fistful of paper towels when I began washing mine. I shut off the faucet, shook my hands over the sink, and turned around. Charlotte handed me her used towels, not thinking. I looked down at them, up at her, and began to laugh. "I've heard of symbiosis, but this is ridiculous," she said and laughed, too.

CHAPTER 7

*I*f there had ever been any equilibrium between me and Charlotte, it was lost the day Sister Roberta announced raises a few months later. I was home with a migraine, a fact that didn't exactly work in my favor. The more I drank alcohol, the more I'd get blinding headaches. Same with coffee. I didn't think of it in biochemical terms, that maybe both sent strangulation impulses to the blood vessels in my head. I thought it had to do with stresses, that when I needed to calm myself or push myself something was wrong, and the headaches came. Sometimes I went to work with them, waiting for them to pass, finding cataloguing books as restful as watching Bob Barker on the TV. That time, though, it was a sick one, with bile coming up when there was nothing else left. The St. Francis library had only one ladies' room, where bad-nutrition shit overwhelmed weak disinfectant; I couldn't have handled it.

Charlotte phoned to tell me that I got no raise. I came right out and asked her: Did you? Yes, she said, after a moment of deciding whether to tell me it was none of my business. You're my fucking supervisor, I told her. Sister Roberta must know how much respect you show me, she said, laughing. The pain in my head went up to the threshold; hold, I said, and I ran to the bathroom and dry-heaved into the toilet. Was that real? she asked. The phone was on a six-foot cord in the back room, and sometimes that was good, but usually not. Chrissakes, Charlotte, I said, you think I'm some sort of maniac? I put you down for a raise, she told me. But not at the expense of your own, I said.

"I'm not your mother," Charlotte said.

"Hey, I didn't learn about sacrifice at my mother's knee,"
I said, laughing though it hurt.

"That's why you're out *looking* for sacrifice all the time."

It was almost closing time; I asked Charlotte to ask Sister
if I could come in to talk to her. Now? Sure, I told her. I
don't think it looks too good to try to negotiate when you're
too sick to work but well enough to gripe, she pointed out.
Pathos, it'll work in my favor, I'm pale as death. Charlotte
put me on hold. Five minutes later, she came back on, said
Sister would see me at the convent in half an hour. What if
I have to throw up? Pathos, Charlotte said. I asked her to
meet me there.

"I'm not your mother," she said again.

"You're my major authority figure."

"In this place you're putting me two steps below God."

"Three," I said. "I don't think Sister reports directly to
the top. At least not on budgetary matters."

Charlotte met me outside the convent. I asked her if she'd
ever been in there before. No.

"I bet they have dead babies buried under the narcissus,"
I said, not thinking. In New Orleans, growing up you got a
taste of Catholicism, no matter what, with half the riders
crossing themselves on the streetcar when they passed the
statue of Jesus in front of Loyola University, and the nuns
riding for free, and early dismissal in public school for catechism on Thursdays. I had a rich trove of myths and truths,
of dead babies and lesbians and whips on the walls and hys-
terical stigmata and bald heads under wimples.

Charlotte gave me a pained look, and I realized what I'd
said. "I'm sorry," I said. She put her arm around my shoulder
and gave me a little squeeze.

It was a tight, spare old-ladies' parlor. Like a room in a
Victorian house where most of the furniture and rugs and
lamps had been sold off over the years to pay the heating bill.
Sister had met us at the door, and she'd asked me if I wanted
a Coke as she ushered us in. I'd seen sisters drinking soft
drinks in the cafeteria and buying them out of the machine

in the administration building basement with dark old quarters, but it hadn't occurred to me that they kept them in the fridge. It was tempting to ask for one just to get a chance at seeing the kitchen, but then I'd have to drink it, and if the kitchen were painfully austere, I'd feel bad if I didn't finish it. "I can't keep anything down," I said, and I saw Charlotte giving me a nice-touch look.

Sister gestured to a love seat, and Charlotte and I both sat on it. Do much courting? I felt like saying. Sister took a ladder-back chair with a chintz cushion, flat and faded with years of fat, frustrated nuns sitting on it. I looked down at my hands, hoping someone else would start the conversation.

"This must be terribly important," Sister said. I looked at Charlotte. She hadn't told her what I wanted.

The pain in my head went past tolerable. Time alone wasn't going to cure this headache; I was going to have it tomorrow. "Money, Sister. It's important to me. I didn't get a raise."

Budgetary constraints, she told me. Arbitrary budget constraints, I said, and I felt the headache dissolve a bit. Not my decision, she said. I told her I was promised six percent, and she corrected me: she *requested* six percent across the board. They only could justify upping administrators this year. Six percent means a lot more when you're making a lot less, I said. Not arithmetically, dear, Sister said.

Charlotte wasn't saying anything. That was fine. She was there, and not protesting; that was all I wanted. She was sitting next to me, not next to Sister; that was a quiet clue, I thought.

You don't really work here for the money? Sister asked. I was about to get the Sisters of the Holy Comforter lecture, I knew it. The Sisters of the Holy Comforter dedicated their lives to helping the poor Negroes and Hispanics. They routinely forgot that there was any other reason to exist. Never mind that there were no Hispanics at St. Francis, and every black kid had a bigger allowance than my paycheck. I knew: I'd worked circulation. They thought nothing of twenty-

dollar library fines. That was what got Brenda fired, all that
happy cash.

"I do work here for the money," I said. "No one takes
care of me." I wanted to say, I haven't taken any vows, I
don't wear a sad silver ring that says I'm married to Jesus
and can cry poor in the name of a higher power.

"Aren't you Jewish?"

"My parents were Jewish, if that's what you mean." To
me, Jewish meant being a member of something, and I wasn't
a member of anything. Never mind the intricacies.

"We're getting a little off the subject," Charlotte said,
then shut up.

"I submit the budget in September; it goes into effect in
March. It's in effect. Now."

I'd taken a course in finance. It seemed to me that there
had to be some elasticity in a budget. They wanted a first
edition of *Cotton Comes to Harlem* for the archives, and they
got it. The air conditioner failed in Sister's office, and she
went only twenty-four hours in minor discomfort, no hair
shirts for her. Brenda had supported half the Fair Grounds
jockeys out of petty cash.

"I'm locked into budget for staff," Sister said.

"I don't need a raise," Charlotte said. "Give her my raise."

The headache stopped. Just like that, the dilation gave,
the blood flowed as natural as could be, the pain went away.
That had happened once before, with a shot of Demerol at
the emergency room.

"You don't have to do that. I understand," I said.

"Next year, for sure," Sister said, standing up. You're a
damn liar, I wanted to say, get the fuck to confession right
now. I have a witness, I said, smiling gently and looking
Sister right in the eye. Sister smiled back. She enjoyed being
secular.

Charlotte and I reached the corner. In the curve of the
cement, following the curbing, someone had written "Sister
Casimir is a fascist pig." It was a campus landmark, a leftover
from the sixties, filled over the years with dirt and grease so

that it was now etched in black. The administration had its priorities, and the message wasn't as bothersome as the notion of getting the paving company out to do the sidewalk over. I ran my toe over the words. "This place isn't going to change until they all die off," I said.

"Which should be any minute now," Charlotte said, and I laughed. Not one of the sisters had died in the five years I'd been there, but there was a good possibility that one morning they'd all have expired at once. They modernized, let a shock of hair show, uncovered a stockinged stretch of hammy calf. Drove station wagons and saw blasphemous films. But they all were drying up at once, fading and hunching and kept alive only by their meanness. One morning it was going to be over, with no fresh troops groomed to take over.

"You made my headache go away," I told Charlotte.

"You need a shrink."

"They cost money. Classic double bind."

"Go home and go to bed," she said, turning toward the faculty parking lot. Halfway down the block she turned. "You can call me in the night if you need me," she called out. No one was on the campus except the security guard. The sun was close to setting over Gert Town, obscured fast by the concrete factory towers. My headache was gone, and I was hungry.

Since Marmee had begun to lose her memory, she could never remember that she had already eaten. Murray would cook her a plate of scrambled eggs, bacon, and grits, and fifteen minutes later, when the dishes were in the sink, Marmee would scream that Murray was trying to starve her to death. Her stomach sent no messages; her mouth wanted pleasures, and she took no notice that she was getting fat as a tick. A hundred fifty pounds, and with age Marmee had shrunk to five-four. Murray dressed her in polyester housedresses from J. C. Penney. Nobody visited, and Marmee peed on herself; the housedresses were Murray's choice. Murray spent most of the day in the kitchen, fixing food that Marmee couldn't remember. Hell, I'd give her TV dinners, I'd said once, watching Murray peel shrimp for gumbo. Murray had shaken her head. It was a matter of principle. So why not put her in a Chanel suit every morning? I'd said. Darby, baby, I got my *limits*.

Every afternoon Murray cut up a bowlful of fresh fruit. She diced apples into fingernail-sized trapezoids, sliced bananas and peaches and strawberries, threw in delicate canned mandarine orange pieces, then added a can of fruit cocktail. Marmee ate the stuff all day, and Murray uncomplainingly replenished the supply. I could sit at the table and watch Murray's knife go at the fruit, expertly, slicing on just the angle I would choose each time. I could eat bowlfuls, never mind that Marmee would run out by midday the next day. Your inheritance, Murray would say, shoveling it into a cut-glass sherbet cup with a cooking spoon.

I had to go down Fontainebleau Drive to get home; instinctively I looked toward Marmee's house as I passed. When I was small and my grandparents went to Pass Christian a lot, I could pass by with Letty and look for their car to see whether they were in town. Letty always looked, taking the back route downtown, and I looked, too, mimicking. No car was parked out front, of course. William had taken away Marmee's license the second time she barreled through the stop sign at Claiborne Avenue and broadsided an unsuspecting passerby. I'd given Murray one driving lesson and quit. I made her too nervous.

I wanted some fruit; it would do exactly the right thing in my empty stomach. I let myself in with my key. The front of the house was dark, but I could hear the TV in the kitchen, applause and laughter, track or live, louder than dialogue. Murray was hollering. Miss Cecile, you out of your mind? I tell you, get *in* here. I walked into the kitchen and saw only Murray, her back to me, her head out the back door. I slapped my feet noisily across the kitchen tiles, not wanting to scare her, and she turned around. "Oh, thank goodness. You mind the baby. Your grandma's out in the yard buck naked." She wobbled out the door, her pink house slippers not giving her much traction. "What baby?"I called out. "In the solarium," came the voice from mid-yard.

I cut through the back hallway to the solarium. The drapes were drawn, and it was dark. I looked on the settee and saw no baby. I edged around the perimeter of the room, figuring there would be no baby there next to a wall, at least not a silent one, and opened the drapes. The room was lit with a tableau that made me forget the baby, wherever it was. Through the crosshatch of panes came a scape of brilliant green, broken only by the white form of Murray in her uniform and the amorphous pink mass of Marmee's body. Murray was half bent over at the waist, hand on hip, fussing and shifting from one foot to the other. And Marmee was sitting on the garden wall, trying to peel a tulip bulb like an onion. She took a bite of the hard flesh inside and offered it up to Murray. Murray took it, looked at it as if she were suddenly going to figure out what it took to make a whole tulip, then pitched it over the side fence. She gestured toward the solarium window and said something, and Marmee stood up. Gravity wasn't kind to Marmee, it pulled her belly down into a flaccid sack, her breasts to her waist, the flesh on her upper arms down below her elbows. She didn't care, didn't cover anything, walked quite proudly. Murray waved to me, said something to her; Marmee waved, the skin on her arm flapping happily.

I remembered the baby. The room was brightly lit now, and there on the floor was a pudgy black infant, on its tummy, sleeping on a quilt that Marmee had hand-stitched twenty years before. There was a kitchen towel under it, ready to catch the worst of any effluence that might dribble out of somewhere. It was wearing a yellow sleeper suit and had no ornamentation in its thick shock of soft black hair, so I couldn't tell if it was a boy or a girl. Watch it, Murray had said, so I sat down in one of the Bergère chairs and looked at it. It looked dead. I got down on my knees, looked it in the face, couldn't tell anything, watched its back to see

whether it rose and fell, saw nothing. I was going to scream
for Murray when it lifted its head, sighed, and turned its face
the other way. Now I could see breathing, the small of the
back moving so slightly, up and down. I sat down cross-
legged on the floor and watched, just in case it looked dead
again. It couldn't take Murray too long to get Marmee back
into a housecoat, maybe some panties, what else? Unless she
fought, enjoying the freedom, seeing no more connection
between clothes and warmth than between food and satiation.

The baby had ragged little fingernails, paper-thin. One
fist was closed except for the index finger, held up as if making
a point. Its skin was the color of Murray's, but I'd been at
St. Francis long enough to know that black babies were born
only about a shade darker than white babies, if that. Mrs.
Nicholas in the archives had brought in her grandbaby one
Friday afternoon to show him off. Mrs. Nicholas's daughter
was the color of a Hershey bar; the daddy would have had
to be white to make a baby so pale, even with regression
toward the mean, if that applied to color as well as to intel-
ligence. Mrs. Nicholas had seen me studying the baby. Naw,
Cooper, she'd said, black babies' *born* white, then the color
come in. They just born before they *done*.

The baby on the floor began to stir, wiggling its little
backside first, then belly-swimming with its legs, then remembering that it couldn't do much and starting to get angry.
Its eyes were still closed, but its face began to redden, and I
looked up, hoping Murray was back by now, though of course
Marmee wouldn't have let her make a quiet entrance. The
baby began to cry, and I ran into the front hallway. "Murray!"

"Pick her up." The voice came from upstairs, echoing as
voices did in the bathroom. Not a good sign; Marmee could
create a grand array of stinks and messes and delays in the
bathroom.

"How?"

"Just don't let her head flop."

"Aw, come on down, Murray."

"What I'm doing you don't want to do." The baby was

crying now, not making TV-baby *laa-uh-laa-uh* sounds, but mewling with small-voiced frustration, sustaining primal damage every second. I tiptoed back into the solarium and knelt down next to her. I slipped my hand under her belly as if she were a warm apple pie and lifted her. When she was about breast level, it occurred to me that I was going to have to maneuver her around or carry her like a pie. I slipped my hands into her tiny armpits, put her up on my shoulder, and caught her head before it flopped back and made her into a quadriplegic for eighty years; she stopped crying. I had a power I didn't know about. This wasn't so magical at all.

I didn't leave the solarium, just walked a bit in a tight circle around the quilt, patting her on the back expertly. "You coming up or what?" Murray hollered.

"Up the steps?" I'd fallen down those steps four times as a child, the straight steep section, but I'd fallen up the rest uncountable times, a sandal catching, up two to the landing, up three to another landing, flat on my face.

"What you think, every baby in the world live downstairs?"

I watched my feet, every step slow, noticing snags in the upstairs hall carpet I'd never seen before. They were in the back bathroom, the one my grandfather sometimes had used, with no dressing table full of half-evaporated perfumes to knock over in a fracas. Murray was toweling down Marmee's body. "She had half the backyard on her butt," Murray explained. She paid no attention to me in particular, as if I walked into the bathroom every day, carrying a quiet, happy baby.

"Where'd you get this kid?" I asked as Murray bent over to put Marmee's left foot into her underpants.

"That my granddaughter."

"Oh?"

"Yeah." She sighed, pulling the underpants up around Marmee's belly, giving the fat a bit of a lift, as if it mattered. I turned my back. I didn't want to watch the rest; it wasn't like cutting up apples or scouring the stove. "You put that

girl through Southern, wiping this woman's ass for forty years
to do it, so what happen? She too good for any of them men
out there. You think Veronica going to get that degree and
come home and marry some boy? No, she got to go out and
make a baby with the blackest man on Telemachus Street.
That baby going to look like a burnt matchstick inside of six
months, you watch."

"Is her daddy smart?"

"Sure, he smart. You don't see him having to pay child
support."

"I love that baby. That's my baby," Marmee said.

"That not your baby. That *my* baby," Murray snapped.

"I mean, a smart daddy makes a smart baby. That counts
for something."

"Veronica got a degree. You got *two* degrees. I don't see
it counting for nothing."

It was the first time Murray had ever acknowledged that
I had more of something than Veronica did. Social lines being
what they were, I'd only seen Veronica a dozen times. She
was born when I was seven, so I always had fresh knowledge
of what I'd had when I was her age. Reported by Murray,
anyway; I didn't quiz Veronica for her mother's lies when
she came to little birthday parties Marmee had for me in her
backyard, infuriating the neighbors. Veronica had a Barbie
when she was three, she rode a two-wheeler when she was
five, she made good grades and was accepted in a private
school that neither I nor the phone book had ever heard of
when she was eight, she had boyfriends in fifth grade when
I was having none in twelfth. Murray would wait until I
came over with news, then trump me with a coincidence. I
hated Veronica, except when I saw her in person, shy and
enthusiastic about seeing new things.

When Murray had snapped the top snap on Marmee's
housecoat, she took the baby from me. Not relieving me, not
distrusting me, but wanting to hold her. She held her up in
the air and looked into her black eyes until the baby's face

registered pleasure, and then she put her on her shoulder. "I think you like that little girl," I said.

"You damn right I like that little girl," she said in a babyish voice, lifting the child up again to let her hear. Murray wasn't supposed to be soft; I was embarrassed.

"Why're you so mad at Veronica?"

"She could've *told* me, that why I'm so mad at Veronica. I didn't have nary a clue, the girl is so skinny. Like you. Didn't show until her seventh month, if that, I swear." Another good comparison. She tucked the baby under her arm like a football, hand gripping its chest, and led Marmee down the stairs. I edged past to get in front of them, expecting them all to fall, as a unit; I could cushion them. But Murray took the steps easily, house slippers flapping.

"Can I have some fruit?" I liked to eat for Murray; I hated to eat for Letty.

Murray shuffled over to the refrigerator, the baby crooked in her arm, took out the fruit bowl, kicked the refrigerator door shut—not my refrigerator, she said—and slid it across the counter. She was using her left hand, getting the serving spoon, the dish from the butler's pantry. "You want me to do that?" I asked. "Naw, you hold the baby." She handed her off to me.

I was sitting across the table from Marmee. It was a butcher-block table too low for the chairs; only very skinny legs could fit under at all. I was angled away to my right; I shifted the baby, turned the chair, ready to eat my fruit. "Last baby you probably held been Veronica herself," Murray said. "And you been a sight less nervous then."

"I was young and foolish."

"You young and foolish now. And Veronica younger and *more* foolish."

Marmee got her fruit first. She filled up her spoon and circled the table toward me. "He's hungry," she said, dribbling the viscous pink juice onto the baby's chin. Strawberries were in season.

"Sit yourself down. That baby got no teeth," Murray hollered.

"All right, all right." Marmee didn't look wounded when Murray hollered at her; she came to the fussing as if it were the final round of an argument in which she was willing to let the matter go for the sake of peace all around. She sat down and finished off her fruit before Murray had mine on the table. Murray refilled her dish. "I'm dying," Marmee said, halfway through.

"You not dying."

"You're very much alive, Marmee."

"My name is Cecile, you know. My name is Cecile."

The morning *Times-Picayune* lay on the table. Marmee picked it up and began reading about an artist who'd been strangled to death, leaving four children. "I know that *whole* story," Murray said. "Miss Cecile, you done read that story a hundred times since breakfast." Marmee reread the first two paragraphs.

"This is my daughter, here in the paper," Marmee said. "I am so sad."

"Your daughter's alive, Marmee."

She ate the rest of her second serving. "I'm dead, I know I'm dead," she said.

"You want to touch the baby?" I walked over to her side of the table. I was getting used to the idea that it wasn't so terribly fragile. Marmee kissed the baby full on the lips.

"You get it where you can get it," Murray said, lighting a cigarette. I frowned at her. She blew the smoke away from the table.

I tried kissing the baby. Her skin wasn't like anything I'd touched on another person in a very long time. Men didn't feel like that; I didn't touch other women. I ran my finger across her cheek, and she turned toward it, trying to suckle. "She likes me," I said.

"They do that, they born doing that," Murray said.

"Oh, I'm dying. I'm dying. I'm dead," Marmee moaned.

"Shut up, you ain't dead," Murray said.

CHAPTER 8

I wanted to see Parker. I had facts, precise observations of his habits and predilections. I tried to be where he'd find me. He went to the R&R at closing time. After my third fruitless visit, Lucille said, He come at lunchtime now. I hadn't asked, I'd just been slow, deliberating at shelves where Lucille carried only one brand of a product. Take it or leave it, that was her merchandising philosophy. She figured me out. I quit going in; I wasn't hungry most nights anyway. I tried the Camera Shop, I cruised Primary Color. I sat on my steps: my street was the best two-way street running all the way from St. Charles. No black Audi. It was in the lot when I took Tchoupitoulas, sometimes in different parking slots. I'd noticed lately that it took a single spot; now that blue Toyota with the WWOZ sticker was parking catercorner across two parking spaces. The Toyota was there a lot; the girl at Import China, who I figured owned it, must have been having an affair with someone. But I was sure that it wasn't Parker; Parker was too talented to screw brainless women.

Friday morning Charlotte asked me if I wanted to go to Burberry Village with her after work. Arthur was breaking ground on a Delchamps out there, a big deal, with half the parish council showing up for a press conference. Important announcement, Louisiana isn't dead after all. We could eat at Subway at the shopping center. Pretend we're suburban, come on. Arthur didn't need to be fed, or even spoken to, we'd have a fine time. I told her I couldn't, that I was eating at Letty's. Sort of a tradition, I told her. We didn't pray over wine and bread and candles or anything, but we remembered that my father had. Every Friday night. He said fruit of the vine, and I heard fruit of the wine, never realizing my mistake until I went to Sunday school. And then I only knew for the moment that I saw it on the paper. I always took my spelling errors as correct, negative reinforcement, the red circle, being stronger than a simple check mark. It was the same with vine and wine. They both fit.

I arrived at Letty's house at six-thirty. She offered me a drink. I knew that meant that I'd be bringing the drink to the table in five minutes, trying to wash down a tough eye of the round with whiskey and water if I wasn't careful. I poured myself a tumblerful of Mogen David. "That stuff is so sweet," Letty said, laying a thick slab of meat on a plate for me. Her tomatoes already were in a wooden bowl on the table, ripening in the heat with their guts out.

"Ever read Proust?" I said, knowing she hadn't. "Sometimes you can bring back somebody if you just drink the right stuff." I took a big gulp. It was Friday night, all right.

"I think it's called hallucinogenics," Letty said. I looked at her, pleased. Letty generally wasn't funny.

"You have time to read my stuff?" she asked. Letty had begun writing poetry; she was now a woman of depth. She met once a week with a coven of other women in the neighborhood who'd come to wisdom with widowhood; everything they wrote rhymed. They rotated houses, making Letty frantic when her turn came that they wouldn't leave when they were supposed to. A two-hour meeting, fifteen minutes of reading and saying How lovely, the rest of the time unloading the feelings that didn't come out in their poetry at all.

> He loves me, he loves me not.
> It's all part of a plot.
> To keep me guessing about his every whim,
> What he forgets is that I do love him.

The phone rang. "Hey, let the machine pick up," I said. Letty had an answering machine and a remote-control beeper for the sole purpose of never having to worry about Eddie phoning and her not knowing about it. She looked over at the machine. It would pick up after the fourth ring; I knew that so well. She gave me a mildly threatening look. I didn't give her permission, I let her grapple with indecision. Third ring, fourth ring. We heard her voice, Hi, this is Letty, I'm sorry I can't come to the phone right now . . . So terribly original, the spiel on the instruction booklet, as if it wouldn't record unless you used the manufacturer's paradigm. Then Eddie. "Hey, babe, looks like I'm strictly out of luck." He chuckled. He had a New Orleans accent, worse when it came through the medium of some technology, in his TV commercials, on Letty's answering device. "Thought having some late dinner at Masson's . . ."

Letty picked up, so I never found out what sort of pitch he was going to make for Masson's. Was it going to be fun? For him to load his plate with chunks of crab in butter, potatoes stuffed with cheese, chocolate mousse, while she nursed a cup of decaf? "I'm here," she sang out. She switched the machine to Off.

"Not a thing. I'd love to." A giggle. "Well, maybe *ten* minutes. Oh, come on, at my age *everyone* needs a little help from Estée Lauder. Yes, you're naturally beautiful, but I'm not." Another giggle, and I left the room.

"You don't mind, do you?" she asked. I had on "Wheel of Fortune." Vanna White was getting on my nerves. Her figure was no better than mine, and her teeth were a lot worse. She had that job because of her attitude. I thought she was okay, and it bothered the hell out of me right then.

"I don't mind. I just wish I'd known, that's all. I could've gone out myself."

"Now, how could I have known he'd call?" she said.

"You couldn't have."

I brushed past her, leaving Vanna cold on the screen and roast beef cold on the plate. "Wait, I made a pie. Take the pie. And your dinner. What am I going to do with your dinner? It'll just take a second."

"No." I went out the kitchen door into the carport. It's

important that I have your blessing, she said. You have my
blessing, I said. All else aside, I want you to have a good
time. Wait, the pie, she said. Hey, don't press your luck, I
said. She'd been funny with the hallucinogens, maybe she
was developing into a funny person. She scowled and put a
hand on her hip. You make this so difficult, she said. I don't
mean to, I said. You're all I have in the world, you know,
she said, reaching through my half-open window and pushing
my bangs out of my eyes. Get home before dark, she said. I
flung my head so my bangs fell back over my eyes and backed
my car out into her street without looking. As I shifted into
first, I saw her shrug a little sadly and turn quickly back
inside. She only had ten minutes to make good her promise
of ageless beauty, and her usual routine took half an hour.
Many mornings I'd sat on her closed toilet and tried to talk,
distracted by my own image in her ceiling-to-floor, wall-to-
wall mirror, while she had gone through Buf-Pufs and as-
tringents and lotions and foundations and a different paint
for each square on the graph of her face. It was different
from watching anything Murray did. Her cleaning the stove
and slicing up foods was soothing because it was so methodical, while dressing Marmee was infuriating because of the
struggle. Letty's toilette was a disconcerting blend of the two:
the comforting repetitions and the annoying interruptions.
The drawers that held her makeup were as big as the ones
that held my folding clothes. What happened to soap? I'd
said once. *Never* use soap, she'd said, this her first piece of
beauty advice, and I had been about thirty at the time.

On the way home it began to rain. Or, rather, I drove
under a brimming-full cloud that sent down sheets of water
as I passed through a dozen city blocks. I still had the Con-
Tact paper in place of my passenger window; night images
were less hazy and dangerous than day images because of
lights. If it was coming at me without a light, it was its own
fault. The rain made the Con-Tact paper belly in, like glass
in a tornado, and then I passed from under the cloud and it
stopped.

I passed my street so I could take Napoleon to Tchoupitoulas. I could have passed his warehouse coming from
uptown, but it would have been on the passenger side, and
through the Con-Tact paper a black Audi was indistinguish-
able from a low oleander bush, one of many dark blurs to
be avoided. Only Import China trucks were in the lot. There
was no curbing in front of my house, only a spread of clam-
shells, no lawn to cut. I pulled up nose-to-steps and made a
dash for the door. No rain, just dusk dangers. I heard a horn
honk and a car slow down, but I didn't look. The horn was
frog voiced and simpy, like a rusty ten-year-old Buick. I
slammed the door. There was no window on the front of the
house; air in shotgun houses could flow from side to side,
but not from front to back, though they were called shotgun
houses because a gun shot through the front door could travel
all the way to the back door without being stopped by a wall.
The breezes couldn't travel as far as a shotgun pellet, so why
bother with front and back windows? I tried looking through
the peephole on the front door, on tiptoe; the previous tenant
had been a drug dealer. A tall one, the landlady had joked.
A huge black car, swelled by the fish-eye perspective, stopped
in front of my house, red taillights. I saw a man move into
and out of my line of vision, return to the car, and pull off.
I took the mattress from my bedroom to sleep in the front
room. The bank of clouds, still full, moved into my neighborhood about midnight and, reasoning that bad people hated
discomfort, I fell asleep.

I carried WD-40 the way some women carried mace, the
vial in my hand, ready to start the day. I had to check the
distributor cap before I even bothered to see whether the car
would turn over; if it was wet, a shot of WD-40 dried it out,
the petroleum not letting the water stay and mingle. I didn't
notice the paper under my windshield wiper until I was inside
the car, though it didn't matter. It was illegible, the writing
washed away in the first minutes of the rainstorm. I turned
it over for clues. The photocopying spirits held better than
the ink on the other side. It was a news release for Altmann,

Inc., singing the praises of Delchamps from the mouths of
the parish president and Arthur Altmann, for release yesterday, words drafted before the men actually said something
else. I stuffed it into my jacket pocket.

Both Charlotte and I had to work that Saturday morning.
I was in before she was. I have to see Sister Roberta, Charlotte
said, flying in, hooking her London Fog on the coat tree, and
running out. There was a derelict in the science stacks, she
told me when she returned. Derelicts and dopers and car
thieves were more scared of nuns than they were of grave-
yards, unless they were hell-bent on raping one. Nun-rape
being rare, Sister Roberta had the odds on her side, and she
could always get one out by talking to him as if he were a
first-grader caught chewing bubble gum in class. I forgot
about the note until ten-thirty, when I put my jacket on to
run over to the administration building for some Chee Wees
and a pecan Danish Roller from the machines. The rain had
brought in a cold front last night; it'd be gone by tomorrow.

"You leave this on my windshield?" I asked Charlotte
when I came back. She shook her head no, extending her
hand for the limp scrap of paper.

"Parker, no doubt about it, Parker," she said.

"Yeah?"

"I told you to come last night. He asked about you."

"Where?"

"He's working on Arthur's account. Stephen Norris liked
his stuff. He was doing the Delchamps photos. You knew
that."

I didn't know that. I didn't know anything about what
might have happened with the cast from Charlotte's dinner
party. I hadn't asked, could easily imagine that each one,
bored and lonely, had sneaked out the back door, in turn,
losing connectedness, knowing they'd be working together
tomorrow. Except Parker, whom I pictured spending his time
shuttling between R&R and the Camera Shop, missing me
by seconds every time.

So what do I do? I asked her. You call him, idiot. I looked

at my watch. Everyone was up by eleven on a Saturday. I knew his number by heart. A male voice answered. Parker? No, Parker's not here. A sibilant, pulled through the teeth: I knew I'd heard it before. I paused, trying to remember, tempted to say, Who's this? Could you tell him Darby called? I said, figuring that if he knew me he'd say so. Sure, he said, not particularly friendly. I'm sorry if I disturbed you, I said. No problem, he said, not meaning it. Any idea when he'll be in? I asked. I was only at work until one. Nope. I gave him the library number, told him I'd only be there until one. Sure, he said.

I walked out with Charlotte at one. She asked me what I was going to do with my afternoon. I was the only one who liked getting the Saturday-morning shift once a month; it meant filling up enough of the day that I could make it to bedtime. I shrugged. Read, I guess. I could take two hours at the public library. Sometimes I camped in nonfiction; I liked the 364.15s, the true crime. Otherwise I'd scan the picked-over popular reading shelf, finding nothing, then go through a chunk of the alphabet in the fiction section. Once the books were out of popular reading, they took on a dull quality, lost their dust jackets, had only ten-point titles on their spines. I had a cardboard marker that I hid on the shelf where I'd left off, *A* through *C* one visit, *D* and *E* the next, go through and start over. St. Francis seemed to have no *books* in its library, only texts. Anything to train its students to become bourgeois: pharmacology guides and accounting manuals. Fiction holdings were limited by what rich, pretentious alumni chose to donate at their deaths, nothing written after 1890, tooled-leather covers that had been decorative and color coordinated. Fiction didn't get you into medical school. Busman's holiday, I'd say to Eleanor when I walked into the public library. She worked reference and had gone to grad school with me.

The Chee Wees and Danish Roller only made me hungrier, and straight from work I stopped in at R&R. I hated to have my stomach growling in the stacks. Lucille made me

a roast-beef po-boy and I watched Tchoupitoulas Street out
the front window. Parker's Audi was in the lot. My chances
weren't bad, and I was jittery. When a black man walked
out Parker's gate, I felt a rush of adrenaline, my response to
phantom realizations of fantasies. Anticipating a phone call,
I'd tremble if a doorbell rang; expecting a robber in the bushes,
I'd make a stopped-heart leap backwards if a neighbor called
my name. When the actual phone call or assault came, and
both did, I was perfectly calm, not fearful, not thinking, just
going on a survival instinct that I thought a person like me
would lack totally. When Parker walked out his gate and
started in the direction of the R&R a minute later, I felt
nothing at all.

He saw me when he walked in and came up behind me
at the counter, saying nothing. I turned around to look at
him. He was studying the postage stamp machine. Lucille
had no impulse items next to checkout; she knew her customers. Hi, I said. He said hi back. I watched Lucille drop
shredded lettuce on my sandwich. I expected some to fall off,
over the edges, but none did. I guess you got my message too
late, I said. He turned away from the stamp machine and
looked at me, as if I might be talking to someone else. My
message, I said. What message? Haven't you been home? I
left you a message. Your note washed off in the rain. I didn't
see any messages, he said, then got quiet. A man answered
your phone. Shit, he said. He sounded familiar, I said. You
know Stephen Norris. I nodded. He was over looking at
slides. From last night? I said. Right. Oh. He got quiet again.
He couldn't go back to looking at the stamp machine. It sold
one stamp for a quarter and two stamps for fifty cents. No
complications. He began watching Lucille. She was wrapping
my sandwich in butcher paper, fast, smooth creases as sure
as an origami master.

"What did the note say?" I said.

"I don't remember."

"Sorry."

"I owe you big," he said. "That's a huge account, your friend Altmann." That's probably what the note said.

"That what your note said?"

"Probably," he said, laughing.

Lucille was waiting for his order. A woman with a giant box of Tide was standing behind him. Parker stepped out of the line; You go ahead, he said. The woman hefted the box of Tide up onto the counter, not saying thank you. Parker looked at me; he couldn't think of anything to say, now that he'd given up his place.

"Burberry Village as lovely as the hype?" I asked.

"If you like suburban plastic. But don't tell your friend that."

"I don't think Charlotte has any delusions."

He fell silent. I waited and nothing happened. I shrugged and left, letting the lady with the box of Tide out the door ahead of me. Parker watched me leave before he turned to Lucille.

In the Latter Branch Library, it was possible to hide in the stacks on a Saturday with a roast-beef po-boy. Not in the fiction section, of course, because the fiction section browsers were idle, looking for entertainment, and turning me in to the librarian would be more fun than finding a two-week-loan best-seller still on the shelf. I could sit cross-legged on the floor by the 364.15s and read about bloody family murders while dripping mayonnaise into a napkin in my lap. I'd read about a hundred thirty pages in this book about an American heiress who'd been shot to death by her Greek husband who married her for her money—you knew it from the outset—and I was thinking about switching to a book about the Main Line murders. Half a sandwich sat in front of me uneaten. I was rationing it: beatings and venality didn't bother my appetite.

I recognized his pants leg. I looked up, liking to have to focus in the field past his crotch. I scooted over against the 355s, the warfare section, in case he was there for a book.

You're not hard to find, he said. Just look for that car and
follow the smell of rancid roast beef. I turned a little pink,
and to cover it I got up, no hands, a trick I'd learned in P.E.;
the effort alone could make a less healthy person's head pop
off. The stack aisles were narrow, and I stood close to him.
I'd just been reading about Greeks, and I was in the mood
for Mediterranean notions of personal air space. Parker edged
back, but only about three inches. You were looking for me?
I said. A little, he said. I laughed. Really, a little. Sort of
fatalistically, if I found you I'd apologize; if I didn't find you
I'd figure out a way not to feel like a jerk. If you're looking
for attention, you should keep that car a long time. I was
parked on St. Charles Avenue, next to an oak tree. You
couldn't park next to an oak tree if you had a passenger; the
roots were so strong that they'd pushed up the sidewalk and
busted the curb. People put For Sale signs in their rear windows and left them along that stretch: it was the most conspicuous place in town.

I'm not looking for attention, I said. I know, he said. We
didn't say anything for a whole minute. I looked down at the
half sandwich on the floor, getting my bearings, not wanting
to step on it in front of Parker. Or worse, to leave it in his
way. I kicked it to the side, and a big swatch of butcher paper
slipped up onto a bottom bookshelf; it stopped when the bread
hit. I smiled. He looked down, kicked it a little the other
way, and I giggled. *Shhh*, he said, this is a library. Right, I
said out loud. No one whispered in Latter Library; too many
rich people went there for niggling rules to be enforced. I
kicked the sandwich again, right past his leg. He stepped
back, intercepted, gave it a smooth shot out into the main
reading area. Your point, I said. He was a solemn type, but
he was smiling. Loser fetches, he said, and I sneaked out of
the stacks, pulled the butcher paper back, leaving a streak of
gravy along the floor. I shelved my books quickly—the computer knew I liked 364.15s—and tiptoed out, leaving the
sandwich. The staff would find it when they shelved; I'd

found a used condom at St. Francis. In the economics stacks, no less.

Parker stood on the library steps, hands in pockets, not finding anything to say. Would you like to come to dinner? I offered, wondering how I'd get something precooked when R&R closed in fifteen minutes. He couldn't, he said, he had to work. I walked off, having too much time again instead of too little. The library steps ranged down a quarter of a block; Latter sat on one of only three sites above sea level in town. I was almost to my car when he came after me. I forgot to apologize. For what? For not knowing what to say in Lucille's, he said. That's okay, I told him and walked off. Seven hours to bedtime, and I'd have some good daydreams constructed by then.

He was getting *two* sandwiches, Lucille told me when I went back in Monday evening. Nobody but a natural-born *hog* eat two of my sandwiches. Especially with two dollar-sixty-nine bags of chips and two cold drinks. He got somebody up there, he don't want you knowing about. He done waited for you to leave, you got to have seen that. He shamed of himself. Aw, Lucille, I said, he was stocking up. I'd do that. I've *done* that. One for lunch, one for dinner. You closed at four Saturday, remember?

"You right," she said. Sometimes Lucille talked to me the way I talked to Letty.

CHAPTER 9

I once saw a documentary on television about continental drift. It was a reversal of time, showing the continents as they are now, in cartoon simplicity, then shifting backwards into a giant landmass, South America nestling into the crook of Africa, the northern-hemisphere continents knitting together, a single plane except for an occasional inlet or isthmus. I wondered at the time what lay on the other side of the map, once the land was massed, perhaps half a sphere of ocean with a lovely error, the Philippines, Hawaii, left over.

That was the way my decision coalesced, great masses of once-separate feeling and practicality drifting together. I awakened one morning and the whole idea was there, locked into place, that I was going to have a baby. If anyone had asked me why, I would have answered, Why not? If I'd been honest with myself, I'd have said that it was a way of getting organized. More geography, a means of finding a center. I would be the Earth, baby Helios the star, and I would have many satellites: Murray, finding me as good and fertile as Veronica, Charlotte, taking the light, too, no eclipses, no black-dead stars. And Letty, shuttled out of orbit; it all made perfect sense. No one asked, of course, not knowing my intentions, and I didn't think about it beyond the abstractions.

It wasn't the first time the notion had crossed my mind. When I was twenty-six, I'd actually mentioned having a baby to my parents. I was in graduate school and selling parakeets and hamsters for three-fifty an hour, and it seemed like something to do. An excellent reason for leaving graduate school and with it the prospect of becoming a dried-up librarian. "You are a virgin, aren't you?" my father said, mocking himself to make it easier. "Was my conception immaculate?" I said. Letty took her plate to the kitchen for a second helping of rice. Letty was eating the same food as everyone else before my father died, a not-so-rich lady eating not-so-poor food. "Letty got pregnant the first try. I was like a kamikaze going for the *Yorktown*," my father said, "a clean strike." I laughed until I choked. "You two are not funny," Letty said.

"I'm serious. I've been thinking of having a baby. By myself. With a little help from a friend."

"Not you-know-who?" Letty said.

"Why not?" You-know-who was Bunny. He played jazz trombone at Tipitina's and made love as if he had been born to it. Bunny had only two liabilities. He had no concept of fidelity. And he was black. Black as if no one had put any white blood into his family since they came from Africa. I pictured a beautiful baby and a very pissed-off Bunny, maybe a committed Bunny, and I didn't think beyond that. "It'll give your father a heart attack, that's why," Letty said. My father didn't know any Bunny facts except his occupation, which kept him in my life when my father was either sleeping or doing layouts for this-week's special on fryer quarters and top sirloin. Bunny pistol-whipped the shit out of his brother-in-law the next week, and I lost interest in him when he went to Parish Prison. I shelved the notion of having babies as long as my father was around. I shelved the notion of having serious relationships with men while my father was around, too, but I didn't think about it. Thinking about why I acted certain ways wasn't something I did.

No thinking this time, either; planning was enough. I had room for the furniture, that was no problem. Astrology didn't matter to me, when whim was so much more important, and in New Orleans no pregnancy could be scheduled without three months of unbearable heat at a bad time. The issue was genes, driving out the bad, doubling up on the good, introducing fresh new talents. Lacking both, art and drive seemed nice to me, and I was sure they could be transmitted.

Green eyes. My failure to have green eyes was one of

those issues that were joked about when I was small and
taking things literally. Like the torn muscle in Letty's abdomen that came of ballooning up to 160 pounds when she
was pregnant, nightly milk shakes, easily rationalized. When
I was a child watching her dress, she'd say, This is your fault,
standing in her slip, her belly folds visible underneath, and
I'd apologize. She let me apologize. The gray eyes came from
the ice man; both my parents had green eyes. We waited for
them to change, get a bit of yellow in them, Letty told me.
But I could dress you in mint green and they'd still move
between blue and gray. I'd tried green eye shadow in junior
high. You look like a slut, Letty had said. And your eyes are
still gray. I could produce a green-eyed baby for Letty with
no problem, just the tiniest dab of yellow pigment on the
chromosomes. Eleanor had green eyes and wished for a blue-
eyed baby; I supposed that Letty liked herself a lot more than
Eleanor did.

It wasn't only that all eugenic markers pointed at Parker.
I wanted something particular out of him, and a baby would
be something, all right. Not long-term from Parker himself,
just take the goodies and run with them. Parker wasn't going
to love me or marry me—one or the other would have been
fine—he couldn't even arrange to see me on purpose for more
than five minutes. For months I'd known him through
glitches, near-misses. I suppose he smacked of safety, but
again, I wasn't thinking about it, just planning. I decided not
to ask him, but to steal from him, take money from Daddy's
wallet when he won't give you any.

The seduction fantasies gave me a whole new form of
entertainment. The daydreams could run all day, with new
tensions. Now the villain wasn't somebody walking up the
detergent aisle in R&R; it was Parker. Or me. There was a
delicacy to plot turns that hadn't been there before, because
an actual plan couldn't go through revisions the next night.
I'd invite him to dinner, he'd say no, and then I couldn't
excise that bit of our history. It would become a fact to be
gotten around. Accidental meetings never worked; almost all

we'd had were accidental meetings. I considered Charlotte as a go-between, manufacturing a good encounter. I let the *Who's Afraid of Virginia Woolf?* fantasy tape roll again in my mind, and I didn't like it. I didn't want viciousness and romance; I wanted success. After a few days of telling stories in my head, during commercials, driving the car, I was tired of Parker and all the imagined rebuffs.

The solution came from Letty. Letty interrupted everything, including daydreams. "Eddie has my picture in his bedroom, where he used to have one of those paintings of St. Louis Cathedral, remember?" she said when I answered the phone, right in the middle of a daydream scene. I was on Tchoupitoulas Street, crushed and helpless, but not bleeding. He wanted me. A commercial for Oldsmobile was on the TV. "Those ridiculous paintings?" I was her chronicler, recalling what she'd seen when I'd never been places she'd been. Eddie had identical paintings of St. Louis Cathedral over his king-size bed. "Even motel rooms do better than that," Letty had told me her first time there, before she quit being critical, before she forgot that Eddie had been my father's boss, and not an easy one at that.

I was interested. "He say anything?" I said.

Letty was waiting for this one. "Just that he has wonderful dreams."

"Where's the other painting of the cathedral?" I hoped she'd say, In the closet, waiting for the old switcheroo, maybe jammed up in front of an old portrait of the late Nat Marino, used for protection. Like the panel in the funeral parlor chapel that had a Jewish star on one side, a cross on the other, easily flipped, depending, like an answer on "Family Feud."

"In the closet," she said proudly.

The solution was this: Parker was going to take my photograph. Viciousness and romance and success. I wasn't going to do it right away, of course. Even played out in my mind, skipping transitional frames, the seduction wouldn't take more than an hour. An hour I expected to save and savor, tell to my granddaughters. I could make up a lot of it in

advance, just in case, take my time, get good sleep thinking
about it. Besides, I knew biology. Or, rather, I knew where
my ignorance of biology could trip me up.

I hadn't read *Our Bodies, Ourselves* since the time in my
life when the notion of pregnancy had been a scary one. For
a few years there, when I was in college and believed one
boy after another, I trotted the book out every few months,
never absorbing cycles and expectations well enough to avoid
going back to it the next time. I alternated among saving for
an abortion, expecting my period, being glad the boy was
college material with pretty eyes, and expecting that now I
would be in love and getting married, not having to stay in
school. The book was water stained and faded from having
been read in the bathroom and on the beach. Sometimes in
private, sometimes in public, depending on my level of panic,
my need of solidarity with other girls, the general politics of
pregnancy.

I went to K&B and bought a thermometer, something I
never expected to own. There was no at-home taking care
of people at my house. While I was at it I bought a pack of
graph paper, a six-inch plastic ruler, and a fine-line felt-tip
pen. I was going to save the chart to show my child, an easy
way to give her the false notion that I enjoyed precision. With
precision, I could get a girl, too. I bought vitamins and calcium
and iron tablets, all in bottles with wholesome wheat sheaves
on the logo and a California distributor named on the label.
Robust-looking bottles. Every morning I took my temperature
before I got out of bed, marked it on the chart, and washed
down five pills with a glass of orange juice. I began to notice
myself; my body might be something more than a vehicle for
carting my brain around.

The chart rose and plummeted the way it was supposed
to. It was funny to discover tracks of normalcy that probably
always were there, unsung, rhythms that other people couldn't
take for granted. I wondered if I'd have an equally splendid
EKG or EEG. I quit going to Lucille's shop; I stayed off
Tchoupitoulas Street; I routed away from places having to

do with film: rolls, negatives, prints, transparencies, changes of original perceptions.

I'd watch the chart, make the appointment. Not say that I wanted to be wearing any particular amount of clothing. It'd be a brisk day. I'd wear a coat. Maybe I could borrow Charlotte's London Fog. I pictured myself in it. Good, she'd let me use it, not knowing the reason. He'd sit me on a stool. He'd wait for me to take off my coat, but wouldn't come out and ask. I'd cross my knees. Black panty hose. And very high heels. No, that would just hold things up. Black stockings on a garter belt. Where do you buy a garter belt, K&B? He'd get behind the camera, and I'd let the coat fall open. No clothes underneath. I couldn't tell whether I liked the idea of the garter belt. I'd try it in front of a mirror. He'd stop, stare. I'd uncross my legs, see if he came closer. I'd step down off the stool, no very high heels to catch on the rung. Glide over to him, coat open just enough. In the coat, we could fuck right there, on the paper backdrop. Or maybe go back to his bed. I'd seen the corner of it. It wasn't far.

The second time the line dropped, I went in to work exulting. Now I could begin counting down, making arrangements. Four more weeks; my body was such an excellent instrument. Charlotte fed into the mood. It was an extraordinary day, a Colorado day; no humidity, no clouds, as if someone, once a year like clockwork, lifted the pall from New Orleans.

"Ever been to the Bright Star?" she asked me. No, why? Arthur was out of town, and this year Charlotte wasn't going to sit at home and eat her own cooking. At least not the first night. This year? Every year, she explained, Arthur went to the shopping center convention in Las Vegas. Why didn't she go?

"I went once. It was hard not to give in to total greed. Talk about too much of too much! Freebies are *serious*. I mean booths where they give you half a fried chicken, so you'll put their franchise in your shopping center. Or a bro-cade carpetbag so you'll put your supermarket in their shopping center at some wagon crossing in Pig's Knuckle, Alabama. The American Library Association, *maybe* somebody'll give you a button that says 'fight the stupids, read,' or something. Let Arthur go to Las Vegas and choke on excess!" Charlotte looked pretty pleased with herself.

"Are you asking me to the Bright Star? I'll pay my way, of course. If you're asking me. Are you asking me?" That was a lot of excitement for the Bright Star. It was a restaurant that looked as if it once had been a neighborhood grocery store or an illegal gambling parlor, the corner lopped off so that the door favored neither street. The cuisine was New Orleans–suicide, nothing kosher, oysters and pickled pork and breaded veal cutlets—things the Jews probably prohibited because they knew that, five thousand years down the line, their descendants would be prone to high blood pressure.

"I'm asking you. I'll treat you. I'll *drive* you. For God's sake, Darby, has it ever occurred to you that someone might enjoy your company?" I shrugged. My father had thought I was pretty funny.

"I want an oyster po-boy with just butter on it; keep the pickles away, I don't like even a drop of pickle juice on it," I was saying to Charlotte, mid-morning. Breakfast was making the last gurgle down the drain, and I was thinking about food, skipping ahead to dinner. The phone rang. Charlotte was in the glue pot, and I answered. "Darby Cooper, please?" A male voice. Mid-month, my bills were paid. A doctor, a lawyer, someone had died. "This is Parker Rutledge, your neighbor across Tchoupitoulas."

"That how you define yourself?" I said. He didn't respond. "My house on fire?"

"Not that I know of. And I do chase fires." I laughed, said nothing. He waited, then asked me to dinner. For that night. I thought of many possibilities. Of eating two dinners. Of telling him I couldn't. I didn't think of asking Charlotte to postpone or cancel. Letty came to mind too fast. She didn't know it, but I'd drawn a line down the center of the earth, putting all Letty's behaviors on one side. Only what sat on the other side was open to me. Oh, I can't, I said, I made plans already. Some other time? he said. That would be terrific, I said, a bit sad, so he knew it wasn't a lie. How about twenty-eight days from today? I thought about saying. I'm trying to get up my nerve to have you take a photo of me, I said. So call, he said.

The minute I hung up, Charlotte offered to cancel. She'd begun waving vigorously at me when she heard me say I had plans, the glue brush stuck in two fingers, giving the impression that she was glue-painting the air. I'd ignored her. No, I said, it'd be more fun talking to you about him than actually going out with him. I find that hard to believe, Charlotte said. You've never had to live vicariously, I told her. True, she said, Arthur is very real and very present. She wasn't complaining at all.

Parker walked into the Bright Star right when I had shoved a forkful of pecan pie and vanilla ice cream into my mouth. Charlotte was in the middle of describing the stranglehold the unions had on Las Vegas, imagining Arthur negotiating whether he could use his own hammer to realign the booth to his satisfaction. I figured I could take a greedy mouthful, enjoy it, roll the textures around, the cold and the hot driving the nerves in my teeth crazy, not being called on to speak for at least a minute.

I smiled at him, chipmunk cheeked, and Charlotte turned around. Come join us, she called, her mouth empty of everything but her own monologue. Parker looked at me, and I nodded my head up and down enthusiastically. I was trying to chew and swallow while appearing to do neither, though it was a restaurant.

"The oysters are huge tonight," I said by way of conversation. Charlotte rolled her eyes at me; this was not going to be easy. She got up with her purse and walked over toward the bar. The hallway to the bathroom was right past it; I paid no attention. Parker said nothing; he was watching Charlotte out of the corner of his eye. "See, I really did have plans," I said. "I never went out to dinner with Charlotte before. But

Arthur's out of town, and she asked me." I remembered the dinner party. "Well, I actually did have dinner with her before, but never *out*. Though you could argue the point, since I didn't really finish . . ."

Charlotte came and stood beside the table. She said she wasn't feeling well, could Parker take me home? I stood up; Charlotte was full of enough cholesterol to have a heart attack or a stroke or something, and no one was at her house. I stood too fast, and the Formica-topped table moved three inches, tipping my iced-tea glass over. "Sure," Parker said, and by the time I'd mopped up the mess with skinny little dispenser paper napkins, she was gone.

The waitress came to take his order. Just coffee, he said. I raised my eyebrows. You didn't come into the Bright Star for a cup of coffee. Rather, you didn't travel all the way from Tchoupitoulas Street for one. I wasn't hungry, he explained, I sort of came here on instinct. Charlotte call you? I asked. For what? I shrugged. I had this sort of psychic message. That never happen to you? Yeah, I said, but usually it's a warning to stay *away* from somewhere. So I never know what I've missed. He laughed.

Charlotte had paid my bill. There was no balance between her and me, and I'd quit trying to create one. Charlotte had so much more money to spare, and to me balances could be tallied on ledgers. "I should've come earlier," Parker said when the waitress handed him a slip and said, "Seventy-five cents; your friend paid for her."

I was trembling by the time we reached Tchoupitoulas Street. I dared not talk; he'd hear the tremor. He pulled into his lot, did a three-sixty with the headlights, pulled up against the building. "I'd like you to come up," he said. I nodded in the dark.

I followed him, my focus on the back of him, not on protecting myself. I padded behind, quiet and proprietary, as if he were a quite splendid sculpture I'd just bought at auction. There was more light in the elevator vestibule. I stood behind him; I wanted to skim my finger over the crack in his ass.

Lightly, to own it. I said nothing. He keyed the elevator, not a word.

A third-floor loft in an empty warehouse is a sinister place at night. Parker put on no lights, but the street illumination, with no curtains, no blinds, nothing, was quite fine. Secure, I nevertheless wanted to cover my back; I didn't want to walk behind him. The structural supports, the paper backdrop for nude Cooper women, the stand of partitions, they hid something.

He said nothing. In his sleeping space was a double futon, with a black cover and a swath of silk draped across it, tropical birds hand-painted on it in night-jungle colors. He began undoing my blouse. He smelled like coffee and Irish Spring soap. I wanted to do this for a long time, but I was afraid, he whispered. It seemed he agreed that something was hiding in the shadows. Why were you afraid? I'm still afraid. That I might not be able to do this. I told him not to be scared, and in the half-light I could see him smile indulgently.

When he had me undressed, he kneeled beside the futon, and I lay down next to him. He still had on all his clothes. He ran his hands over my body, much more gently than I'd have touched him. He pressed my knees apart, easy, I wanted it. He licked my clit, back and forth, as if I were making it up the way I wanted it; I closed my eyes and imagined myself imagining him doing this. I came so fast, and he knew I came, and he stopped for a second and made me come again. One more, I said, and he teased me with his fingers, then gave me one more.

The idea of getting pregnant didn't occur to me until after Parker had come, too, his clothes still on, like in the Hubig's pie dream. He slipped a pillow under me to keep the globs and dribbles off the black futon, and that's when I realized that it was staying inside me. I had a sense that I'd done something right, that there had been no interference, that this was supposed to happen. The night when I was full of peanut oil and oysters and cane syrup and butterfat, a New Orleans beginning. I'd ask Charlotte tomorrow, make sure she hadn't gotten in the way of serendipity.

CHAPTER 10

I think there is a life passage that no one talks about. It's when fantasies shift. I know mine shifted the first time when I was in fifth grade. Up until that point my daydreams had been grandiose, full of free-floating adulation. Usually I found a cure for cancer; "it's spit, I'm simply surprised no one ever thought of why it was there before," I'd say to the reporters gathering on my parents' front steps. That was the general stuff of go-to-sleep fantasy, once I'd gotten over thinking about death and trying to pretend that one day I'd go to a place of eternal chocolate. In fifth grade my breasts began to sprout, tiny hard lumps that I covered with spit, just in case. I began to dream myself to sleep with stories of my teacher Mr. Erskine, the two of us huddled in a lifeboat, touching, not doing anything because I didn't know the mechanics of it all. Mr. Erskine turned out to be gay, of course; this was New Orleans in the sixties. But I didn't learn that until I was grown, heard he hustled guys in the bars on Carrollton Avenue. Sex was my dream substance from that time, until the night at Parker's. Then I shifted back to grandiosity, on a small scale, if that was possible. As I said, I think it's a life passage, though I've only asked one person. A quite beautiful girl in my sophomore psych class at Newcomb. Don't you have fantasies? I'd asked her. I *live* my fantasies, she'd said. I thought it was because she was so beautiful. She was found stabbed to death in her apartment five years later, having gone too far, it seemed.

I didn't sleep at Parker's that night. He dozed off, and I slipped out. It was easier getting out of the warehouse than into it; Parker hadn't locked the security gate, and the elevator would go to one for anybody. Tchoupitoulas Street was less traveled late at night, with trucks having nowhere to go with their cargo. I saw three dogs and four cats in the half-block walk; they were moving slowly, unafraid, no wonder they got confused in the circadian rhythms and got run over so often.

I went to bed thinking about Charlotte, that now I was going to save her, and she was going to be grateful. I'd bring my baby to work, and Charlotte would hold it, soften up. She could share it, have someone in her life when Arthur was out of town, it could sleep over. If I died, it could go live with her; whom else? Letty had no use for the child she'd already raised, and Marmee had no brain at all. Murray screeched the time I said I thought Marmee needed a kitten. I wasn't going to do a Sydney Carton, though I could let Charlotte think I might, write a will and tell her about it. Charlotte paid for so many of my meals and ate along with me; Charlotte let me disappear all the time and told me that being with me might be something a person would actually want. If I died, Charlotte would be a good mother substitute for my baby.

I began spotting two weeks later. A few red-brown stains in clean white cotton, unexpected or I'd have been wearing pilled blue nylon. I came out of the bathroom in the library, and my plans began to shift. Parker had phoned the day after the conception, and I hadn't been at my desk. I hadn't called him back, hadn't answered my phone that night, even after Letty came driving over, honking her horn in front of my door. In a mostly black neighborhood. Honkie bitch, they probably joked when she did that. And I'd told her never to do that. When he called the next day, I said to Charlotte, loudly, genially, Tell him I'm in the middle of something, I'll try to call him back. You're nuts, Charlotte said an hour later, when I was still in the middle of nothing. Arthur came back late that night, and Charlotte tied our line up half the next morning; Parker didn't try again, as far as I knew. He wasn't going to get involved; it was scary that he might. The spots meant I had to start over again. I picked up the phone.

I'd make an appointment to have him take my photograph. But, wait, did I need the London Fog? The chart, the chart wasn't working. Reopen contact. I saw some baklava at the Greek bakery on Willow Street last week when Charlotte took me there to buy pita stuffed with goat cheese and olives. I'd get him some baklava. There were no tampons in my desk. I went back into the bathroom and put toilet paper in my underpants. It was late morning. Charlotte, I've got an important errand. Go. I'd never had an important errand before. I had a new solenoid switch on the car, and a new passenger window; the brake-tag inspection people had laughed when I'd driven in, hadn't even taken my registration form, told me I was wasting my time, come back when I had a whole car. A lot of money, but now I could go around town and get back on time, not have to park on inclines, of which there were maybe three in the parish. I got to the bakery before the lunch rush, got to Parker's lot just as a dozen Import China chicks walked out the gate toward Lucille's. No one in the elevator going up; it went to three when I pushed the button. The security gate was locked. I held the Door Open button and called his name. No answer. Again. I waited. The elevator would close if I let the button go. I put the cake box on the floor, reached in my purse for a pen, switched hands, put my elbow on the Door Open button, picked up the cake box and wrote From Darby on it, switched hands again, dropped the pen, began turning the box sideways, gently, to fit through the wrought iron gate. I didn't see Parker until he was almost to the elevator. Hi, he said, neutral, no joy in seeing me. I had the box and my right hand through the gate, down at the bottom, ready to set it delicately on the floor. This is for you, I said, it says From Darby. It's from Darby, that's me. He took the box, my elbow came off the Door Open button, and the door began to close. He didn't move, so I hit the three button, and the door opened again. Thanks, he said, can't let you in; I'm in the darkroom, see you later. I didn't believe him exactly, though I wasn't sure why. The door closed, and I went down. I hadn't even gotten pitas for me and Charlotte, thinking something might happen. I should have known that buying a perishable food-stuff was the best way to plan on altered plans. I picked up the pen on my way out. When I went to the bathroom at the library, there were no spots on the toilet paper. No more came after that, and it was just as well.

I liked the anonymity of shopping in big places, of getting prescriptions filled where the druggist changes by shifts and never knows your name, supermarkets where the grocery checkout women are so numerous and transient that you never get the same one twice. For my test, I could have gone to the doctor and gotten a very personal lecture. Usually I went to what I referred to in Letty's presence as a JDPS—to aggravate her. JDPS: Jewish Doctor on Prytania Street. They were a breed, all Letty's age, half Letty's high-school mates, all about as smart and up-to-date as my cousin William was as an attorney. Men—all men—whose mommies coddled them through the Depression and pushed them to medical school on mediocrity, men who grew up arrogant and never read a text or journal after 1950. I might have had to go to one soon, but only after I had the fact of the pregnancy and, with it, the resolve to answer all his questions with a look that said he was unthinking and crazy. I went to Delta Women's Clinic instead.

Delta Women's Clinic was known for two things: one, the picketers who showed up pretty regularly to protest abortion, the clinic's reason for being; and two, its lemon-sherbet-yellow facade, with its name in slightly uneven two-foot letters over the door in black. Ride the streetcar uptown from Canal Street, and you couldn't miss it. Free pregnancy tests. It wasn't fair, I knew, to go in for a test when they weren't going to get my two hundred dollars in business afterwards, but that was the merchant's gamble. Give away balloons, customers will come in to browse, maybe buy the next time.

Brimming with human chorionic gonadotropin, I went there first thing Saturday, not having peed, nervous anyway. The picketers were out, I supposed because Saturday-morning trade was brisk, dump the baby and get back to work Monday morning, miss only a couple of cartoon shows. You know you're going to commit murder, a man said to me. He had no chin, probably very little spine, a polyester plaid shirt, shiny dark brown slacks, lace-up black shoes on a Saturday morning. I'm going in for a test, I told him. I thought it would make him feel better. No, you're not. I *am*, time me. I'll be out in ten minutes. And then what? he said. Then I'll call up for the good news. What if it's bad news? Your idea of what I think is bad news is way off, I want it, I said. Another woman walked up, skinny and nervous, wearing no wedding ring but accompanied by her equally skinny boyfriend. My evangelist left me for less ambiguous prey. I was the first customer, a numeral one on my cup, call back at noon. I called at noon; they put me on hold for five minutes. The results aren't ready, call back at one. I should have known, my adrenaline was pumping, a sign that I knew nothing was going to happen. At one I was calm, expecting nothing. Positive, do you want to make an appointment? I have to think it over, and I'll call back, I said. I didn't want to hurt anyone's feelings, not hers, not the man's on the picket line. I didn't believe in anything in particular, about abortion, about politics, about religion, about ethics. It gave me the neutrality to want everyone to feel triumphant. I always bought the books from the Jehovah's Witnesses. No harm done; everyone was dealing in statistics. Their statistics made them feel good, so I swelled as many ranks as possible. Positive, a bit of data for someone. For me a huge globe of a fact, if I could hold on to it.

With most matters I never particularly liked being alone; I thought it would be natural and right to put them to someone else. I wasn't lonely with this new fact. It was a private joke with myself, out smug in public places, no longer bothered by pairs of people. I stood behind a couple at the Winn-Dixie checkout. She was tiny, less than five feet, with bleached permed-tight curls. He was a foot taller with beer on his belly and on his breath, and he kept nuzzling her neck. I smiled at her. I liked my fact.

I began throwing up the next day. Suggestible, probably; the book said that the more tenacious the pregnancy was, the sicker I'd be. Signals made full circuit in my body, fulfilling their own prophecies.

It took Charlotte only a week and a half to figure out what was going on. She eyed me suspiciously when I brought in a thermos, a recent purchase at K&B, plaid with a red cup. It cost more than the ones with GI Joe and Strawberry Shortcake; it was station wagon tailgate picnic style, stolid and settled. The type a mom would have. I filled it with orange juice, smelled the orange juice, imagined it coming right up again, rinsed it well, and filled it with milk. Charlotte watched as I filled the little red cup, all pleased with myself. Someone just tell you that you have a terminal disease or something? she asked. She'd never seen me drink anything that wasn't full of carbonation, sugar, or caffeine, preferably all three. No, I said, I just see myself differently. The milk didn't stay down, came up curdled and foul an hour later. I made it to the bathroom, and Charlotte didn't know that day for sure. But I lost my lunch every afternoon, and the bathroom spies brought the word back to Charlotte. The ladies who worked in the library were messy; that was their word for themselves, used proudly; messy meant looking for a pile of shit to poke a stick into and stir around. Except for the sisters, and Charlotte, and me, everyone in the place had dropped a handful of babies into the fifties, and they knew what all the puking meant, now that their daughters were marrying and having little sons and getting divorced and coming home and getting pregnant with no husbands this time and reminding them. When I came back to my desk, pale and smelling of Aquafresh, Charlotte grabbed my arm as I passed. Charlotte would have made a good third-grade teacher. Hold on, she said, you have some explaining to do.

I let her hold on to my arm, and I looked down at the

floor. I'd done a lot of thinking about how I was going to
give this news to Charlotte, and the place wasn't the cataloguing office at the library. Her house, sitting neat on a
regency chair, some restaurant, with wineglasses. "Would you
like to be a godmother?" I said softly.

She let my arm drop, swiveled in her chair until her back
was to me. I stood still, I could have walked around to look
at her face, but I didn't. She stayed that way for a while, and
I went back to my desk. I had a stack of OCLC cards, and
I went through them, seeing nothing, went through them
again. When Charlotte turned back in my direction, she kept
her face down, her focus on some books on the floor that she
went into and out of over and over, not finding the information she needed, though it was right there up front. When
she looked up, her face was fine, schoolteacher-inscrutable.
Are you aware of what you're doing? she said. I nodded. I'm
almost thirty-five, I said, I know what I'm doing. In some
measure, she said, her tone a bit mean. Somehow I thought
you'd be happy, I said. Charlotte shrugged. Do your work,
we'll talk later, she said.

I waited half an hour. I set myself a goal, a half hour,
and I did my work that way, checking my watch. What's
your maiden name? I asked her when the half hour was up.
The words startled in the silence, and I expected the phone
to ring right then, take away the impact. Honoree, she said,
why? She was okay now, thinking this was old prattle, questions from the blue. You ever been aware of your breathing?
Your fingernails? Your tongue? I'd say out of nowhere. Ever
wonder about colors you can't see? Who was your best friend
when you were twelve? *Honoree*, that's French, right? Yeah,
but why? What's it mean? *Honored*, she said, but what's this
all about? I thought honor was *honneur*, I said. *Honored*, she
said. I'll be in Reference, I told her.

All the foreign-language dictionaries were on a single
shelf, *Cassell*'s, one of each—French, German, Italian, Portuguese, Greek, Russian, Latin—and a thin little volume of

Esperanto-English. No Spanish. Spanish must have gone out under somebody's jacket last winter, Spanish was the most popular foreign language. Even with no Hispanics. Practicality, don't study anything that you can't use in the marketplace, that was the St. Francis credo. No Japanese; they were only thinking of the New Orleans marketplace. I looked up *honoree* in the French-English dictionary; Charlotte was right, of course. It was her name, though she hadn't had it now for most of her life. Honoree was too pretentious, like Desiree. Girls who now were having babies named Latonya and Shellonda had names like Desiree; I read the birth announcements. No husbands, except at Southern Baptist Hospital, of course. I plucked a few more dictionaries off the shelf. Honored wasn't in them, just honor, spelled *honour*, something at St. Francis geared to the world marketplace. Italian, *onore*, Onore Cooper. Too African sounding. Portuguese, *honra*, not bad, but a pronunciation problem. Russian—all in cyrillic script, not worth teaching myself in one afternoon. Same with Greek. German, *ehren*. Not bad at all. For a boy. Though in uptown New Orleans everyone would think it was Aaron. Or Erin. Spelling problems, but worth thinking about. Esperanto, the deciding vote. Honor. Honor Cooper. I would try to have a girl named Honor Cooper. Classy. Even if it did rhyme a bit.

"What do you think of the name Honor Cooper?" I whispered when I walked back into our office.

"I think you're crazy," Charlotte said. She wasn't so angry now, I could tell.

"Oh, God, the puns," I said. "A tribute to you. An *honor*. I have to be careful, you know. Jews don't name babies after living people. They figure the Angel of Death might be checking his list and see Charlotte and come down and get the baby instead of you."

"Sounds like a great reason for having a baby named after yourself," she said.

"Jews are into generations and begats and stuff," I said.

Charlotte slapped her forehead. "How'll you survive?"

"Either I will or I won't. And if I don't, you can have it."

"Oh."

"If you want it, that is." Here's a million dollars, I'm saying to a Zen Buddhist, after he's figured out how to go through the rest of his life free of desire.

"You have a long time to think about this," she said.

"I'm not a godly person, you know, I wouldn't expect it to be Jewish or anything like that."

"You want an ungodlymother, so you pick the most ungodly person you know," she said, smiling sadly.

"I mean that in the kindest sense," I said, and she laughed.

CHAPTER 11

I dare any woman, that is any woman who is not pregnant this very minute, to say that the process of having a baby is anything but an abstraction. You get the fact of a positive test result, and then you expect that you will go into a short-lived dream state until one morning at 3 A.M. someone hands you an extra person. In reality, of course, as soon as you thicken you become slow prey for everyone else's fantasies. In my case, all their fantasies were litigious. Maybe it was that finding villains is more fun than finding layettes; probably it was that they all just wanted to be angry.

I turned out to be like Veronica, skinny enough to keep it to myself for as long as I needed to. Unfortunately, Veronica had keened up Murray's senses for impending disaster, and in my fourth month she noticed. What happened to your titties? she asked. Then, Wait, I *don't* want to know. I'd only put on five pounds, all in my breasts, fine with Dr. Avvie Cohen. He expected that a Jewish girl wanted to leave the hospital in her Cacharel jeans, that little weight gain was fine, never mind that I was a cadaver with giant breasts for three months. Not you, too, Murray said. You don't know what kind of trouble you getting into. Veronica seemed like she had to go halfway to the Supreme Court, and she *black*. A white girl, where you going to prove discrimination?

"That's all you can say?"

"What you want me to say? You pregnant, right?"

I nodded. Marmee looked up. You're pregnant? she parroted. You're thirsty? she might as well have said. Marmee was locked into the second, like someone smoking marijuana, forgetting the beginning of the sentence before the end was

out of her mouth. The meaning never had a chance to stick
around.

"They going to throw your total ass out that school,"
Murray said. "Veronica went four years to Southern, and
she'd be selling chicken legs at Popeye's if not for your cousin
William. And I swear he got her back on with the School
Board because she black. Got the *union*. You got no union I
know of. And come to think of it, you got no particular
cousin William, either. He might want to help Veronica
run around with a bastard, but he ain't going to want to
help *you*."

"I'm not worried." I had reciprocal privileges at the Tulane Law Library. Which of course was nothing like a real
library, but I knew two people who worked there. Librarians
know that the only questions they will ever get are stupid
questions, though they tell you the opposite in graduate school.
Anyone with sense can find the answer to a smart question
with no help. I want to read about the Equal Employment
Opportunities Commission, I had told my friend who was
on the night shift. She knew I worked at St. Francis: You
haven't got anything in your library on the EEOC? she'd said
incredulously. Hey, I'd said, the EEOC wasn't even *invented*
the last time St. Francis acquired a book. You must have a
snap of a job as a cataloguer, she'd said, and I'd laughed. St.
Francis got federal money, St. Francis lived and breathed
federal money. The statue of the Virgin outside the president's
office bled federal money. They couldn't fire me. Besides,
abortion wasn't exactly a *sacrament*. I could practically be a
campus hero if I played it right. I am truly not worried, I
said to Murray.

"That what Veronica said. I'm not worried. Shit, you
don't think them sisters going to take this so easy? They want
something poking in they dried up holes so bad they can taste
it. You walk in there advertising that you no virgin, they
going to make you pay. You know better than to think they
holy women." The poor Negroes of Gert Town had been the
Sisters of the Holy Comforter's stepping-stones to salvation

for probably thirty years. Murray had watched them float through her neighborhood, fearless and arrogant, for as long as that. She'd seen them caress the big men's biceps and cuff the little boys' heads, and she knew they had bad passions worse than most women.

"Sister Roberta can't touch me."

"Maybe not direct, but she can sure touch you with a ten-foot pole. You *don't* lose your job, you may be damn sorry. You come back with a baby, and every time that baby sneeze, she dock your pay. I know. I worked for this old cow forty years."

"I'm hungry," Marmee said, aware of the focus shifting onto her.

"Yeah, you hungry all right. You don't know about being hungry." Murray pulled the cut-up fruit bowl out of the refrigerator, even though she had a pork chop frying on the stove. The piggy grease smell and the cigarette smoke were getting to me, but I knew better than to complain. "You want some?" she said to me, and I shook my head no.

"Can I take some home?" It would taste good in my house. Murray slid the glass cup across the table to Marmee like an old-time saloon keeper. She filled up a margarine tub with fruit, snapped on the lid, and dropped it into my purse. I tried to think of what might be ruined by the syrup.

"It ain't going to leak," Murray said, reading my mind and peeved. "You told Letty?"

"She's out of town."

"By the looks of you, you had ample time to tell her *before*."

I looked down at my waist. I'd moved the button over an inch, but I couldn't see a difference.

"I'm leaving it up to fate," I said. Letty was on a month-long trip to Europe with Eddie. She'd been gone almost two weeks. I figured that telling her when she was across the ocean was a top-notch plan. She could get a lot of mileage out of the news with Eddie: poor me, she'd say a dozen different ways in as many cities, and there was a small chance that she would sit on an airplane or a train for a stretch of time and think. So far, though, fate wasn't making matters easy for me. Letty hadn't called.

Murray ignored me. "She going to teetotally kill you."

"It's not going to cost her anything," I said.

"Veronica ain't cost me nothing, either. But I'm not exactly walking around town bragging about her. What you think Letty going to tell people?"

"Hey, Murray, she's going to love it." The minute the words were out, I knew they were true. "She probably'll wish she'd had the nerve. She won't say it, but she'll think it."

Letty phoned that night. She was in London. It was the middle of the night there, and Eddie was asleep. Letty had pulled the phone into the bathroom. "Can you hear me?" she hissed. "Yes," I hissed back.

"He's driving me out of my mind," she said. "We go to grocery stores. Or what passes for grocery stores in this godforsaken part of the world. He looks at olive oil bottles. He dives in freezer cases, looking for God-knows-what. I've quit going out with him."

"What do you do?"

"Stay here, what do you think?"

"I think if I were in London, I'd get on the underground and go look at stuff."

"Well, it's a good thing it's me here, and not you. I'd be worried sick if I thought you were running around strange places unescorted."

"I live a half block off Tchoupitoulas Street; I'd take terrorists any time. At least they're not so personal."

"This is costing me money," Letty said.

"Want me to call you back?" The last thing I wanted was the power Letty would gain over me if she paid for hearing my news transatlantic.

"No!" she whispered. "He's sleeping."

"You're not having fun?"

"You know I'm not having fun. The whole purpose in

my life is to avoid food, and Eddie's whole purpose in life is to look at it. We go into a restaurant, and he goes into the kitchen and checks out the produce. That's not exactly romantic."

Watching someone nibble on a lettuce leaf in six different languages isn't exactly romantic, either, I wanted to say. "Eat; you'll get his attention," I said.

"Get off my back, Darby."

"I'm serious. If you show him you love food, he'll love you." I wasn't thinking about Tom Jones sort of love, lust built on dribbles of food and tongues and teeth visibly busy, spittle advertising its aphrodisiac powers. Tom Jones the singer? she'd have said. I liked pictures of Letty when she was poor and chubby. Eddie would, too, I was sure. "Didn't you go to the Uffizi? Eddie's Italian; Christ, he looks at olive oil bottles, doesn't that tell you something? You see any skinny women in the Uffizi?"

"I don't know what you're talking about."

"Aw, soften up, Letty, just soften up."

"I didn't call for this kind of aggravation."

"I'm pregnant, Letty." Compound the error.

"You're what?" The whispering was over. But it wasn't shock; it was an instantaneous chance for attention. Not from me, from the sleeping Eddie.

"I'm in my fourth month. I decided if you phoned, I'd tell you."

"So you could ruin my vacation? Thanks a hell of a lot."

"You weren't having fun, anyway."

"I was, too."

"Okay, you were having fun. Sorry."

"Get an abortion. I'll pay for it, and you can pay me back. I'll call William this afternoon, nine o'clock your time. You can go pick up a check at his office by ten, I'm sure. Just call."

"I did this on purpose."

"Then undo it on purpose."

"Why do you care?"

"Because you don't do things like this. Veronica I can understand, but you? What're you trying to do to me?"

"Nothing. I'm old enough to know that I'm still going to have a kid to raise long after you get over this phone call."

"I'm not talking about this goddamn phone call. You can leave New Orleans if you feel like it. I can't. I'm going to have to live with this. I don't deserve it."

"Jesus, Letty, you are not the center of the fucking universe."

"Don't talk to me like that. Especially on my nickel." She was getting shrill. It was a matter of seconds, I was sure, until she'd get Eddie's attention. Unless Eddie was as out of it when he slept as he evidently was when he banged women. I heard a male voice in the far background, or maybe muted through a door, though Letty probably had opened the bathroom door a crack, enough to let out a fat slice of light and a blast of her voice. She covered the receiver. Her nickel. She uncovered it, now for my benefit. "Let the girl alone," Eddie said. "I'm coming home this afternoon," Letty said. "I'll switch my reservation. Same flight as I was coming in on on the twenty-fifth. I'll call from the airport."

"No!" I hollered, but she had hung up.

I was in Charlotte's car when I heard the news story. I was an eating fiend at odd hours of the day, and Charlotte was willing to go along, never mind that half the time I threw up and she had gained four pounds. We were driving up Carrollton to Cuco's, and I was imagining fajitas and flan. "Why don't you just throw five bucks in the toilet and avoid the middle man?" she was saying. Charlotte liked WAJY-FM 102; it was playing low, but key words came through. Heathrow. Turn it up, I told her, then reached for the knob myself. A suitcase bomb in Heathrow 3, at a Pan Am gate. I felt nothing, and that meant something had happened. Letty's there, I said. You have to take me to a phone. There was a pay phone at K&B on Claiborne, and Charlotte pulled in the exit drive, angling against the grain. I don't know what to do, I said, sitting in the car next to the pay phone. Call her hotel, Charlotte said. She's checked out, she's coming home. I couldn't sequence. Her friend, too? No, I said. But I don't know what hotel. So who knows where he is? One of them must have left an itinerary. Letty just left her flight numbers, going and coming, nothing in between, figured maybe I'd bother her. Which I'd never do, of course.

Call the airline, Charlotte said. I fished for a quarter, couldn't find one, Charlotte scooped one off her dashboard. No phone book. I used the quarter, got the number, mumbled it all the way back to the car. Another quarter, I said, one-eight-hundred, two-two-one, one-one-one-one. Toll free, you don't need a quarter. You do to get a dial tone; this is a fucking dial phone, nothing fancy, one-eight-hundred, two-two-one, one-one-one-one. The line was busy. I dialed again. More frantic, glad it was a dial, the ones and twos were fast, it felt as if I was getting away with something. Finally, a recording. No information available at this time, please call back. I got the quarter back. I'd call Marino's. They had to know where Eddie was, what if there was a fire? I didn't know the number. Take me to Marino's, I told Charlotte as I bounced in. No seat belt, this was an emergency.

Charlotte drove with demonic speed, daring someone to pull her over, though police in New Orleans never pulled people over; it didn't occur to them. "I haven't felt like this since I was very small," I said. "It's like being homesick. You ever feel like that? Where you wanted your mother, where a letter from her, or a pair of socks she rolled up for you make you want to cry? I sort of thought I was past that."

"It's your mother, for God's sake," Charlotte said.

"I haven't thought about her that way for a long time," I said.

I jumped from the car as soon as Charlotte pulled into the parking lot, tore past checkout, past the butcher's counter, the smell of sawdust and disinfectant. The office was down a narrow corridor at the back; I only knew because a small sign, like you can buy in the drugstore, OFFICE, was tacked

on the wall, always had been, even when there were two
drinking fountains at the back, one white, one colored. Both
spewed clear water, no rainbows, a mystery to me for all the
years it took for the signs to disappear. The office was paneled,
with low ceilings, soundproofed, vinyl and pressed wood the
theme, ochre and pea-green the color scheme. Are you Evelyn? I asked the woman at the desk. She was about seventy
and had flaming red hair and tiny rhinestones on her glasses.
I'd never met her; my father believed in my visiting the store
only as a customer. She nodded. I'm Darby. She gave me a
blank stare. Darby Cooper. She smiled with apprehension
and recognition. Letty's in London with Eddie, and maybe
they're both dead, there's been a bomb in the airport, and I
think they're both in the airport. Evelyn blanched, her face
as white as her hair probably was naturally. I don't know
what to tell you, she said. Tell me the name of their hotel, I
said. She went over to another desk, a bigger, messier desk,
and rifled through a stack of papers until she found two pale
pink sheets stapled together. The Savoy, she said. A phone
number? I said. She shrugged. More than a quarter for di-
rectory assistance to London. I could call the travel agency.
But what the hell, this was an emergency; Eddie could pay
for this, especially if he was dead. I got the number, got the
room for Eddie Marino, it rang. He wasn't dead, he was still
checked in to the hotel, unless he took Letty, distraught and
clinging, to the airport. Five times, no room was that big. Six
times. Finally, a hello.

"Letty?" I began to cry.

"Darby? What's the matter? What's the matter with
Mother?"

"Nothing."

"Where are you? It's the middle of the day over there.
We're going out to dinner in half an hour, you almost
missed us."

"I'm at Marino's. I thought you were dead."

Letty began to laugh. "She thinks we're dead," she said
to Eddie.

"There's been a bombing."

"At the airport, Darby. London is a very big city."

"At the terminal that Pan Am goes through. Where you'd have been if you were coming home today."

"I'm not coming home for two weeks, you know that."

"You said you were coming home today." I was beginning to scream, and Charlotte walked in. She put a hand on my shoulder, and Evelyn looked relieved.

"I forgot," she said. "Eddie got up, and it was almost morning, and we decided to explore when it was just day-break, and I forgot."

"Oh."

"What're you doing at Marino's?"

"How else was I going to track you?"

Letty covered the receiver. Okay by me, it was Eddie's nickel. She was going to figure that out next. One minute, two minutes. "You shouldn't have done that."

"I thought it was an emergency."

"Well, it wasn't. Those people know I'm here with Eddie?"

"Of course. What was I supposed to do, ask for Eddie's number and not give an explanation?"

"You could have told them you needed it for me or something. Are you in the room with Evelyn? Yes or no, just say yes or no."

"Yes."

"And she knows everything?"

"I guess." I was really crying now.

"Sometimes you don't think, Darby."

"No, sometimes I don't. Like when I think my mother is lying splattered all over an airline concourse. Letty, I thought you were dead."

"Well, I'm not," she said and hung up.

CHAPTER 12

When I was a freshman in college, my parents made me live in the dorm. Half the point of going to college is to grow up, Letty said when my father chafed at the cost. I wouldn't know, he said. Well, I wouldn't, either, Letty said. Letty went to Newcomb, too, lived right in Marmee's house, drove her own car to campus, made a passing attempt at being a good AEPhi. While my father was alive, Letty admitted freely that she'd never grown up. After he died, of course, she was owed something, and she happily switched the blame over to him.

My roommate, Tikki, was from Baton Rouge, and all she had in common with me was that she was Jewish. From New Orleans going to Newcomb is no big deal, only one girl from my school ever got turned down, and she married a rich Tulane boy anyway. From Baton Rouge, you had something to prove, and Tikki was frantic with worry. Only she had the mission to excel in college; why anyone else was there was a great solipsistic mystery to her. She rattled into the room at 3 A.M. reeking of cigarettes, flipped on a lamp, lit up a Viceroy, and tore through pages looking for something she didn't know. By November I despised Tikki, and my mission was to avoid her. Not to sleep or study or even eat. I camped on friends' floors, left my tray in the UC if she walked in, skipped assignments if my books got caught in the room with her. Spaces got smaller and smaller as the year wore on, at the time in my life when my world should have been seeping out over its edges. Instead of poking and probing the far reaches of the campus and town, no parents watching, I found a handful of refuges and darted furtively among them. Tikki never knew I despised her. I saw her in Winn-

Dixie once when I was twenty-seven. She had a curly-headed little boy, raspberries, and red peppers at two-fifty a pound in her basket. She'd only made it as far as produce and had spent ten dollars on nothing. She hugged me and kissed me, and I smelled day-old garlic on her breath. A rich bitch, no halfway measures for Tikki.

Avoiding Parker brought back all the stealth I'd learned at college, having absorbed little else. It was a matter of time more than place, lucky for me, living as I did a half block from him. My hours of coming and going had little to do with the way he lived his life, and I even could cruise past the warehouse to see whether his car was there. About when I was hitting the six-month mark and feeling a little poochy in the belly, I noticed his car was almost never in the lot. Intermittent reinforcement, a trained pigeon performs a task better when he only gets a reward some of the time. The car was there just often enough to keep me driving by again and again. All I had to do was make it until the baby was a few months old. Men couldn't gauge how old a baby was, at least not in the first few years. He wouldn't say, Hey, that kid looks five months and three days old, must be mine. Though later, when it was seven or so, he might say, Hey that kid looks seven, might be mine.

It was the litigious bent of everyone around me that tripped me up. Murray wanted to haul Sister Roberta into court, though the poor old woman hadn't said a word yet. Letty wanted to get the name of whoever did this to me so cavalierly, then slap him with a paternity suit. And Arthur, who knew everything Charlotte knew, thought all the flaming legal possibilities were a hoot.

I was over at Charlotte's nibbling peanuts and watching her kill a bottle of Cold Duck by herself the night Arthur came back from Dealmaking in New York. I could measure my pregnancy by the shopping center industry, whose members met exactly once every six months and in between sent all the retail phonies back to do battle with one another at all the major suburban intersections. I got pregnant when

Arthur was at the convention, a night I'd chronicled in flat
detail in a spiral notebook, the anecdote the kid might want
to hear one day. You weren't due in until noon tomorrow,
Charlotte giggled at him, not noticing at first that he had
Stephen Norris with him, each carrying a suitcase. We cleaned
up, got four Burger Kings and a goddamn Wal Mart, Arthur
crowed. I left the rest to Sid. I'm pooped. Want a drink?
Charlotte said to Stephen.

"So how's the little mommy?" Arthur said. He'd only
seen me three times in his life, but he had a lot of familiarity
with me and my case. That, plus two scotch and sodas on
the plane and two more at home, gave him certain liberties.

"*Shhh*," I said.

"Aw, you can tell Stephen. He knows about these things.
Love 'em and leave 'em, he's had one or two in his time, I'm
sure."

"Arthur!" Charlotte said, as if she didn't mean it. She
upended her glass and laughed.

"Come on, you tell the daddy yet? I think your mama's
right. Drag him into court. Make him pay for the rest of his
natural life, or eighteen years, whichever comes first. Of
course, I'll have to have the little daddy do all the photos for
my centers. He'll need the money. Right, Stephen?"

Stephen looked as if he were quite sober, observing the
rule of keeping steady while the client gets sloshed. Probably
Arthur's nonsense had been escalating for the past couple of
hours, and Stephen was ignoring him the way I ignored
Marmee. He had no reaction to the news, so Arthur happily
spelled it out for him. "Your friend Rutledge. I'll have to
give him all my business. Nice-looking guy. I'm sure you've
noticed."

"Arthur, shut the fuck up," Charlotte said. Finally we
were getting a glimpse of George and Martha, right when I
didn't want it.

Stephen was staring at Arthur; his eyes got a faraway
look, and he didn't turn when Charlotte spoke. He looked
as if he had just taken in too much information, as if he were

waiting for someone to process it for him, to chew it up like a mother bird and push it down his gorge before he could feel it.

"Babe, I know what I'm doing," Arthur said.

"Like fun you do. You come out in the kitchen."

Arthur shook his head no, slowly, keeping his irises dead center in his eyes to avoid vertigo. Charlotte stood up, hands on hips, but Arthur paid no attention. He leaned forward at the edge of his chair, his left elbow and most of his weight balancing precariously on his left knee. "There are secrets it's not fair to keep," he said to me.

"That's a philosophical issue," I said. "You can't just make that pronouncement."

"It's my house," Arthur said, and I smiled. He looked at Stephen for approval, but Stephen wasn't reacting, no please-the-client-at-all-costs all of a sudden.

"I want to talk to you," Charlotte said to Arthur.

"I know you do." He didn't move. Charlotte stood up, tipsy but knowing exactly what she was doing now, and squeezed herself in between Arthur and the arm of the sofa. "Miss me?" he said and laughed. She began whispering in his ear. I could see her head bobbing, emphasis on every other word. "Oh, shit," he said. "Why do you know things like that and I don't?" His vision was narrowed by alcohol; he didn't know Stephen and I were in the room, except in the vaguest sense, shadows reminding him to be cryptic.

"Because I pay attention. There are details *you* don't like to notice."

"I'll take you home," he said to Stephen giving him a fatherly pat on the shoulder. No, Charlotte told him, you're too drunk. I'll drive him. *You're* too drunk, he said back. I don't drink, I said, I'll drive him. Stephen looked at Arthur the same way I had looked at my father once when I was about twelve, when he thought he was doing me a big favor by introducing me to a fourteen-year-old boy who would take me out and buy me a hamburger. It was a miserable first date: all I could think about was being tongue-tied, and I had been too nervous to say much of anything. Full of a hundred sips of Coke, I had practically peed in my pants rather than excuse myself to go to the bathroom. Stephen nodded, no other options coming to mind.

"Charlotte is either going to have to get over this baby stuff, or she's going to have to fire you," Arthur said to me when he walked us to the car. His tone wasn't mean at all, just sort of sad. He opened the driver's door and let me in. I rolled my window down fast, but he already had walked back toward the house.

Stephen gave me an address on Prytania Street, not far away. We rode in silence. "If you see Parker, please don't tell him," I said when we reached Jefferson Avenue. We only had a few more blocks left. Stephen shrugged, I could see the motion out of the corner of my eye.

"Thanks for the ride," he said when he got out, not meaning it, but reverting to good behavior: Did he say thank you? Arthur might ask. No? Well, then we'll have to take away the account. He had to get between two parked cars to reach the sidewalk. Prytania was lined with small, cheap foreign cars in that stretch, transportation for apartment dwellers. Bumper to bumper parked, a dozen to a block, I wondered how he'd get through. The VW Beetle was touching the Toyota in front of it, and Stephen gracefully walked across on the Toyota's bumper, as if he owned it, his suitcase up over his head.

It was the blue Toyota with the WWOZ sticker on it. It was in Parker's lot sometimes when I left for work in the morning, and other times when I cruised by as well. I was sure the Import China receptionist was having an affair with her office manager. She didn't look the type to live on Prytania Street, though: she was too downtown, stupid poor instead of idle poor. But the Toyota couldn't be Stephen's: sometimes it was in Parker's lot nights and weekends, and Stephen was not the type to take his job that seriously.

I decided to call in sick the next morning. I phoned early, before Charlotte was due to arrive. Sister Roberta answered;

it should have occurred to me that at that hour no real person would be in the library. You must be quite ill, Sister said, sarcasm exorcising any leftover goodness from Reading of the Offices. Just a little flu-ish, I told her, why? You've been able to come in sick for months now, she said. Oh, I said. Might you be better later today? I might, maybe around suppertime. She wasn't going to get me to show up until Charlotte was gone. I think it would be a good idea for you to come by the convent for a little talk, she said. Five o'clock, all right? I tamped down an urge to say that I was feeling better right now, that I could meet her at the convent right now. Sure, I said, and pushed it out of my mind. I took the phone off the hook, buried it under a pile of laundry so I wouldn't hear the irritating noise warning me to put it back in the cradle, or the dial tone that would come a minute later. I knew these things.

I lay on my mattress, my hands resting on my belly as if it were a crystal ball. I decided I would think for eight hours, just lie there and think. I would make a list; a mental list was okay. I saw a movie once where the uncle is going to lose custody of the little boy unless he gets a job. He worries that the boy will be adopted into a family of listmakers; he doesn't want him to become a listmaker. I figured listmakers used pencils and slips of paper. Mind lists had to be okay. Charlotte, Parker, with maybe some time left over for Sister Roberta. Though she wasn't so necessary. She had an agenda, probably had had one for some time. I'd been at St. Francis long enough to know that you didn't try to outsmart the nuns. They had more idle time to plot than even I did. They were listmakers.

The dialogue from last night returned, and I found myself mentally alternating between what Charlotte said and what Arthur said, making it easier to take. And less confusing. I imposed chronological order, though it was hard recalling exactly what had been said, in what order. Charlotte had told Arthur to shut up. But what had he said? Backtrack. He'd named Parker. Well, sort of, your photographer friend, he'd said. Did he say Rutledge? To me or to Stephen? Must have been to Stephen, or why would I have asked him not to tell? Charlotte whispered to Arthur, what? I couldn't do this for eight hours.

Maybe I should focus on what was going to happen. Charlotte would phone. Parker might phone. That was simpler, all speculative, ready to have wishes imposed. Why do you want to fire me, Charlotte? Take it from there, see what she says. She doesn't want to fire me, Arthur wants me fired. Maybe Sister wants me fired. Sister has the power, so why worry about Charlotte? Keep the phone off the hook. Before nightfall I'll know if I have my job. Parker, Stephen would definitely tell Parker, or he'd have said something to me in the car last night. If I were Parker, would I call? Probably. Didn't Arthur say that my mama wanted to slap a lawsuit on him? He'd want to marry me, right away. He'd want to kill me, right away. From that it was easy to segue into daydreams, I wanted him again, no more rescuer dreams, I wanted sexual dreams, where my little round uterus would harden up into a mean, happy ball when I came. Lying on my side, as I now had to do, I fell asleep.

There's something about a person ringing your doorbell that's different from someone ringing your phone. Your car is out front, you're breathing, and it's plain mean not to answer. Especially in a shotgun house, where they can cut up the alley, peer in each window until they find you, walking brazenly or huddled quietly. I let it ring twice, as if I had a reason to be home, then opened the door.

Parker walked right in. Not fast, just expected. He looked around the living room, which had no furniture. I thought he wasn't going to speak, that he had come over to wait for me to say something. His hands were in his pockets. "I want to sit down," he said finally, and I followed him to the back room where the rusty patio table and chairs were. He sat, I stood, arms folded. I had on my flannel pajamas, white with tiny pink roses on them, the elastic at the waist pulled up so that it followed the line of my diaphragm, the top hanging loose. I looked pretty much the way I always did in pajamas. His eyes flitted over and past my abdomen, unsatisfied by the evidence. He waved a hand toward a chair, and I sat at the table. "You want something to drink? Something to eat?" I hoped he'd say no; all that was in the refrigerator was a carton of Donald Duck orange juice and half a loaf of Orowheat Honey Wheat Berry bread. I'd finished off my jar of peanut butter at lunch, and I figured I'd stop at Burger King on the way home if I had an appetite after Sister got finished with me. A sack of hamburgers, ketchup only, I craved dark red stuff. He shook his head, no.

"What do you want from me?" he said quietly.

"I didn't even want you to know."

"That doesn't answer my question."

"Sure it does. I don't want anything from you. Don't you think if I wanted something you'd know it by now?"

"You live a half block from me. You haven't moved. You didn't have to do anything. You knew I'd find out one day."

"But not until it was way too late. By then you'd have no idea it was yours."

"You told people it was mine."

"No I didn't," I said. "Charlotte figures things like that out."

"I know."

"Oh?"

"Yeah, I know. She's figured out other things that have gotten me in a world of trouble. Never mind."

I was curious, but I had my mind on finding out his feelings about me, and I wasn't going to let him sidetrack me right then. I shrugged. "I wanted you to like me."

"I like you. I *did* like you."

"I suppose I wanted you to love me."

"That wasn't exactly possible." I raised my eyebrows, not imagining what he'd say next. "For a million reasons. And *you* were half a million of them."

"Thanks a lot."

"Nothing personal, it's just the way you act."

"That's nothing personal?"

"With you, no. You ever notice how you have this tendency to hit and run? Like a little girl on a playground, you come up and tag me, then run in the girls' bathroom."

I laughed. "*Little* girls are pretty smart. You wouldn't have loved me anyway."

"Probably not."

I shrugged again. This was like an anticipated death, like my grandfather's. When something comes slowly, inevitably, it's easier to take. "See?" I said. The tears were going to start if I wasn't careful. I flung my hair back.

"You're going to take me to court," he said.

"No."

"That's what I heard."

"You heard wrong. Honest."

"Maybe you want me to help out a little? I could give you some money or something. Pay your hospital bill."

"You Jewish or something?"

"Catholic."

"Same thing."

He smiled. "I need a drink," he said.

"Vodka and orange juice?"

"At two in the afternoon?"

"Not much conventional around here, sorry."

He took the drink. I poured myself a glass of orange juice, something to fiddle with. I sipped at it slowly, no more wanting to have to excuse myself to go to the bathroom than when I was out with that boy at age twelve. Pregnant women were sieves; it was a joke, and I didn't want him to see me in that way. The pregnancy wasn't an abstraction for me, but it could be for him. Clean, a fact and nothing more. Nothing involving me; a child would show up one day, with green eyes and a bonnet. That would be fine, no blood and puke and assorted effluence from every hole in my body. Nothing personal.

He busied himself with the drink, stirring it with his pinkie finger, dunking an ice cube and watching it pop back up to the surface. "Why'd you come over here?" I said.

"You knew I'd come over here."

"Now you're not answering my question."

"Trying to figure it out. There are no accidents, you know."

"But there are deceptions."

"Not really. Not unless a total fool's on the short end."

"Well, thank you for your active participation." I smiled at him. He didn't look me in the eye.

"Is this a setup?" he said, scanning the room, as if a hidden microphone were right out where he could see it. The room was barren. The rusty table, the chairs, a black pole lamp from my dorm room. The table was in a lattice sort of pattern; you could see your knees right through it. He reached for me, frightened to touch me, it seemed, but he must not have been able to resist. He ran his hands over my shoulders, feeling no bra strap. I stood up, backed away. It was important that he not touch me, not know this was real. His hands went for my rib cage; I tried to pull away. One hand touched my belly, only for a second, but long enough. Parker pulled back. "You want proof? You think I'm crazy, that some lawyer wants to get you on tape so I can seize your assets? What do I want with a goddamn Leica and a Japanese mattress?" I unbuttoned my pajama top and threw it off. Then I slipped off the bottoms, leaving on only a pair of bikini underpants. Even with the melon in my belly, I was beautiful. I was going to have a girl. My father had taught me that, that the old women in Stuttgart would say it was a girl if the mother was looking wonderful, a boy if she looked deathly, no other options. For a few years there, my friends were all getting baby brothers and sisters, and my father was right every time. When a girl came, he would say, See, I told you, I knew it would be a girl, remember how beautiful her mother looked?

Parker began to cry. Good soppy tears that made me smile and cry at the same time. He reached out gently, touched me on my tummy, so delicately. A twinge, it hardened up, relaxed slowly. He wouldn't know what he'd done.

"I'm sorry," I said. He nodded.

He was probably right, that the pregnancy was no accident. When he made love to me that afternoon in my sixth month, it was different from the first time, when the baby was conceived. I don't know why I could tell that he was unafraid the second time, but it was surely true.

"You won't see me," I said. We were walking to the door. "But I have to not be angry with you. What if I have to look at someone with your face every day for a long time? I can't hate it; that's why I stayed away. When you're married, you can't escape the person you're angry at."

"Married people don't hate each other."

"Oh, I think they do."

CHAPTER 13

I considered not bathing, leaving the ripe smell of sex on me. I knew a boy in college who swore he could smell if a girl was horny, and I often thought about whether that was true. Sexuality was probably out of Sister Roberta's range, dog-whistle pitch, an infrasmell, ultrasmell, bloodhound scent. My clothes were loose, and the faint odor came up through the middle trough, around my belly and up out the cleavage. I didn't want to spend the rest of the day thinking about it, so I took a bath, the soapy water ebbing between my legs, semen leaking out onto the washcloth. Valuable stuff at one time. I wondered if men measured potency by volume. Women had no such gauge; so what if an orgasm lasted half a minute, producing nothing?

I reached the staff parking lot at five to five. The campus was no bigger than the one where I attended high school; I could make it to the convent by five. I scanned the parking lot the way Parker scanned his, only he was always checking the periphery for people hiding, while I was looking for Charlotte right there in the lot. Her car was still there. I thought she'd be gone, a slack day when she didn't have to deal with me. I cut across to the green, taking a vector as far from the path between the library and her car as possible. She was sitting on the back steps of the administration building as I passed. I tried to pretend I didn't see her, even though I was protected by the excuse of my five-o'clock appointment with Sister. I kept my eyes down, my brow furrowed, as if I could avoid seeing a woman with pale hair and paler eyes sitting alone on that dark campus.

"You stop, Darby," she said when I was almost past her. I told her I had an appointment with Sister at five o'clock;

I looked at my watch. "Why do you think I'm sitting here?"
she said. I told her I didn't know. Maybe I was going to be
fired, and she was there to watch. She shook her head no.
"I'll be here when you get out," she said. I looked at the sky.
We hadn't gone off daylight savings time yet, and it was
going to be dark by six-thirty. I wasn't counting on Sister
letting me out before dark. Though Sister was a fast one with
words, and she had a regimented life. Maybe if you missed
dinner at the convent you got nothing to eat, I didn't know.
I thought firing me might take some time, since I planned
to argue in my own behalf. It'll be dark, I told Charlotte.
"Then I'll wait in our office." It didn't occur to me not to
show up.

Considering they were people set apart from the secular
world, most of the sisters sure were schizzy, a persona for
every occasion. One afternoon Sister Roberta had been shrill-
ing at a workman who'd dropped his Barq's can into an
excavation site behind the library. The president, Sister Theodora, had walked past. Sister Theodora was black and char-
ismatic and a crackerjack administrator. She was about the
same color as I was, but she made sure everyone knew she
was black. "Good afternoon, Sister Theodora," Sister Roberta
had sung out, her voice full of piety and cheer. As if Sister
Theodora hadn't noticed that Sister Roberta felt quite free to
holler at anyone darker than a brown paper bag who made
less than four dollars an hour. I wasn't surprised when she
offered me something to eat or drink. "A glass of milk?" she
said, and that could have been a good sign. After all, milk
was kind stuff, but I knew better. People who give birth to
babies and bury them under the narcissus are not the nur-
turing sort. I didn't want a glass of milk, but I was curious
to see the kitchen. I nodded.

At five o'clock there was only one sister in there, and she
was peeling potatoes. Sister Ignatius, Sister Beetle Bailey. The
only thing remarkable about the kitchen was that it was so
clean and ordinary. Like a dormitory kitchen, all stainless

steel. Loaves of white bread, boxes of lime Jell-O, an entire sacrificial chicken. Gospel bird, that's what Murray called chicken, at least on Sundays. The refrigerator was big enough to shove an entire nun inside, dressed. They used 2-percent-fat milk. And squat glasses like the ones in the cafeteria. I thought they probably all lived so long because they were so generally uncautious. It was food, it was there: they ate it without thinking about it. Sort of the way people thought in the fifties. Or didn't think.

The parlor was dark, not good for clever negotiating, reading faces. "I've been waiting for you to talk to me," Sister said. "I suppose I could have waited indefinitely." No more milk of human kindness.

I said nothing. The best defense is a good offense, my father would say. And the superlative defense is to do nothing, I'd say back.

"I have to accept this, but I don't have to like it," Sister said.

"Then do we really need to talk?" She'd used up my civil-rights and equal-opportunity-employment and mortal-sin arguments in one sweep.

"Yes, dear, we have to talk." I folded my arms across my chest. Careful, practiced, nothing to show contours. "What you've done is disgraceful. Particularly on this campus."

"I bet there's not a married mother within a mile of where we sit," I said. St. Francis was surrounded by a car dealership, a dying shopping center, an interstate, and Gert Town. With fresh, careful students and the Sisters of the Holy Comforter thrown in for emphasis. Gert Town was full of women like me, only they were black, making only slightly less money from welfare than I made with my master's degree. They reached certain junctures and, having nothing better to do, had babies. Without husbands. Veronica went to Baton Rouge for her education, then came right back and picked up some seed on Telemachus Street. There were more men than women on the streets of Gert Town, but no one knew where and when they perched indoors. Useful, on a temporary basis, just like Parker. The women thought they loved them, too, for a while.

"Precisely my point," Sister said.

"Hey, these kids are going to mess around if they feel like it. And I'm not exactly visible. When's the last time a student came into Technical Services?"

"You're visible. You walk around this campus, and you're as conspicuous as if you were green. As white women, religious or not, we're here to set a better example. You think about it."

"Oh." I never saw myself as the drop of buttermilk in a bowl of flies, unless I walked past a mirror. Which wasn't often, not on an old campus, where the only mirrors were the stainless-steel ones in the bathrooms.

"You know your rights." I nodded. "Well, there are rights, and there are rights." I nodded again; don't let her think she's baffling you. "You tell me what I mean by that," she said.

Sister Roberta previously had taught high-school math. That was the beauty of the religious life, having a sequence of empty lives, one upon the next. Unfettered by having to take care of anything, they could take one degree, have a profession, go back for a different degree, get a new profession, go back still again. The lines between professional identities crossed sometimes, and there was that math teacher, sitting right in front of me, forgetting that she was a librarian now, an open seeker of information.

"I have no earthly idea what you're talking about. Sounds like *Animal Farm*. 'All animals are equal, but some animals are more equal than others.'"

"This isn't the time to smart off, Miss Cooper."

"Okay," I said, remembering that she hadn't fired me yet. And might not do so at all.

"I don't like what you've done."

"Do you believe in abortion?" Ah, a chance for my old script.

"That's not what we're talking about. I understand this was intentional."

"Charlotte had no business . . ."

"I didn't talk to Mrs. Altmann."

"Then why's she sitting on the steps out there like some carrion bird?"

Sister smiled, switching lives again; now she was nineteen, unschooled and jolly. The image of Charlotte, pale eye holes, hanging off the administration building like a gargoyle, was pretty funny. I giggled. "She's your supervisor, and you're lucky at that. I told her we'd be meeting. Personnel policy, something you'll be learning about in spite of yourself."

"Who told you?"

"No one at the university."

Letty. Had to be Letty. Though Letty's biggest fear right now was that she would go out for the newspaper one morning and find me on the stoop, destitute and wanting money from her. Letty liked toying with her greatest fears. "It was my mother, wasn't it?"

"I don't think you understand. You're not here to play Twenty Questions." A pause, then, "No, it was not your mother." She paused. "I'm giving you a copy of the personnel manual. Something I'm sure you pitched in the trash as soon as you filled out your W-4. I can strangulate you with it. And I will."

She handed me a slim booklet. Half of it was insurance benefits, which already had done me significant harm. I carried no maternity coverage. If I'd been confident and patient and had seduced Parker a month later than I did, I'd have switched to a family policy. And gotten coverage. Those are not the matters you think of in the heat of passion.

"No maternity leave, no disability leave. You never asked for it, and now it's too late. Check page forty-three. Three months' notice. If I'm not mistaken, you don't have three months left."

"I'll have it over a weekend."

"How very convenient."

"Then I want leave three months from today."

"That's not how it's done."

I flipped open the manual, skimmed page forty-three. "No reason why it can't be," I said.

"This is not a very good start." Her mouth formed a thin line. I'd never seen a nun with lips; maybe it was chromosomal.

"I'll stick to the letter of the law."

"No absences, unless you're sick. And I have the right to ask for a doctor's letter."

"No problem." I was thinking that it was time to talk to Murray about leaving the baby with her. That part hadn't occurred to me. I was sure I'd be fired, go on welfare, collect food stamps, be all outraged and sorry for myself. I was feeling good.

"I'll monitor the quality of your work."

"Nothing's wrong with my work."

"Not now. But I've seen women in your condition asleep at their desks. I cut them some slack, but I don't feel sorry for you."

"They did it on purpose, too."

Sister stood up, indicating she'd had enough. At the door she said, "That's a boy you're carrying. Women carrying boys get snappish. That's what my mother told me. And she had nine."

"Nine kids?"

"Nine *boys*. And two girls."

"No wonder she was snappish," I said, but Sister didn't laugh.

Charlotte wasn't on the steps anymore, but her car was in the lot. I found her in our office, doing absolutely nothing. She was sitting at her desk, standing a pencil on its end, letting it fall over, lifting it by the tip, sliding her fingers down the shaft until it fell over again. "I didn't get fired," I said from the door. Charlotte was alone in the building except for the night clerk downstairs at the circulation desk. Dinnertime in the dorm.

She tipped the pencil over again. "I knew you wouldn't be."

"Why didn't you say so?"

"I did, you just weren't paying attention." The pencil was point-down now; Charlotte began a staccato rapping on the desk.

"Why'd you tell her it wasn't an accident?"

She looked up. "I don't know what you're talking about."

"Everything'd be fine, if she thought it was an accident."

"I doubt that."

"Then what'd you tell her?"

"Nothing. She told me. You kind of went over my head, you know."

"I didn't go over your head, I went around your body."

Charlotte didn't smile. "I've never mentioned your pregnancy, let alone implied that it was on purpose."

"Somebody told her."

Charlotte studied the pencil. It was your basic La. Schools pencil, nothing to look at. "Someone out there does not have your best interests at heart. I have my suspicions, but it's not my place to tell. It's something you need to figure out for yourself."

"Thanks a fucking lot." Charlotte could see through things, Catahoula-laser eyes. I didn't think it was because she was old enough to have accumulated wisdom; it was more that she'd had a gift for some time. She'd share or she wouldn't, as if she could impart wisdom simply by making me think it through myself. You're not my psychiatrist, I'd say when she gave me that costly taciturn silence. You can't afford me, she'd say back.

"I want to talk to you," she said.

"Fire away." I felt like saying, You won't get the attention you deserve, it's been too much of a talking sort of day.

"Have you ever thought about the fact that this is not an act in isolation?"

A yes-no question. No, I haven't thought about it. Yes, this is an act in isolation, it fairly reeks of isolation.

"You affect other people."

"You sound like goddamn Letty. 'How will I ever be able to walk into the synagogue again?' 'People are saying you did this because I sleep with Eddie. Do you realize what that's doing to my relationship with Eddie? Not much, I'll tell you.' 'Don't expect me to baby-sit Saturday nights, you hear me?' She even drags my father into this. 'If your father were alive, he'd be dead by now.' I love it!"

"Forget I mentioned it."

"This affecting you? I'm fucking sorry. In six months, I've been out one day. One day! That's better health than you'll get in any other department in this library. You don't see me taking a week off for a dead aunt in Waterproof, Louisiana, or a weekly hangover or blood pressure of four hundred over three hundred. I've missed one day. And it doesn't look like it was a particularly busy one, either."

Her lips were pursed as if she were about to cry. Charlotte had an upper lip defined by a roller coaster line, no nun-chromosomes. She tossed her hair back, but it was earlobe length, stick straight, not needing rearranging. "This was a bad idea," she said. She stood up and restacked the books on her desk.

"I did this for you," I said quietly. "I thought it'd make you feel better."

"Well, it didn't," she said and walked out.

CHAPTER 14

I tried to move in with Letty when my navel started getting clipped by the steering wheel on my Karmann Ghia. I'd make a turn, and the spokes would tweak it; it stuck out and invited every small child's nightmare. It was right after Thanksgiving, and Letty lived six blocks from Touro. I'd given it careful consideration over the four-day weekend, with the library closed and nothing to do, no way to sleep more than two hours at a stretch. Maybe I could have gone to Marmee's, but her night sitters went bonkers one after another. Ora Lee was sitting for the priest at St. Rita's this time, and for some reason he was taking forever to die. Days would have been fine, with Murray knowing half the White Fleet cab drivers in town, but I figured this baby would arrive at night. A Friday night, as I promised Sister Roberta.

I took Letty to dinner, a test of how much I could stand. We went to Nature's Way. I didn't tell her that most nights I drove through at a different Burger King, grabbing a Wimpy-Jughead sack of burgers, sometimes with pickles so I could say I was eating something green. Letty saw the bowls heaped with vegetables of every hue but blue. Nothing to rebel against. I ordered brown rice with cheese and mushrooms, textures and good grease. "I'll have a salad like that over there," Letty said, pointing at a woman's dinner. "And this Red Zinger iced tea. With diet French dressing, and Sweet 'n Low for the tea." The man behind the counter got a wild look in his eye and turned to me for help. I wanted to say, Goddamn it, I knew it.

"This is a health food restaurant," I said.

"I know that," she said and looked at the man behind

the counter the way she used to look at dress salesladies when I wanted the organdy dress with the hot-pink sash.

"Skinny isn't healthy," I said. "I mean, it's not *synonymous* with healthy."

"We have rice vinegar. And honey for the tea," the man behind the counter said.

Letty looked at him as if he had no understanding at all of what he was in business for. "Rice vinegar would be fine," she said. "Let me taste that tea." He gave her the tea, and she examined the glass before sipping from the rim.

"People don't wear lipstick in a place like this," I whispered loudly.

"I like it," she said, and I saw the counterman's vertebrae sink comfortably back into place.

I poured soy sauce over my rice. "You're going to get toxemia. Or at least look like a balloon," Letty said.

"Which is worse?" I said, and she smiled.

"It means a lot to me, that you invited me to dinner."

"I figure I owe you one."

"More like three times three-hundred sixty-five times twenty-seven," she said.

"But, hey, who's counting?" I said, wanting to cry.

"That wasn't very nice of me."

"That's okay."

"Eddie's out of town for a few weeks."

"Where?" Who cares where, unless it's a combat zone?

"He's visiting Linda. She had another baby a few months ago."

"Oh." Linda Marino Whatever-Who-Cared? was Eddie's dream daughter. She was very tall, very busty, very blond, and very adopted. Eddie's sperm must have died even faster than they jumped. Linda won first prize at the day camp talent show by singing the Marino's jingle in a nasal, Patsy Cline sort of voice. My prejudice against her was born in the thick of childhood, and couldn't have been eradicated by anything less than an actual conversation with her. Linda lived in Atlanta and thought that coming to New Orleans was like visiting a Third World country; she needed shots or something. At least that's what Letty said.

"Eddie gets a kick out of being a grandfather," Letty said.

"Oh." I was reading about Parent Effectiveness Training, getting ready to listen to my kid, who couldn't even blow air over its larynx yet. Listen, nonjudgmental, and you get it all out of them. It was a hopeful respite from the Lamaze books, where I was scared each time I read one that I wasn't going to have control. Once the baby was there, you didn't need a partner, but you needed one for the actual getting there. Charlotte wouldn't take classes with me; I wouldn't ask Letty. I tried Murray, who said, "Shoot, they give you gas, you out, you got a baby. Trust me, it better than all that grunting and groaning and knowing what going on. You don't *want* to know what going on. And I sure don't. Changing your diaper was one thing. This is entirely another."

"He goes up there a few weeks," Letty was saying, "he gives the kids presents and buys them ice cream, makes them love him, then gets on a plane and comes home."

"I can't wait to be a grandmother," I said. It was true, I wanted to get right down to the business of being nurtured in my old age, skip all the in-between stuff.

"Linda lives in Atlanta, though."

For Parent Effectiveness Training practice, Letty was a good subject; her emotional age was really only about sixteen. "You like the idea of distance," I said. This active listening was so totally phony, she was sure to call me on it.

"Yes," she hissed. It was working. "But that's not fair, I know it."

"I can't move to Atlanta."

"I'm not trying to run you out of town." Letty filled her fork with a rainbow of fiber, stuffed it into her mouth, rice vinegar dribbling down her chin. The woman was starving; that's probably why she never ate anything good in public.

"What do you want, Letty?"

She was chewing noisily. The greens and reds and purples were merging into brown in her mouth. She spoke before she swallowed. "I *don't* want responsibility."

"I've left you alone."

"And I appreciate it."

I wanted my money back. I wanted a place to stay, and I'd just spent eight dollars on food that was too healthful to be wasted like this. I should have taken her to Burger King: they had a salad bar now. I kept eating, trying to enjoy my food enough for eight dollars.

Stephen walked in right at the good point, when I had more mushrooms and cheese than rice left. "Stephen Norris," I whispered to Letty. She was content to have her back to the door in Nature's Way; no one she knew was going to walk through the door. And if they did, she wasn't sure she wanted them to see her.

The eating space in the restaurant had six wooden spool tables and twice as many chairs; it was about the size of my living room. Letty turned around to look. Hi, I sang out as he approached our table. He was looking the other way. He stopped as he passed, for a second, and looked at me, as if he had something saved up to say and didn't know if this was too small a place to say it in.

"You're a fucking asshole," he said. Out loud, the people at the two other occupied tables could hear him. He walked up to the counter, but no one was there.

I stood up to walk over to him, and Letty grabbed my arm. "Don't make a fool out of yourself," she said. I jerked my arm away. I went and stood next to him, as if I was second in line. He didn't look at me; he was rapping with his knuckles on the countertop. No one came. He picked up a Xeroxed menu from the stack and studied it, looking up hopefully a time or two.

"Why'd you say that?" I said.

"God fucking dammit," he said, slamming the paper down on the counter, wanting it to be a sledgehammer and looking stupid because it wasn't. Then he looked me in the face. "I hate your guts," he said softly, so only I could hear him. Then he walked out.

On Christmas Eve, I was alone in my house. The baby was due in only two weeks, and so there had been a chance that my house would have a little family of two in it for the holidays. I'd decorated in case, hanging all of Letty's old blue glass balls on a gnarled tree branch I'd found in the park. Letty always had had Christmas, no matter that my father had come from a strict Jewish home. But for some reason, in her pursuit of Eddie the Catholic, Letty was pretending that she was a moderately observant Jew. It shows respect for tradition; I'd think he'd admire that, she'd said. She didn't go so far as to do Hanukah, I noticed. I was careful with her ornaments: if she didn't snag Eddie, she'd go back to having a tree.

The branch was anchored in a bucket of sand, the sand carted in a cupful at a time; I'd taken fistfuls and flung them into a cardboard box in my car one night where developers were doing some site work at the new shopping strip on Tchoupitoulas. There were only two gifts left underneath. A copy of *Horton Hatches the Egg* for the baby, in case it arrived early. I thought that should be its first possession, boy or girl. And a bottle of gin for the garbagemen. Wrapped. I was going to put it out on the can when they picked up on Friday.

The doorbell rang just as I was getting into bed with a book. Parker was visible through the peephole. I was in the same pajamas I'd had on when he'd seen me three months ago. I opened the door far enough to stick my head out. His car was behind him, the lights on, the motor running. In his hand he had a flat gift in silver wrapping. I asked him to come in. No, lots of deliveries to make, he said. Oh, I said, disappointed. He handed me the gift. I have a gift for you, too, I said. I waddled over to my little tree with as much grace as I could and tried not to look as if I was hesitating. Horton or the gin, it was hard to decide. Then I remembered that he had a lot of deliveries to make. That was awfully impersonal. I chose the gin. He gave me a kiss on the cheek before he ran off to his car, and I started to cry.

I didn't open the gift until the next morning; it was all I had. Inside the flat box was no store-bought gift. It was a photocopy of a typewritten hundred-page Rutledge family tree. A personal gift after all. I read it all Christmas day, never getting out of my pajamas. I found three reprobates who'd married Jews. All in the twentieth century, too.

CHAPTER 15

*A*s far as I can recall, Honor's only accommodated me once. And while I needed her to do so then more than ever again, she gave me a false sense that she was going to be easy.

I had my oil changed after work Friday afternoon. My baby was due that day. I knew almost to the minute; I'd only had sex twice that whole year, a waste of safe time. I thought an oil change was a good thing to do since I was going to have a serious passenger soon. I went to the Exxon station at Lee Circle, where they didn't know me. I could read and snack and not have to tell them my business the way I did at the Texaco station around the corner from Letty's house. Letty sort of owned one of the guys at the Texaco station. He'd come wash her car on Saturdays and pick it up when it was due for a tune-up and clear the storm drain when Letty complained about it. She'd give him fifty dollars at Christmas, and he didn't mind. His kid had cerebral palsy, and he was happy for any money that came his way. I had to say one nice thing about Letty for every gallon of gas he pumped into my car.

I went through the vending machines, and that should have told me something. Crackers and cheese. Crackers and peanut butter. Fritos. 7-Up. Baby Ruth. I ran out of change three times, but the cashier didn't say anything when I kept coming back. I had a wonderful bellyache by the time I pulled on my seat belt and left for home. When the spasms stopped and started, I thought nothing of it, chalked it up to the vagaries of the peristaltic process. It wasn't until the ten-o'clock news came on that I figured it out. I phoned Letty, and her answering machine came on. I left no message, because I would have wanted her to save it, and she would have erased it by morning. The pains were three minutes apart, and they were intense. I went out onto the porch, expecting someone would come along now that it was the right time. But the street was empty and darker than usual. One of the boys down the block had shot out the streetlight last Saturday with his BB gun. I doubled over with a pain, there on my steps, with no audience. When it passed, I ran inside, knowing I had just so much time to get ready. Less time than in a fire. I grabbed a Marino's bag, threw in a nightgown, grabbed everything familiar in the bathroom. Another pain came, and I sat down on the closed toilet until it passed.

I had a tiny undershirt and sleeper that I'd bought at K&B a few days back. Into the bag. My payment receipt from Touro, cash in advance, unless you had a welfare card or insurance or a Jewish doctor for a husband. Into the bag, with my driver's license and all the cash in my wallet. Eleven dollars and change. I put on the bathroom light and walked gingerly to the front, as if I would pee in my pants if I walked more quickly. Warm fluid ran down my leg, nothing I could do to stop it. Straight down, I waddled back for a towel, fresh underpants. Threw an extra pair into the bag. Front again. I locked the door and sat on the steps. I'd wait for the next one to be over, then drive to the hospital. Tchoupitoulas to Napoleon, Napoleon to Prytania, where to park? Louisiana Avenue, lots of residential, but three blocks to walk. Three minutes, three blocks, I could do it. The pain came, I started to sob, the pain finished, and I dashed to the car. Tchoupitoulas, Napoleon, missed the light at Prytania, passed the hospital, no parking spaces except at meters, Louisiana Avenue. Dark, but no one would hurt me, no one was that low. Another pain in the car. I couldn't stop crying now. The pain stopped, I got out, saw the headlights were still on, reached back in to turn them off. A block and a half. Another pain, I doubled over, perfectly ready to push the baby out onto its head on the concrete. Into Emergency, shave off a block. Would it be fifty dollars extra to come in this door? I asked.

The nurse smiled, No. Honor was born less than an hour later. At eleven-eleven, on one-eleven. The numbers were good, but the timing was more excellent. Not only was it a Friday, not only was St. Francis closed for Dr. King's birthday on Monday, but Friday was three days short of three months since I'd put in for leave. Honor gave me a mighty mistaken notion.

She was the worst-looking thing I ever saw. For a minute there in the delivery room, I thought about giving her up. She was covered in brown glop, but that wasn't it; I wasn't that foolish. It was more that she was so misshapen, spindly limbs and a giant softball head. The books said she was supposed to look that way, but I thought that I'd gone to enough trouble, the least she could do was come out ready for loving. It wasn't until Dr. Cohen moved her from lying on top of my belly so she could root at my breast that I felt something for her. A matter of minutes, but you remember those minutes. I thought she was so sincere, her eyes closed, her mouth sucking so eagerly. Though it probably wasn't sincerity so much as greed. Still, I loved her right then for knowing what she was supposed to do and going at it with such verve.

I'd seen the hospital commercials on TV, the pretty mommy and the five-o'clock-shadow daddy and the baby in his own jammies, all checked in to what looked like a high-class hotel room, champagne and everything. You didn't get that when you paid cash. I was on a ward, all by myself, more square footage than the hotel room. The service was better, really: they took the baby away and brought her back every four hours. Only trouble was, I was in bed A, and the bathroom was next to bed D. I felt as if my uterus, viscera, and various vital organs were all going to fall out the bottom; it was a long walk.

I phoned no one all day Saturday. More than anything, I was curious as to how long I'd be missing before Letty tracked me. Letty was born in Touro, I was born in Touro, probably with the same pair of forceps, I told her. She knew

I was coming here, JDPS, I'd said, got you here, got me here, can't be all bad. I was so sleepy. I had a pink-iced cupcake at lunch. I didn't need anything to read, didn't need fantasies for drifting off to sleep.

By eight in the evening, I was wide-awake, bored, and I thought about making some phone calls. Murray was the only one who came to mind. She'd be home on a Saturday night, and I thought I knew her number. I dialed, a white uptown lady, hello in three syllables, answered; sorry I said, I've transposed two numbers. Whatever, dearie, she said and hung up. This time Murray answered with her at-home voice, an octave lower than the one she used at Marmee's. Hey, it's Darby, I said. Where you at? Touro. Yeah? expectantly. A girl, Murray, just like I told you. I began to cry. Why you didn't tell Letty? she said. How'd you know? I said. She call me at work, ask me if you at the house, tell me if you show up to call her, she be out just tonight. Don't call her, I said, let her find me. Shit, Darby, right now you need your mama. No matter if you got six husbands, you need your mama. She said she didn't want any responsibility, I said. Well, she *got* responsibility, Murray said, time she face up to that.

Letty burst into my room an hour later. It wasn't Murray's doing. Letty had Eddie with her, and she had enough important news to make tracking me worthwhile. Letty knew how to have her excitements, to draw everyone in, as if she were six and it was her birthday, and all her friends had to put on their mommies' dresses to come sing to her. "We're getting married!" she said, rushing over to my bed and giving me a very wet kiss on my cheek. You could smell a New Orleans restaurant on her, hot bread and cigarette smoke and fine wine and subtle garlic. Eddie was standing in the doorway, the great purveyor of peppers and pasta, suddenly shy. I looked at him and felt sorry for him, and was glad I didn't hate him. I told him to come in; Sorry I can't sit up, I said. He had two dozen daisies behind his back. "He opened the store to get those for you," Letty said. I gave her a look that said, What, am I supposed to be impressed? "We'd have gone to the florist, but they're all closed on Saturday nights," Eddie explained, and then I liked him. When I said thank you, I actually meant it.

"Well, aren't you curious as to why I'm here?" I said, when Letty went silent.

"Aren't you going to say congratulations?" she said.

"That's bad luck," I said.

"Not when you're almost sixty."

"Especially when you're almost sixty," Eddie said, and I laughed.

"Okay, congratulations."

"We saw her, Darby," Eddie said.

"And?"

Letty was silent for a moment, and I began to feel light-headed. Honor was so goofy-looking, with tufts of pale yellow-strawberry hair and blue eyes. Not as pale as Charlotte's, but a translucent blue that made her seem even less substantial. "She's beautiful," Letty said quietly.

I sat up in bed, didn't feel a thing, right down on the stitches. "You're not just saying that?"

"No," Letty said. "You looked just like her."

My hand went up to my cheek involuntarily. I felt the cheekbones, the symmetry, the proportions. I pulled a wisp of my hair up in front of my eyes. "Could be worse," I said.

"You and Letty make beautiful babies," Eddie said.

This was going to be good.

I heard the noise in the hall, incubators on wheels, like dessert carts coming, you don't get your pick. Eddie knew and began backing out of the room; I was in bed A, as far from the door as from the bathroom. We just got here, Letty said, not knowing. I supposed the last time she'd had to deal with new babies was when I was born and nurses carried babies in their arms, not thinking about liability. Letty wasn't the type to knit fancy bunting and bring it to the hospital so she could gossip about someone's ugly grandchild afterwards. She'd get a birth announcement and pitch it in the trash. They'll never have a chance to reciprocate anyway, she'd say after I turned thirty. Lately she'd been saying, They'll never *consider* reciprocating.

The nurse came to the foot of the bed, and Letty peered down at Honor. Tentative, one hand covering her mouth, she moved her head down an inch at a time. Honor's skinny little rump was up in the air; she hadn't given up the notion that she was in a confined space. She was wearing a disposable paper shirt. Like a middling restaurant, hushed voices and no decor, linen tablecloths with paper napkins, you go home vaguely satisfied. Let me do it, Letty said, lifting her up past the nurse. She was quite expert at it. She handed Honor to me. You don't forget, she said, pleased. She looked at the nurse. Where's the bottle?

"No bottle," I said, patting my chest.

"Oh, God, Eddie, let's go," Letty said.

"We'll wait in the hall, how about it?" he said to me. "Linda's done it with all three; Nat grieved because you can't do it when you adopt," he tried to explain to Letty.

"Hey, it takes about an hour, it's okay, really," I said. The milk was in and my breasts felt like leaky rocks. A drop on my gown was spreading like an ink stain with the touch of the rough fabric.

You ought to rethink this, Letty said. Not now, Letty, I said. How're you going to leave her with anyone else? Please? The tingle of letdown was actually painful, a reflex I didn't know I had, like orgasm. The first time I ever came, I thought I had peed in my pants, it was so close to that sort of relief, release. Honor didn't know about any of that yet, except that sucking made the discomfort go away. I thought about whether I had any sensations left to discover. Maybe extreme pain over more than an hour's duration, maybe paralysis, maybe suffocation; other than that I knew it all.

She offered to buy formula. No, it costs money, I said. She looked toward Eddie. He shrugged. Wholesale? she said. Let her get diapers wholesale, Eddie said.

Letty was satisfied with that, the power of being Mrs.

Eddie Marino: wholesale was stronger than an engagement ring.

"Please?" I said. Letty came over and kissed me again, twice in one year now. If Eddie had looked, he'd have seen she didn't know how to do it, her head weaving and bobbing, aiming for the wrong side, not wanting to come at me full on the mouth by accident. She was left-handed; maybe that had something to do with it. Eddie was quite sure of himself on some counts. He came over and kissed me, too, Canoe driving out all the Letty smell, my olfactory processes on overload, like trying too many perfumes at the department store all at one time; you shut down. The pink scent of baby nursery was gone. I couldn't believe primitive mothers could tell one baby from another by odor; they could predict when the baby was going to pee and hold it out over the arable ground. Missing the cue branded them. I'd have liked to have been that natural, not to take my share of some Louisiana landfill, but you can't dangle a baby out a car window, even if you actually know when it's going to pee.

Letty and Eddie got married the following Saturday. Letty and Eddie, what an awful combination: in American English they rhymed. Leddy and Eddy. Letty wasn't taking any chances; she had Eddie at the doctor for a blood test on Monday morning, took me back to her house that afternoon, showing off for Eddie. I went home nights; what'd he know?

With money you can do about anything. Especially grocery store money. Flowers by Marino's, catering by Marino's, guest list by Letty. It didn't matter to Eddie who came, but Letty had this great desire to flaunt it at all the women with dead husbands who couldn't get another. She'd been left a young widow, my father not even having had the decency to let his heart valves rot away slowly like most other Jewish men. But she'd waited a number of years, worked her way up through her fifties, then showed them all. She invited the women Eddie had screwed behind her back, she invited Evelyn. I was at her house, nursing Honor, listening to her editorials in between. "Just in case she has any doubts," Letty said into the air, calling up Evelyn, who'd probably creamed her pants over Eddie until she dried up twenty years ago. I watched her call Linda, whose last name was Trevor, as unethnic as you can get. Marino was gone now, not even an *M*. Linda Carol Trevor. Her stint as an Italian was over: she was blond and plastic and living in Buckhead, using olive oil only because it lowered cholesterol. "You and Darby will be practically like sisters, you want to talk to her, she's right here." I clapped my hand to my forehead, and for a second I felt like Charlotte. I waved frantically at Letty, almost dropping the baby. The stitches weren't healed, and I still lay down to nurse. Honor was half off the sofa. Letty didn't notice; she thrust the phone at me. I scowled; I shook my head vigorously no. Letty dropped the receiver into my hand and walked into the kitchen.

"Let's not talk and say we did," I said.

Linda laughed. "How've you been?" Sincere, she still had a brain, even living in Atlanta.

"You mean over the past quarter of a century?" I was nobody at day camp, except that I threw up my Delaware Punch next to the pool one afternoon and gained more notoriety than I realized. Linda's country rendition of the Marino's jingle, Stephen's affair with Mr. Garland, my Delaware Punch being soaked up by white towels, such was the substance I shared with all the other people who didn't get away from New Orleans when they were grown, or didn't get far away enough.

Honor made a pleasant tiny-girl sound. Usually her noises were loud and demanding. "That child cry like a *boy*," Murray had said when I brought her over to show. Marmee had pawed at her and heaped candies on her belly until I had been crazy with fatigue. Marmee was a great-grandmother, but not like my great-grandmother, who came on the Panama Limited in her purple dress with candies from Fannie May, hard sucking candies. We'd walk around the block: the winner was the one whose candy lasted longer. She always chattered, open-mouthed, and she always won. I never figured it out. A genetically transmitted trait, piling candies on the babies. Marmee was a spayed dog nursing a washcloth, her residual impulses going nowhere.

"That's the baby?" Linda said. I told her yes. I knew what that meant. Not a baby. The baby. The freak. The little bastard. Everyone wanted to see her, like my friend's baby that was born with arms like little chicken wings and a truly gigantic noseless head, needing a trach tube until she died. The wedding's Saturday at my house, Letty would say on the phone. Then, Yes, it'll be there. Not looking at me, pretending she was fooling me. You could announce a bad-luck baby by rumor; for a wedding you had to call everyone. A full house was set for Saturday, curiosity seekers. They could get by with a gift for Letty. Are you into hand-me-downs? Linda said. My third's a girl; most of her stuff was new, nothing from the boys. Except in winter, they all wear overalls. Linda was prattling, nervous, terrific. You mean she's going to get bigger? I said. Believe it, Linda said. You sound sad, I said, drunk with the newness. I guess so, she said.

"If Honor had been a boy, we'd have had to have a bris today," Letty said Saturday morning. Honor was in a white smocked gown, Letty's treat, eighty-five dollars at the Peterson Shop, looking more ready for a christening.

"Nah, I signed for it to be circumcised in the hospital."

"Your father would have wanted a bris," she said. Theirs had been as mixed a marriage as they come, battles between Jews often more acrimonious than battles between Moslems and Christians. The subtleties were harder than the chasms.

"This is not a good day to talk to me about my father, I said.

"Eddie was always very good to your father."

"I don't want to hear it."

"You better be nice to Eddie."

"That's not the goddamn point."

"I'm entitled to a little happiness."

"You mean you're entitled to a little money."

"What's that supposed to mean?"

I looked at Honor's new dress, my new dress, gray and inoffensive and costly, and I considered backing off. Letty was on a spree, getting ready to give me some stock and some furniture. "It means you were born rich and you're going to die rich, and the time in between with my father was a fast-passing nightmare."

"In a way that's true," she said.

"Shit, Letty," I said, ready to cry. The wedding was in half an hour. I began taking off Honor's dress. Letty said nothing: dressing and undressing babies was playacting, make-believe. I put her into the K&B sleeper. I took off my dress, flung it onto Letty's bed. Now she noticed something. She asked me what I was doing. "I don't want these clothes," I told her. She waited to see what I'd put on instead. I had a green jersey shirt and skirt I'd bought at the Council of Jewish Women's Bargains Beautiful sale year before last, the only white person with all her teeth shopping there, horrifying Letty as she walked around in her smock, happily willing to work dirty, as long as it was only for half a day. I went on her shift. "Still won't make your eyes green," she said. I shrugged. "Dress nicely, or I'd prefer you don't come."

"Suit yourself." Letty saw a minute snag in her panty hose and took them off. "If you think about it for half a second, you *have* to have me there. People'll want their money back."

"Do whatever you want. You generally do anyway."

"To say the least." I danced around in front of her, jester antics, until she smiled. I gave her a hug, and it felt quite fine. She was wearing a thick knit white dress and it gave her a little substance, a supercutaneous layer of fat. I liked Letty best in coats.

Linda didn't come. She hired a string quartet as her gift. Letty came down the steps to the strains of Pachelbel's Canon in D. "Sounds like a G.E. commercial," I whispered to her as she passed. She was too nervous to smile; her heel twisted inward for a second. I backed into the dining room, holding

Honor. In case she made a noise, there were chairs; I could sit down and nurse her. Couldn't have done that in the gray dress, zipper down the back, stains easy to see on the front. Murray was chasing Marmee around the buffet table, smacking her hand when she reached for the platter of cold cuts, so neatly arranged, as if someone's job had depended on the precision. "You *not* hungry, Miss Cecile," Murray said too loudly in the middle of the ceremony, and a ripple of laughter carried halfway to where Letty stood. "Let her eat, it's her goddamn money," I said, and Murray happily sat herself down on a dining room chair, arms folded across her bosom, while Marmee stuffed a fistful of roast beef into her mouth.

Honor slept until Letty cut the cake. People walked past me, put their fingers to their lips, gulped in a great big stare, and walked on. The single girls pulled the strings from under the cake. Me and the widows and two divorcees, whose ex-husbands had died anyway, tough luck. I got the thimble, and Honor let out a piercing scream. The room went silent. "This is goddamn funny!" I said, waiting for a laugh, but it didn't come.

When Letty threw the bouquet, a path cleared to me. Eddie's girlfriends were there vying for it, all right, each with more stake in winning than I had. Honor was in my left arm, my handicap. Letty aimed straight and true, Evelyn lunged so that it ricocheted off her hand. And landed right on Honor's tummy. She began sucking on an orchid. "Letty's been cloned, I'm just the middleman," I said, and Eddie let out a great drunken guffaw.

CHAPTER 16

'd have thought that all accidental children would be boys, all on-purpose children would be girls, as simple as that. They know that now, that boy-making sperm swim faster and die sooner; girl-making sperm take it easy and last for days. It starts that soon. But Honor and Veronica's Indira were conceived deliberately out of rhythm, take it when he's hot, while Linda's little girl Inglish was an accident. I think some spirituality was at work to make all three, but it could have been nothing more than the sheer force of will.

Linda came home to Eddie when Inglish was six months old. She left the two boys and most of her clothes, so it seemed to me that she wasn't quite ready to ditch Robert Trevor in any serious way. She called him Bob. His name Robert? was my first question, though she was roundly defaming him when it came up. Yes, she said, knowing, I think, what was coming next. A palindrome, his parents didn't like him very much, I said. That was the first thing I said when I met him, she said, liking me. He's the fourth; it's come down through enough generations. Robert Trevor, I through IV, starting out at a deficit.

Inglish was crawling around Letty's house eating lint. Linda paid no attention. Eddie was at the store, and I was at the house, I thought, because Letty was scared of Linda. Not that Linda was going to insult her or snap at her, but that Linda was going to let her make a bad impression. I could see that Letty had funny little fantasies about being a mother to Linda, maybe as a way to winning Eddie, in case she hadn't already, maybe as a way to finding motherhood pleasurable. Linda's outfit was from Benetton, and Inglish was crawling around like Swee' Pea in a pink dress very much like the one Letty had bought for Honor to wear to her wedding, black patent leather shoes scuffing at the toes. There's a Benetton at Canal Place, maybe we could go to-morrow, Letty had been saying when I let myself in the back door. An advance apology, expecting that I'd have on jeans. Not my fault Darby dresses that way, implied before Linda could think otherwise.

"She was an accident," Linda said, waving a hand toward Inglish, as if she were a puddle of Kool-Aid on the floor. "Bob doesn't believe that, the bastard. Says I can't control the ones I have, I have no business popping out any more. What the hell does he know?"

Letty took a quick glance in Inglish's direction. I was holding Honor on my lap, sensing Inglish would scale her head as if it were an easy obstacle if I lay her on the floor. Inglish was not exactly under heavy supervision. Linda poured herself three fingers of bourbon. She'd only been there since mid-morning, and already she knew where the bar glasses and liquor were. I'd lived in that house fourteen years before I'd noticed.

Eddie's presence in the house was limited to the contents of the bedroom closet. Letty had attacked his apartment vi-ciously. Take what you want, she'd said to me. I offered to pay for it, but Letty said, It's just going to go to the Goodwill anyway. So I'll pay you thirty-seven percent, that's the bracket you're in now, right? Another person might have slapped me. Letty was pleased at the thought. I got the king-size bed, mattresses flipped for the first time, overstuffed chairs, a sofa, a glass-topped kitchen table with imitation Breuer chairs, a bookshelf that had never sported a book, and the privilege of burning the naked photo of Letty. Don't you think Linda's entitled to some of this stuff, I'd said. Oh, Darby, please, she'd said, as if I were begging for an insult.

"Bob is a total fascist," Linda said. Linda went to LSU; I was impressed that she'd learned the word. It was on the sidewalk at St. Francis, but that was another story. " 'Your kid's taking the sofa apart,' he says. I tell him he's building

a fort, let him alone, and Bob smacks the kid." Inglish had
one hand atop a home-delivery glass gallon bottle of Ozone
spring water that Letty stored next to the refrigerator. Top-
pled, it would be a wet mess of cruel thick shards of glass.
Linda did nothing, waiting for something bad to happen.
Letty didn't move. I waited until Inglish began rocking the
bottle back and forth, the arc of its cap widening, and dived
for it in time, Honor tucked into a little cave formed between
my chest and my lap. "See what you have to look forward
to?" Linda said. Honor let out a scream, though nothing had
harmed her. "Inglish sounds like a half-drowned kitten com-
pared to *that*," Linda said. I lifted my shirt and let Honor
nurse. A doughnut-shaped bottle that babies can hold themselves sat on the table. If Linda nursed all three, as Eddie
said she had, then she probably quit as soon as she found a
way to make them independent. These days it was possible
quite early. I saw a bottle in K&B with a straw in it.
    "I miss her already," I said, shaking my head. In two
more weeks I had to go back to work. It was like an anticipated death; I was that close to grieving. Honor soothed me.
I was with her more than I'd been with Letty as a child. Letty
believed in baby-sitters, thirteen-year-olds with no sense and
lots of bubble gum, Murray in a good mood. "When you
turned nine months, all of a sudden you got into screaming
your head off when we went out," she told me, a reminder
like the story of her split stomach muscle, my fault, some
innate evil in me that sucked in a demon when I couldn't
talk yet. It wasn't as though Dr. Spock hadn't written his
book by then. In fact, it was the book everyone else was
reading; Letty wasn't one for going along with a trend. Especially if it involved reading small, repetitive print. She bored
easily. He mentioned crying alone in eighteen different places.
I'd read them all. Nowhere did he mention girl babies who
were so sure of themselves that they screamed as loudly as
boy babies.
    "Be glad you work," Linda said.
    "*I'm* glad she works," Letty said, looking to Linda for a

conspiratorial smile. I'm tired of my responsibilities, too, was what she was saying, but Linda wasn't ready to make that leap. Grown children were for being taken care of this week; they had nothing to do with preverbal people whose job was to build their own realities over the next few years. Even if they had to build them on torn sofa cushions and shattered glass bottles.

"You could go to work," I said.

"What'd I do with my kids?"

"Same thing I'm going to do with mine."

"That's different," Letty said.

"Oh, right, my kid's lucky to be alive instead of sucked down a tube, she should take what she can get."

"That's not what I meant," Letty said. "Linda has three kids."

"Pretty lame recovery, Letty," I said, and Linda smiled.

"You read *Roots*?" Linda said to me. She pronounced it *Ruuts*; she'd been in Atlanta too long.

"Long time ago."

"I read it when Robbie was a baby." Robert the Fifth, I presumed. "Something to be said for primitive societies, the father has his own hut."

"But he stays in the village," I said. Linda laughed.

"This is ridiculous," Letty said. Pleased, now she had two badly behaved daughters.

I didn't see Linda any more during that visit. Linda suggested we go to lunch. Linda wasn't one for sitting in a corner of Burger King and letting Inglish slam bits of inedible meat down on a high-chair tray. Letty refused to baby-sit for Honor, though Eddie was willing to take Inglish to the store with him, pass her around. "It's one thing, when Linda's going back to Atlanta, it's another with you living here," Letty said. "I don't want to set a precedent, I told you that." "You want to come with us if I can get Murray to keep her?" I said. "Sure, that'd be wonderful," Letty said. I knew Murray could do it, but I didn't call her. "Murray's got a cold," I told Letty. Eddie took Inglish, and Letty went shopping with

Linda. I didn't ask who paid, not even for lunch. Linda left a Marino's bag full of size-six-months clothes. Bob had called, swore he wouldn't smack the kids. "It's a start," Linda had said. "Your father never hit you," Letty said proudly after Linda was gone. "Nobody's going to hit Honor," I said. "I won't have to worry about that. Think about it."

The morning I went back to work, I left Murray with two bottles of my milk, pale and blue and weak-looking, one saved in the freezer, the other fresh that morning. "This child need red beans and pork chops," Murray said, holding one of the bottles up to the light. "Naw, don't," I said, not ready to face the fact that Honor was going to have a life of her own, spun outside my control. "Maybe a little bean gravy, how about it?" Murray said. I began to cry. I was still holding Honor, and Marmee was stroking her hair, her index finger flat against Honor's skull, maybe remembering that the fontanel wasn't closed yet. Marmee could still read and recognize numbers; maybe this was one final bit of knowledge, equally important. "This stuff look *pitiful*," Murray said. I was paying Murray three dollars an hour, above what William paid her. The deal was that we wouldn't tell William I was paying if he ever found out Honor was there. Murray would just tell him she was keeping Honor for a few hours as a favor; he'd never know the difference. "She's my kid, Murray," I said, surprising myself.

Overprepared, I got to work too early. Only Sister Roberta was there. She looked at her watch, a Timex; "Good, good," she said. She thought she had me where she wanted me. "I took a faster route," I said.

I hadn't seen Charlotte in ten weeks, and I had only spoken to her on the phone once. When Honor was four days old, the umbilicus still stained violet, I'd phoned her at work. It was early in the day. I told her she was a godmother when she answered. Darby? she said, as if she didn't know my voice. Yes! Your leave starts today, right? Yes! I had the baby, Charlotte. I figured that, she said; Honor had begun to fuss as soon as the phone had answered. Don't you want to know?

Know what? It's a girl, I said, seven pounds exactly, twenty inches exactly, all her parts. Darby, she said, yesterday was a holiday, and I've got to switch all of Technical Services around until you get back. I've got to go. I asked her if she wanted me to call Sister. No, she said, this time you did the protocol right. I'd had no drugs, but also no sleep, and nothing was too keen to me that week. By the time I thought about Charlotte, the library was as distant to me as anything I'd known ten years ago.

Charlotte walked in ten minutes later than I did. "Oh, shit," she said when she saw me.

"Thanks," I said.

"You could have let me know you were coming back today," she said. "Now I've got to shuffle everybody around, and I've got better stuff to do."

"Ten weeks, a leave's ten weeks, I came back when the form said I would, you're so *managerial*, you should've looked." It was better than crying.

Charlotte let out a whoop, her great cackle grown exponentially. "What'd you say you were in the hospital for?"

"Why?"

"Somebody must've attached some electrodes to your head."

"Maybe you just don't remember me."

"No, I remember you."

During the morning, one at a time, the ladies of the library slipped in, each with a crumpled paper bag from a downtown store, edged up beside my desk, and sneaked a wrapped gift out, depositing it at my feet. Welcome back, each said, then balled up the bag and disappeared. Charlotte watched. A half hour before lunch, Charlotte left. She returned with a crisp, uncrumpled bag from Hausmann's, sidled up to my desk, and slipped a small wrapped gift onto the pile at my feet. Welcome back, she said. I stayed at work until after six, feeding time at the convent, then carted the gifts out in a garbage bag. My breasts were about to burst; when I got to Marmee's, I ripped off my shirt. Marmee watched in fascination. "I did that with you," she said. "And I fed the baby today." She began unsnapping her housecoat at the throat. "No, you don't," Murray said. I opened the gifts that night. Charlotte's was a silver cup with HONOR engraved on it.

"You got this wholesale," I said when she answered the phone, not identifying myself to see what she'd do.

"Right off the shelf," she said.

"I can't figure you out."

"You ought to try. Your having a baby has been painful for me. You're old enough to know better, but you're not wise enough."

"Meaning?"

"Look, I'm not going to tell you to go sit in bars until you find out what goes on in other people's minds, but I am going to tell you that you ought to try doing something."

"Like what?" One thing about Charlotte, I'd known for a long time that she'd done thinking no one else had done. That was how she saw through people. She'd been in the same bars as Arthur for thirty years, but she saw more.

"Like paying attention."

"I pay attention."

"You've never noticed how I felt. *You* walk around like you're in some tunnel designed exclusively for you. Everybody else is just a security guard stationed along the wall." I pictured the Holland Tunnel, where my parents and I had gone once when we visited my father's cousin in New Jersey. I was seven, my big trip to New York, where I caught only the sights and smells of first-generation immigrants, low-ceilinged apartments with plastic on the furniture and chicken boiling in a kitchen pot all day. It was all claustrophobic, the onion steam, the exhaust fumes.

"That's the way Letty is, not me."

"You can't blame her forever."

"Sure I can."

"Pay attention," Charlotte said and hung up.

Honor was six months old when she drank the lemon oil furniture polish. It was in a clear plastic bottle and looked delicious, like thick lemon syrup. Honor, of course, would suck on anything; it was Marmee who thought she was doing her a favor.

Murray found her not breathing, smelled the gasoline smell on her mouth, saw the bottle, did CPR the way she'd seen Cagney do on TV the night before when her father died, not so rough, Murray knew better, Honor was an infant. She called nine-one-one and they talked her through it, got out the crash truck; Honor was still not conscious when Murray called me from the hospital.

I didn't have a reaction; it was one of those facts that shut the adrenaline down, along with everything else. Okay, Murray, I said, then I put the phone down. It was only one in the afternoon. Sister would fire me if I left, Charlotte would hate me if I left. I have to go, I told Charlotte.

"Uh, uh," Charlotte said, shaking her head vigorously from side to side. She didn't look up from her work.

"Honor's in the hospital." I was already in my jacket, digging in my pocket for the car keys. Charlotte looked up. "She drank furniture polish, she wasn't breathing." Matter-of-fact, no tears, no more feeling in the telling than in the hearing.

"I'll go with you," Charlotte said. "Just walk out casual, like we're going to lunch. We won't explain. Unless we have to. Later."

Honor was at Baptist; she didn't have a JDPS. Dr. Amos Brown was a Rockwellian drawing, practicing out of a gingerbread cottage on Magnolia Street, sending his patients to Baptist, a brilliant diagnostician who saw everything in terms of *Gone with the Wind*. Girls were Melanies or Scarletts, boys were Rhetts or Ashleys; Honor was a Scarlett before she had her Apgar. If a person has a Melanie or an Ashley, do you actually tell them? I'd asked him when he'd visited me in Recovery. Sure, he'd said, people usually get what they want. Dr. Brown knew she was out of danger by the time we arrived.

Murray didn't have time for me; taking Marmee to the

emergency room was like taking a toddler, only much taller
and not as cute. She walked into the examining rooms, pulled
aside curtains, scaring people who already were scared if they
were conscious. A woman older than Marmee was in the bed
next to Honor's, a tube in her nose and moaning. "I think
she's dead," Marmee said, peering into her face. The woman's
eyes opened. "You're supposed to be dead," Marmee said,
and the woman's eyes became frantic. "You going to be fine,
just fine," Murray said, jerking Marmee out into the hallway.

"We came to Baptist when our little boy died, though of
course it was too late," Charlotte said.

I looked at Honor. Tiny electrodes were stuck to her
naked chest, and an IV in a fine needle ran into her scalp.
The feistiness was all in the belly, heaving angrily. I kissed
her on the forehead, and she smiled expectantly at me, wanting liberty. She could tolerate pain, but not frustration. Or-
dinarily, she'd have moved by now, but she was waiting,
passively, to be freed. I began to cry. "How'd you stand it?"

"I didn't stand it. Now are you paying attention?"

"This is hard for you."

"It's been hard for me for over a *year*. Don't you get it?"

I told Charlotte about the movie I saw when I was seven,
where the father chose to let the mother die so the baby could
live. Seven was a memorable age, at my father's cousin's house
in New Jersey I saw a movie where they protected all the
people in a hospital from a psychotic killer by pulling sheets
over their faces as if they were dead. I slept with a sheet over
my head from that day on. Fear enveloped in a closed space,
different from a tunnel. "Who could feel anything for a
baby?" I said. "It wasn't as if they were real people, you
know. I don't think I'd cry now; the father made the right
decision."

"You didn't have to sit in a bar after all," Charlotte said,
and she put an arm around me.

"You can't enjoy Honor through me, can you?" I said
after a while.

"Not unless you're dead," she said, and I laughed.

That night I phoned Letty to tell her what happened. I wanted her to feel bad. "There was no good choice on who'd stay at the hospital," I said. "Marmee's too useless, Murray's too tied up with Marmee, and I'd have gotten fired. So Charlotte stayed."

"You could've called me," she said. "I'd have come and gotten her."

"She was barely conscious," I said.

"Not the baby. Mother. You're paying Murray to take care of that child. She should've stayed."

"Forget it," I said. When I'd gone back to pick up Charlotte, something had switched over in her. She held Honor on her lap, and I let her, reasoning that Honor was going to survive to make me old and crazy, that she wasn't going to die today, smashed into a Karmann Ghia windshield. Charlotte let her straddle her knee, facing her, pale eyes focused on greening ones. "You scared the shit out of us," she said to Honor. Honor didn't smell like a filling station anymore, more like an antiseptic hospital. She batted Charlotte on the breast. "They had to give her a bottleful of sugar water," she said. I told her I didn't care.

CHAPTER 17

*T*he truth was, I'd read about AIDS and wonder about Stephen Norris. I figured he kind of deserved it. Certainly not because he was gay, or even because he was generally vicious, but because I'd childishly wished it on him for telling me that he hated me. There was a book about bad things happening to good people and I thought there should be a book about when good things happen to bad people, basically a treatise on the capitalistic way of life. But there'd be no irony in bad things happening to bad people, so I kept it to myself, this wish I had for Stephen. Had he not been high risk, I'd never have thought about him again. I wouldn't have sat around thinking, for instance, about how he deserved to be hit by a car; those sorts of stories weren't on the nightly news. AIDS was across the canal in Gert Town, Murray told me that, but the closest I came to anyone in Gert Town was when the faculty parking lot was full or Murray needed a ride home after we went off daylight savings time. To me AIDS meant Stephen.

When he actually showed up on a documentary on Channel 4, I believed I'd done it to him. Mind-body connections, across time and space, they're possible with that much disgust, I thought. The show protected me from feeling sorry for him, focused as it was on the waste of such a valuable life. Stephen himself was willing to attest to that, "Here I am, thirty-seven years old, making a significant contribution to the local economy, and I'm going to die, and Washington didn't care until it was too late." All I heard was the arrogance, that he was infusing on-paper dollars into the city, hyping shopping centers that were losing money for big northern investors and giving false notions to people who should have been putting

their money into 5 percent savings accounts instead of buying
geegaws at the Hallmark store. New Orleans was more ter-
minally ill than Stephen. And more responsible for the purple
blotches on its own skin than Stephen was for the ones on
his. I could see his: he was stripped to the waist in the doctor's
office, blotchy naked legs dangling, for realism. Color TV,
blood would be a nice touch; sure enough, they cut to the
vials in the lab. He was helping to kill the city, he wasn't
worth a damn, we'd be better off without him, unless he was
replaced with someone with more drive, who could go even
farther in the wrong direction.

Honor didn't like the news. I switched to the Disney
Channel, eight-ninety-five a month. She went to Newcomb
Nursery School, and she was a costly child to keep. A school-
mate named Amanda visited one Saturday afternoon. I
offered her ketchup for her hamburger. "This is a forty-five-
dollar dress," Amanda said indignantly. She was still wearing
diapers, as was Honor, but Amanda was going to be a mean
uptown matron, I could feel it. Weekends I catalogued and
appraised libraries for rich people afraid of fire. They tended
to buy by color, shelves of rich brown leather, some maroon,
gave the study a good scent. Though lately New Orleans was
bringing home writers who liked the Truman Capote smell
of things: signed books were all the rage, worth saving, or at
least declaring for insurance purposes. Honor had a Nintendo,
and she was still small enough to think her house was as good
as anyone else's; she more than held her own. All my extra
time was gone, keeping up with the parents who registered
their children at birth, expecting that they'd stay in New
Orleans and repeat the cycle. The Carnival attitude, narrower
than any tunnel I'd ever built for myself, nothing existing
outside the thoroughly familiar. They inherited their money,
but no one in my family in the right position was kind enough
to die.

I charged the parents of Honor's friends a thousand dollars to make cards and a floppy disk and an insurance ap-
praisal for all their books, in a fireproof metal box: they

thought they had something quite fine. Their children were getting educated, learning social protocols, little girls kicking little boys in the groin or teeth, and they thought books sounded like smart people's investments. I'd come back next year for a hundred dollars to update, like a washing machine warranty, or termite maintenance, a hundred dollars to add in books worth maybe half that much.

I dreamed about Stephen that night. Thoughts truncated in the day played back at night, like a song you cut off with the motor in the car: it comes back, and you're sorry you didn't just sit in the car until the fade-out to the commercial. I was working in the hospital, I don't know why. Stephen was in a semiprivate room, next to the door, probably because that was how they always picture people in the hospital, good camera angle. He was naked, with a sheet draped across his privates. The sheet was dirty, everything was dirty. Kaposi's sarcoma covered him, like a burn victim; he was thin and dangerous-looking, but he wasn't weak. A thin plastic tube came out of his abdomen, like a straw, half-filled with blood. I was supposed to suck on the straw. No one else was in the room. Stephen kept screaming at me; he was strong, he grabbed my head, forcing my mouth down near the straw. I pressed my lips together, shook my head, pulled away. He chased me down the hall, droplets of blood trailing behind. I doubled back, slipped in the blood, catching myself with my hand. My hand touched the blood; I looked at it for open cuts, found none. After that I was home, but I was worried, and I kept inspecting my hand. Stephen didn't die, but I became sicker and sicker, thin and breastless and covered in purple lesions.

Honor woke me by smacking me on both cheeks. That was the way she got my attention, moving my head. "You are not looking directly at me," she'd say, cupping my chin in her hand and pulling my face up from a book in the daytime. Honor said "directly" as clearly as if she'd been saying it for years. Where she got language, I didn't know. She talked like me, not like Murray, with whom she spent

her afternoons, delivered to Marmee's in Murray's husband
Isaiah's taxi, while I still worked at St. Francis. I wanted to
quit, but it was so secure, rent and food in case the frills
money dried up. "I don't want to get up," I said. "Get up!"
she shrilled. "I want to watch 'Noozles.'" "*You* turn it on."
Honor could do anything: she could flip through the cable
channels, she could make herself a frozen waffle. She couldn't
use the toilet yet, but that was a power play. It made Murray
crazy. "Bad enough your grandma can't do it, but this child
know better, she got more sense."

The doorbell rang, and Honor screamed that she would
get it. She could do that, too, when the key was in the lock,
and only because she had an uncanny survival instinct did
she not unlock the front door and go trooping out on a whim
every now and then. I'd have wakened and found her like a
dead dog on Tchoupitoulas Street, her silky pale hair black-
ened by tire tracks. I tore behind her, straight from the bed;
the squalor could come right in the door.

It was Parker. I shoved Honor behind me. He wasn't
going to see her, because I wasn't ever going to have to tell
her that he'd seen her and not come back. She was almost
three, and for over three years he and I had had a tacit
agreement on the streets. I knew he still lived in the warehouse
because the Audi often was there when I passed. I figured
he knew how to avoid me, because he was succeeding at
doing so.

"What's the matter?" I said. I had to restrain Honor; she
could tolerate anything but frustration. My hands were behind
my back, and my nightgown was gaping at the front. She
spun around and crossed my wrists, dancing away until I
thought she would rip my arms off if I didn't let go. "One
minute, please," I said to Parker and kicked the door shut.
"You stay on that sofa and you watch TV," I said. She gave
me a look of an asylum administrator who'd just seen an
inmate wielding a meat cleaver. I slipped out onto the front
steps and pulled the door closed behind me, key in hand, just
in case. Honor had locked me out once before, in my night-

clothes, a freezing wet morning, 6 A.M. There had been no way to break in, no way to get an extra key; I'd had to offer to buy her a Cherry Merry Muffin before she'd turned the key.

"I think I owe you an explanation," he said. I laughed, short and loud and almost ugly. He gave me a wry smile.

"Why?"

"Stephen was on TV last night. You see it?"

I nodded. I owed *him* an explanation, having wished Stephen dead, slowly and painfully, no shot to the head for him, make it last much longer than his words had that night in Nature's Way.

"I want you to know I didn't sleep with him until after I slept with you."

This is why people faint, the blood goes down to your feet so you can escape, though I don't know why being all sloggy and tumescent with blood would make feet move at all. My head emptied out, and right away I sat on the step, putting my hollow head between my knees, fill it up. I had low blood pressure; it wouldn't have taken much to drop me into shock.

"I don't want to know about this," I said. It had never occurred to me before. I put my hands over my ears. I thought about Honor's body, which I knew better than my own. No flaws, no marks, the strawberry stain above the nape of her neck long gone, I assumed. All her systems worked fine. Did that mean anything? I hadn't paid attention to what the TV narrator was saying last night; I was too busy watching Stephen, trying to see whether he was suffering. They'd shown a baby at Charity, his mother probably back on the street, shooting up and spreading disease. He looked fine to me, but he was only six months old.

Parker didn't leave. "You can't come in," I said.

"You sure?"

"I haven't thought a lot of things through, but *this* thing I've thought through."

"You ought to talk to me."

"That's why he hated me," I said, putting it together.
"How do you know?"
"He told me."

Honor began banging on the inside of the door. "I want to watch 'Jem,'" she said. I looked at Parker. "Jem" was plastic trash, slut fantasy thinly veiled, cat fights, saccharine triumphant over imagination. If he was going to get a set of images to take away, one smell, one vision, one sound, one bit of culture, I didn't want "Jem" to be part of it. "Peer pressure," I said, and he looked at me blankly. She banged again, scratch another image. At least she was beautiful, if he had to see her, and maybe he ought to see her, register a good image, balance the rest. I didn't want her to see him seeing her, that was the problem. "Come back when she's asleep," I said. "When's that?" I told him nine.

Honor was a terror, mostly because her instincts were so fine. They worked well sometimes, when she was favorably disposed toward me. She knew when to keep a secret, and she only divulged it if she was angry. When I walked back into the house, and she asked who that was, and I said, A man, and she said, Maybe he was a daddy, I knew I had to keep her from being angry at me. Which wasn't easy, because I was the one who shampooed her hair at night, and when nine o'clock came, she was wide-awake. Go to bed, and I'll take you to K&B tomorrow, I said. She wanted to go right then. K&B's closed, I told her, it's dark out. Uh, uh, she said, you took me there in the dark when I had an earache. That was an emergency. *This* is an emergency, she said, clear as a bell. Walk to bed, or I'll have to put you there. She wanted a book read. One, I said. She pulled out a Richard Scarry book, with all the anthropomorphic little characters scattered all over the page with bits of commentary in four-point letters under each picture fragment. No! I said. I pulled out *Good-night Moon*. She had to find the mouse on every page. It was ten after nine. My hands were shaking. The fucking mouse is on top of the bookcase, I said. I *know* that! she screamed, Now we have to do it over again! The doorbell rang. You

stay put, I said, and she bounced out of bed and followed
me. I picked her up by the shoulders. "This time you are
going to listen," I said, my tone like Murray's, as if I meant
what I said. I put her onto the bed, and she began to wail.
But she didn't move; the wailing stopped, a few snuffles, then
silence. I pulled the door closed behind me and ran before
Parker could ring again. I'd have thought he'd have done so
by then, but he hadn't.

I think there is a certain point in life when you recognize
that you may not see a person or place again, that you can
know a floor plan or a personality very well, but you won't
actually be there even one more time in your life. It happened
to me early, the first time when I was in fourth grade, leaving
public school. The screaming white trash at the downtown
public schools had caught the attention of Steinbeck, the
networks, and even Letty, who made up her mind that I
wasn't going to be a political experiment. Marmee went
down and demonstrated at Frantz School with the other
Cadillac liberals. Save our schools, they chanted, then jumped
into their fancy cars and drove off, all breathless, while
the fat, tight-permed hags of the neighborhood stayed until
nightfall, screaming, two-four-six-eight-we-don't-want-to-
integrate. The smell of my school, of cooked green peas and
chalk dust, the music teacher with the huge black mole on
her neck, the pink disinfectant dust on the bathroom floor,
the loudspeaker with the lozenge pattern in the center circle,
I knew I was never going to see that again. Private school
was quietly clean, scoured after hours; loudspeakers weren't
needed to tamp down the teeming masses of poor people's
children. Different.

After that experience I took a measure of many encounters, whether to save them if they were final. Parker was
probably dying, so this didn't need to be the last meeting. A
last meeting was guaranteed.

He tiptoed in, looked around the living room. I told him
the coast was clear. He asked me why he couldn't see her.

"Because if you never see her again, there'll be the fact of it. When she asks, I'll have to tell her."

"I want to see her more than once," he said. Maybe, I told him.

"Nice place you have here," he said, and I rolled my eyes back in my head, expecting something better of him. I had furniture in the living room now, an Early American table from Magazine Street, Eddie's sofa and two of his chairs, an art deco desk Letty handed down to me for my birthday last year, a rattan love seat I'd found at the Goodwill in perfect condition, not tacky enough for most Goodwill shoppers, a dhurrie Charlotte let me have for twenty dollars, bookcases that I'd sneaked out of the library one Saturday afternoon, fine old wood and out of use, now that there was metal sectional shelving instead. All the holes were filled with plants: that was another beauty of a shotgun, light from both sides, river and lake.

"Real people live here now," I said. He nodded. I could tell he didn't know what I meant. "I'd offer you a drink, but I don't want to wake her up. Unless you want something straight. You want something straight?" I opened the bottom of the desk, and there was most of Marmee's liquor. Every Friday I'd give Murray a hundred twenty dollars cash, and she'd give me something from Marmee's larder. Your lagniappe, she said sometimes, your inheritance, she said other times, her guilt cutting both ways, that she was taking money from me, that she was taking food from Marmee. I had a freezerful of meats that were too tough to cook unless you poured MSG all over them, the way Murray kept Marmee puffed up, tenderized from the inside out. I cocked my head to the side. Parker passed on the drink. Maybe he was into health: the first stage is denial, before you go off and spend the rest of your life eating raw cookie dough, knowing you're doomed anyway.

"You could have gotten away without telling me anything," I said. "I never put you and Stephen together."

He stood up, shoved his hands into his pockets, and bent at the waist toward me. "You've got to be joking."

I shrugged. "You were a pretty terrific lover," I said, looking him in the eye. It was the sort of thing you can say only when you have power.

"I wanted to be."

"You can't fake that," I said, though for all I knew you could. Women certainly could fake just about anything.

"I liked it," he said, looking at the floor. I patted the sofa, and he sat down again. "You could have won out, you know, you just didn't have any fighting spirit. Stephen was so *driven*; he had to have me, wouldn't let me alone. You were some sort of fucking fatalist: it was as if you were saying, hey, if he doesn't come groveling at my door, so what?"

"I didn't know it was a goddamn contest."

"How could you miss?"

"Charlotte says I don't pay attention."

"Charlotte pays attention. Almost cost me my biggest client."

"Arthur?"

"Taking pictures of shopping centers is big bucks. And easy, as long as it doesn't rain, and there's always one day a week when it doesn't rain. Shopping centers don't move, they don't talk back. And I'm goddamn good at it. But she told him and then he decided that Stephen was giving me business because he was in love with me, and only because Stephen threatened to quit working for the agency did he keep me on. Great way to earn a living, having your lover lying on his client's floor kicking his feet in the air until you get the job. Does a lot for the ego."

"Why didn't you tell Stephen I didn't know?"

"Because I assumed you did know. When you're trying to hide something, you figure everyone's seeing it."

"I've never tried."

"Like fun. You hide a lot."

"What'm I hiding now?"

"That you want to see me again."

I didn't know why that was true. I didn't need more babies from him, and I couldn't let him make love to me; I wasn't that crazy. He was distilled down to essence, and I liked him. Besides, he was Honor's father, a stranger she'd brought home one day from her other life, as if she were an adopted child, and now I could explore her origins, find out why she could roll her tongue into a trough or paint pictures with a tri-part balance like perfect photographs shot through a jelly haze or go crazy after eating a chocolate bar. If Honor was like me, and if AIDS was as swift as I thought it was, he was going to die before she reached the age of recall. I remembered places from when I was three, but people didn't imprint themselves on my memory until I was six, except the ones who cheated by showing up in photographs. He was a picture-taker, no risk there.

I could hear the phone ringing, all the way at the back, insistent. Four rings, then a hang up. Seven rings, a hang up. Then it began ringing without stopping. Parker heard it, too. "I have to answer that, or my mother will be over here in ten minutes."

"I'll leave in nine," he said.

"I don't want her here." All the doors through the house were closed, making compartments, one for the phone, one for Honor, one for us. But with each ring the phone became louder. I told Parker I'd be right back. I slipped into my bedroom, closed the door behind me, leaving no light, slipped into Honor's room, making more noise than I thought was possible. It was like decontaminating from a radioactive chamber, this passage, room to room, vault to vault. Honor stirred, then sat up. She talked through a soupy sleep; she'd remember nothing in the morning. "What are you doing, Darby?" "You're asleep," I told her. "The phone is ringing." "You're asleep." She flounced back, squirmed like a puppy, and was quiet. The phone was still ringing, and now I rushed. My luck, Letty would give up right before I answered. I opened the door to the back room, and the phone went silent. It was on the floor, I kicked it across the room, rented equipment, take it in and they give you a new one, reconditioned, but without Honor's marker scribbles. It didn't break. I decided to phone her back. She picked up on the second ring. "Letty, what's wrong with you?" I said.

"*Shhh!* Eddie's asleep! I've told you never to call this late, the phone rings right in the bedroom."

"Were you just calling me?"

"Yes, I'm so excited. Listen, I just wrote the best poem, I've got to tell you about it, I was halfway into a dress, I was coming over there, you make me sick with worry when you don't answer the phone, makes me think something's happened, particularly at this hour, I know you're not out with that child, not at this hour, I'd hope. Listen, I've got it right here, ready?"

"Letty, I have company."

"It's only eight lines."

"No, goddammit, this is important."

"This is important, too. You're lucky, most girls your age have mothers who don't do anything, they have to drive them to the beauty parlor and everything, all I ask is for you to listen every now and then."

"I have to go," I said and hung up. Before I could get through Honor's door again, the phone was ringing. I didn't answer.

When I reached the front, Parker was gone. A note lay on the sofa, scribbled on the back of a Whitney Bank deposit slip. I opened the front door, in case he'd just left, but he wasn't anywhere on the street that I could see. "I want to take you both to the park. Tomorrow, 1:00. Cancel only if you have other plans, please? P." It seemed Letty had done me a favor, but I certainly wasn't going to tell anyone.

Usually only Honor fretted over the way she dressed. She was almost three, but she could read labels as well as Letty. She wasn't a prodigy, just an uptown child, knew Liberty meant Wal Mart, knew Esprit meant approval. She had an eye for fashion, let the rest wear pink, she wore green, saved the inborn love of pink for bedsheets and crayons and birthday cakes. Honor had green eyes that were so translucent and oceanic that they made Letty's look small and dull and bilious. She chose a sweatshirt and miniskirt and matching socks, and when she willingly let me do battle with her hair, I knew that she thought it was important to look especially fine today. Her instinct kicked in; wanting something overrode any wish to make me frantic with arguing. Her hair was down past her shoulder blades, fine and shiny and straight, none of the Cooper-women wave, still strawberry blond. Most children her age missed the cues, the ladies on the street, in the drug-store, addressing their remarks to the proud mother: Such a beautiful child, they'd say, and Honor would say, Thank you, and they'd fall all over themselves; Hey, sugar, come over here and see this little woman.

I told her that my friend the man who rang the bell yesterday was coming to take us to the park. "He might be a daddy," she said, very matter-of-fact, but for a second I felt sorry for her.

"Some people have daddies, and some people don't. Some daddies last forever, some stay a little while, some you barely see, and some you don't see at all," I said. Already two of her friends were fatherless: four years into a marriage their daddies had had enough, and their mothers seemed just as glad of it.

"I want to ride the camel," Honor announced. I stuffed a ten and a five into my pocket.

At one o'clock, my heart was beating so fast that there were no downbeats, all flubs, no dubs. I combed Honor's hair until she grabbed my wrist and pushed me away. I found bits of lint on the dhurrie; I picked them up, had nowhere to put them, slipped them into my jeans pocket. The palm plant had a lot of brown undergrowth I'd never noticed before; I began plicking off dead leaves with my fingernails. Nowhere to put those, either. The doorbell rang; I dropped the leaves at the bottom of the pot, good cannibal mulch, for all I knew. "I'll get it," Honor shrilled. She stood on a chair, and I knew he could hear her fiddling with the key. Manual dexterity, independence, good impressions.

"I'm Parker," he said, bending slightly, but not crouching, not insulting her.

"I'm Honor, pleased to meet you." Parker gave me a broad grin, and I looked at Honor; I didn't know she had it in her. "Murray told me that," she said.

When we headed downtown, the evil fantasies began to spin. When he cut over to the bridge approach, the center failed to hold; I was sure we were being abducted. The West Bank was the Fischer housing project and levees and Popeye's chicken outlets on every corner and big weedy lots where you could dump a dead body. At least that's the part that showed up in the *Times-Picayune*.

"I thought we were going to the zoo," I said. The zoo was uptown.

"The park."

"There's no park over here." We were at the pinnacle of the bridge; Parker went back into overdrive.

"There's nothing but park between here and the Gulf practically," he said.

"Darby, do you love me?" Honor said from the backseat.

"Of course I love you." Nothing but park between here and the Gulf, bayous so covered over with algae, they'd never find our bones.

"Darby, do you love me?" she said again.

"Yes, I love you."

We hit Barataria Boulevard. "Pirates hid out here," I said. I remembered Louisiana history, in third grade and again in eighth grade, full of idiots battling yellow fever and snakes and the British so they could live in the hottest, muggiest place in the northern hemisphere. Jean Lafitte was a sneaky little shit, getting away with his crimes simply by knowing how to ply the backwaters and get out when the getting was good. A terrific model for whatever Parker was up to.

We were in the country, though we were only twenty

minutes from my house. Bait shops along the road. White people walking along the highway, skin burnished brown and precancerous by the sun. They looked like the types who always found the dead bodies back in the swamps, poking sticks around, looking for excitement, maybe a snake, preferably something worse. I was trembling. "Mommy, do you love me?" Honor said. " 'Mommy'?" I said. I'd only called Letty Mommy maybe a half dozen times in my life; this was Honor's first attempt at the word.

I saw national park markers and sat back in the seat. "We'll see alligators," Parker said to Honor.

"Then I want to ride on the camel," she said, the fear switched off.

We passed the ranger station, and I began to get nervous all over again. "Where're you taking us?"

"I'm taking you to a dark swamp to hack you into tiny pieces and feed you to the alligators."

"Mommy, is he joking?"

"Are you joking?"

"You see an ax in the car?"

I looked on the backseat and saw a camera bag. Less than a mile up from the ranger station was a sign, Bayou Coquille, and we turned in. The parking lot was full of late-model cars. A good Sunday afternoon, a dozen children in detergent-commercial bright stripes, forty-dollar tennis shoes. I was ashamed of myself.

Anywhere else in the world, snakes knew winter was coming and had burrowed underground. But I'd been to Mississippi with my grandparents often enough as a child to know that Delta snakes have no sense, that they flop around in the marshes a week before a drop into the forties. They were too lethargic to do anything, but they scared me anyway, primordial fear, dating too far back to spring from actual experience. We took the boardwalk, and I watched the ground along either side, part fascination, part terror. "Are alligators reptiles?" I said. Parker was walking first, then Honor, then me; the words sailed right over her head. "You work in a

library, don't you know taxonomic classification?" "It wasn't
in the course work," I said. Parker stopped; there was a little
family of cypress knees, stair steps alongside us. He crouched
and took a photo.

"They're not fish," Honor said, about the cypress knees
or the alligators, there was no knowing short of asking. Honor
wasn't thinking about snakes, and I hadn't brought up the
subject. She was waiting for the camel. She wanted every
flower, and I let her take a fistful of Bishop's-weed before
Parker turned around and saw her. "They want to save every
flower, every tree; you're not supposed to take any," he said
gently. "I think they're beautiful," Honor said. "Well, then
don't let anyone see you," he said. He opened his camera bag
and pulled out a plastic Ziploc bag full of unused film,
dumped the film into the camera bag, held open the Ziploc,
let her drop in the flower, slipped it back in next to the loose
film.

The bag filled quickly, yellow, white, blue, lavender, scar-
let of creeping spotflower and tickseed, lemon mint, pick-
erelweed and asters, Indian fire. But Honor wanted a water
hyacinth. The bayou was covered with them, but they were
all out beyond reach, unless we waded, and no one would
wade where there were alligators, under the water making
little whirlpools, the same color as the murky water if they'd
surface. "I want the big purple ones!" she screamed. "Then
go get one yourself," I said. Honor stepped off the boardwalk,
and I grabbed her arm. "You said I could go."

"How about a picture of one?" Parker said.

"Your camera doesn't make pictures right away. Letty
has a Polaroid," Honor said.

Parker shrugged. I told her to keep walking, that maybe
some were closer to shore farther on. "Where's the camel?"
she said. I told her this wasn't the zoo. "You said we were
going to the zoo."

"I said to the *park*."

"The park's the same thing as the zoo."

Right then a boy ahead of us found a snake, and I was glad of it. A king snake, Parker said, its blunt nose edging along the ground, as if it were drunk; he took a picture. Honor bent over it, transfixed. Parker sidestepped around her gracefully, took another shot, Honor looking at the snake. She reached out with one finger, tracing the snake's slowly undulating form. I stayed back until the crowd had dispersed; the snake had lazed off into the underbrush, and I ran past the spot. "They have snakes at the zoo," Honor said, hand on hip. "But they're in glass cases," I said.

The pontoon boat passed, aggravating everyone; so far no one had seen an alligator surface, except on the far bank. "It's eating my flowers!" Honor hollered. "Don't you do that, man, you're mashing up my flowers." A grinder on the boat was sucking them in, chewing them up, making a pile at the back of the boat. It was a tiresome sort of job, like mowing the levee, back and forth across a vast stretch, finishing in time to start over again, Sisyphus pushing the rock up the hill, watching it roll back down. He saw Honor on the boardwalk, jumping up and down, face red, little fists clenched in the air. The motor cut, and he drifted over toward us. "You're eating my flowers," Honor said.

He smiled. "You want some?" "Yeh," she said, fists loosening at her sides. He looked at the pile, all torn, putted out to the middle, plucked three, and putted back to her. "Put 'em in your backyard pond, you'll have thirty-six thousand in a year—times three," he said, then dumped the pile of shredded flowers on the bank, revved up fast, shot back to center. I told Honor to say thank you. "I hate saying thank you," she said. "Give me the flowers then," I said. "Thank you," she whispered, though the man couldn't have heard her if she'd shouted by that time.

Parker stopped at an ice house along the road back and bought Honor a pack of Ho-Ho's and a Coke in a frosty glass bottle. "Thank you," she said, and gave him a kiss on the thigh. She fell asleep while we were still on Barataria Boulevard, the Ho-Ho's open and crushed and uneaten, the Coke held perfectly vertical, though she had flopped down on the seat.

I carried her into the house, chocolate crumbs trailing me, Coke left on the front steps, Parker following with my purse. When she was exhausted, Honor sometimes slept with her eyes partially open, a tiny slice of the bright green irises visible. I lay her on her bed on her back, and she looked dead. Parker bent over closer to see the small rise and fall of her chest. I told him she was alive, remembering when I'd watched Indira. I walked back to the living room, expecting the front door to be open. It was always open when I came in with Honor asleep, a minor risk I had to take: getting her to the back without awakening her outweighed the possibility that right then someone was going to pass and see the door open and walk in and rob me and rape me and leave me for dead. Every time I came back to close the door, I had that familiar rush of adrenaline, expecting a strange man to be standing in my living room. This time it was closed; I'd never come in with another person before.

Parker brushed a wisp of hair off my face and bent over to kiss me. I pulled away. The intellect kicked in, though sexual hunger and self-destructive tendencies were so strong. Go to bed with him, I'd come for an hour, remember it all the time I was dying. I wasn't so self-destructive now that I had Honor. I was expected to make her survive, though for Honor survival sometimes rested on a hundred-dollar toy, and in the process I had no choice but to stay alive. I had to do my job and eat my food so I wouldn't get sick, and sometimes I thought that I had Honor not so much for companionship but so I'd have a reason to behave right. I remembered that the day I took my pregnancy test I'd begun drinking orange juice.

"I know what I do to you," he said. His voice was low; the green of his eyes was soft, bedroom green. He didn't take his hand away from my face.

"I'm not into risks," I said. He smiled. "Serious risks, you know what I mean."

"I don't have AIDS."

"Sure you do." We were together because he had AIDS, he was going to die, he'd seen Honor, and later on I could tell her he'd seen her and he'd loved her and now he was dead and it was too sad.

"Trust me, that's something I've paid attention to."

"I don't get it." I stood back, arms folded across my chest.

"When's Honor's birthday?"

"January eleventh."

He began counting on his fingers. "January's nine months after April, right? I met Stephen when we went to that dinner. And there were a couple of months in between the times I saw you. So I met him in January or February."

"That dinner," I echoed. "February. *That* dinner."

"That dinner. I won't go into the confusions, you can figure them out yourself."

"I've been great at that so far."

"Hey, Darby, I was torn." He shoved his hands into his pockets.

"See, Stephen knew that, but I didn't. Not fair game rules."

"True." He gave me a wry little smile. "He hated your guts, and he wrote his own rules, I guess: expect the other guy to play along without all the necessary information."

"Like the basics, like that we're playing at all. Shit, I thought it was terrific that I brought you over there, that you got the account."

"It did make Stephen rather appealing. Money can do that."

"So I've learned from my mother." We're doing this on your grandmother's money, Letty said whenever we did something costly. Letty phoned Marmee every morning of her adult life, until Marmee forgot what a phone was, never saying anything, just doing her duty, earning her right to

another generation of handed-down money. I gave her back
the gray dress for the wedding, Honor's dress for the wedding. She wore the gray dress herself, probably sent the baby
dress to Linda, though it never came back in the hand-me-
downs bag.

"Now you're going to die," I said.

"I tested negative. I was careful."

I laughed. He didn't wear a condom with me; he knew
what to be afraid of, what to try to make happen. He proved
something to himself, making Honor, but his belief that he
was straight didn't last long enough. Stephen's anger would
have been persuasive; I could imagine him telling Parker how
diffident and useless women were, offering him job after job
when I offered him nothing except perhaps responsibility.

"He's in love with me, that counts for something," Parker
said.

"I saw him on TV. He's got six months, tops. What're
you doing, looking for a replacement?"

"That's mean."

"That's true. Goddamn you, I can take a lot, but I am
not going to be first runner-up."

"Maybe I made a mistake," he said. "I'm sorry." His hand
reached for me again, and I backed away.

"I want you to leave." Emphatic, no begging for arguments; I meant it.

"I want to see you both again."

"No."

"What'll you tell her?"

"Nothing. She won't remember you. I'll throw away
the Ho-Ho's, and that's what she'll holler for when she
wakes up."

"And ten years from now?"

"I'll lie."

"No, you won't."

The door opened, and Honor walked in. Her face was
pink on the side she'd slept on too hard, and her eyes were
droopy. "You're still sleeping," I said, picking her up and

putting her head on my shoulder so she'd go back to sleep. She saw Parker. "Where's my cake?" she said to him.

"It was smashed. I put it in the trash," I said.

She pushed away from me and slid down to the floor. She ran to the trash basket and saw nothing, darted into the next room, found it and came running back, trailing crumbs. I snatched it from her. "No!" she screamed. I held it high. She jumped like a miniature basketball player.

"I could get you another one tomorrow," Parker said to her. The bouncing stopped.

"No, he can't," I said, opening the front door.

"Chocolate," she cried out after him. "I only like chocolate!"

CHAPTER 18

T hree weeks later I moved into Marmee's house, not a permanent sort of move, just clothes and toilet articles and toys. I stopped the *Times-Picayune* and had my mail forwarded. It was like rooming with Tikki all over again, taking refuge, costing me something, costing Tikki nothing, in fact gaining her quite a bit. Tikki had had the sense of having a single room for most of freshman year: I was a specter who'd roomed there, maybe that year, maybe in 1940, for all she knew. Running from Parker was different, because he searched for me. I could have handled him, except for Honor. Possibly I even could have welcomed him, except for Honor.

He came by Monday night, not with a pack of Ho-Ho's, but with a box of Doberge squares, all chocolate. Honor knew quality, knew that a sharp white box that smelled of a bakery was finer than something wrapped in plastic in a convenience store. The bell rang at eight-thirty. Honor was in her jammies, diapered up for the night, her hair in sweet damp tendrils falling down her back. When I read to her, she snuggled as close to me as she could, it was the good part. Horton the Elephant, hatching the egg, I read with derisive little *hmphs* all through. The work was all done, now she wanted it back. *Hah!* I said. Poor Maysie, Honor said. Hey, I said, the point of the story is that Horton did all the work, he sat on that egg for fifty-one weeks. Maysie doesn't deserve squat. But she looks so sad, Honor said. I shrugged. There's room for discussion, I said, more to the air than anything.

I didn't let Parker through the door. He slipped the box to Honor, the way I'd slipped the baklava through his security gate: go down low, get it through. The box was taped shut, and Honor couldn't get it open. I told her no, that chocolate would make her crazy, and then she'd make me crazy; I could see the Doberge through a plastic window in the top, six little squares, icing shiny. I thought I might steal a few after she went to sleep. Honor couldn't count objects, just singsong one to ten, but she knew a broken pattern when she saw one. Maybe I could pass five off for six, but that was about it.

Parker pulled a pocket knife out and cut the tape. He was crouched down on one knee, halfway across the threshold. "I said no, and no to you, too," I screamed. Honor put her hand on her hip; the movement came straight from her Letty genes. "Can I have one?" she asked Parker. "Your mother said no," he said, painting me the villain with his tone, not backing me up at all.

"I hate you, Darby," she said.

"*Oooo*, that's really going to make me want to give you a cake," I said.

"I love you, Darby," she said and patted me on my bottom.

"Can I come in?" Parker said.

"No!"

"Can I have a cake, please?" Honor said.

"I have something for you," Parker said to me.

"No!"

"Please?" Honor said, kissing the hem of my skirt.

"You wait here, you don't move, I mean it," I said to Parker, and I took Honor into the back room, seated her at the table, and opened the box. "Have at it," I said. She couldn't eat more than one anyway, though she might very well lick the icing off all six. I wasn't going to sleep tonight, I knew it now.

Parker had stepped just one step into the living room. That was fair; it wasn't a great neighborhood. "I know what you're trying to do," I said. "And I'm not going to be the one to let you do it."

"I want to see you and Honor."

"You want to fucking justify your existence. Know what

my father always used to say? Too late!" My father would put two handfuls of change in front of himself, palms up, tell me to take one. I'd try to do a fast count, though I was only five or six; what did I know? Ten seconds, the change went back into his pocket. Too late, he'd sing out.

"It's not too late."

"Isn't it? It's too late for somebody to figure out a way to give your friend Stephen his immune system back, ever think of that? Then what, you going to go running back to him, take your first best option, quit settling for me and pretending to be fucking normal?"

"I haven't seen Stephen in months."

"I admire your loyalty." He was going to make me cry, he was going to have to get out of there.

"Hey, I can't win for losing here."

"To tell you the truth, I can't either," I said.

He handed me a manila envelope, "For Darby" written on it, not "To: Darby." "Aw, no, you've got to go now," I said.

"See you later," he said, and took the steps the way long-legged people can do, a shuffle down an incline more than actual steps, barely hitting with the balls of his feet.

It was the photograph of Honor at the park, black-and-white, so her hair took the tone of the pale markings on the back of the snake. Her hair hung down around her face, sinuous, beckoning the snake, her finger reaching out; you could see he was motionless, not threatening at all, the way he lay. Honor was as unafraid as Letty, a trait that clearly skipped generations. Was it a boy snake? Probably, all snakes were boys. When I was very small, I thought all dogs were boys, all cats were girls. Some nursery rhyme, a dog and a cat were dancing together in the accompanying illustration, though I don't think that's where I got it. I was glad English didn't have masculine and feminine nouns: it left my perceptions up to me.

Good warm glycerine tears started, and I brushed them aside, locked the door. I expected a major mess at the back, no napkins, lots of chocolate; Honor would have to be bathed all over again. She was sitting at the table, a decorous smear of chocolate on one cheek, her hands and jammies perfectly clean. I looked into the cake box, five cakes left, a row of three, two side by side. "Chocolate makes me crazy, and I make you crazy," Honor said. I spat on my finger, wiped the smear off her cheek, kissed her on the wet spot.

"Why are you so scared of Parker?" Honor said. I pulled back to look at her. Where did that come from? That from a child who still wore a diaper? She put her skinny arms around my neck, and I held her. I let her sleep in my bed that night, and she kicked the daylights out of my kidneys until I moved to the sofa at 3 A.M. But I liked having her there, didn't consider picking her up and moving her at all.

Parker phoned, Parker left gifts. Honor was no shield, Charlotte was no shield, silence was no shield. "That kid could stand having a father," Charlotte would say, her hand covering the phone, then passing it to me. Honor spent some Saturday afternoons at the Altmanns', sometimes without me. Or I'd kill a bottle of Cold Duck with Charlotte, while Arthur made raspberry ice cream with Honor. She stood on a kitchen stool, wearing Charlotte's apron and a stained purple-pink mustache. Through a good afternoon drunk I'd watch the two of them, cranking and licking, Arthur seeing a mean jay in the yard, telling Honor that sometimes he thought the squirrels were pesky, to tell the truth, maybe they deserved what the jays handed out. "Animals with fur are mammals, they're the best," Honor said back. Charlotte and I were the audience, not trying to hide after a while, laughing at Arthur and Honor, mean as jays ourselves.

"I won't talk to you, you blew it," I'd say into the phone, then hang up. Parker wasn't obnoxious, he wouldn't dial right back; I'd find a tiny Hello Kitty purse in the mailbox when we got home, wrapped, with a pink ribbon.

"Letty owns a piece of this house," I announced to Murray Monday morning, showing up at the door with Honor, two suitcases, a box of Huggies, and a garbage sack brimming

with toys. Newcomb Nursery was closed for the holidays:
Honor got a college-sized vacation. "I'm just using her forced
portion."

"Come in, *child*," Murray said, quite pleased. She couldn't
wait to see William, I could tell. Murray loved mess better
than eating, and she hadn't had much in a while, nothing to
natter over with her friends on the phone since they'd doubled
up Marmee's Haldol. Marmee ate and babbled and drooled,
and no one came to see her except Honor. Murray was
having to stir up conflict with Veronica, claiming Indira ought
to be getting support from her natural daddy, anything for
Murray to rant about until the soaps came on. William was
going to have a fit about my moving in; William was as
bored as Murray, and he didn't have afternoon television to
distract him.

"I don't care what you do, just don't mention my name
in all this," Letty had said when I'd told her I was moving
in to Marmee's. She still remembered Linda's staying three
years back: a week with a small child in her house, tipping
glass bottles and stinking up the garbage. She knew I could
visit next if she wasn't careful. I didn't tell her my reasons
for running away from home. She'd have begun planning a
wedding.

"Just one thing," Murray called out as I walked to the
car, my stuff still lined up in the foyer, visible from the street.
"You can stay, but *these* got to go." She gave the Huggies a
boot half out the door for emphasis.

"Saturday, I'm off Saturday, I'll do it Saturday," I said.
William I messed around with, not Murray.

I bought the book on training a child in one day. I got
a doll at K&B with a hole in its crotch and a crude baby
bottle, only three-fifty-nine. Three cans of Pringles, a liter of
Gatorade, a bag of Brach's assorted candies. Murray was on
duty Saturday. I told her I needed three hours alone in the
kitchen. She called Isaiah, told him take her to Winn-Dixie;
she could pass three hours, watching Marmee lift stuff off
the shelves, try to cram it in her underwear, fight Murray

for it. "Shoot, I hate to be the one buy cake mix she done stuffed in her drawers," Murray had said the last time she'd taken Marmee on such an outing. Murray enjoyed getting sympathy while she gently beat up on Marmee, all in the name of honest shopping.

I followed the book, followed the clock. Filled Honor with chips, candies, made her drink until her bladder was as puffed as an adder, sat her on the potty. Filled the dolly with water, let her spritz into the potty, gave her a candy, Honor rolling her eyes in disbelief. Half an hour, an hour, an hour and a half, not a dribble. Finally Honor peed, a great puddle in the middle of the kitchen floor. "Damn!" I shouted, to hell with the moderate tone of the book. Honor picked up the soggy doll and batted me over the head, an arc of water flying behind it. "This doll is stupid," she screamed. I popped her back into a diaper and went to wait on the front steps for Murray.

"Where your drawers?" Murray said to Honor when she came back, lifting Honor's skirt. Honor shrugged. "*I'll* do it Monday, you watch," Murray said. On Monday when I came home, Honor was in white eyelet-trimmed panties from J. C. Penney. She never wore a diaper again. "Murray chased me with a newspaper," Honor said when Ora Lee came on duty that night. "Well, it worked, didn't it?" I said. Ora Lee laughed.

Ora Lee was gentle and indifferent with Marmee, and Ora Lee was a sneak. William paid her every two weeks, William was her boss, and she told William everything. As it turned out, he had no particular complaints about my being in the house, figuring, he told Murray, that having an extra competent adult in the house was a fine idea. "May I let Ora Lee go?" he asked me in front of Murray. "Then what?" I said. "Then you look after your grandmother." "Honor's potty trained," I said, "I'm not into wiping people's asses." He walked out. Murray told Ora Lee what had happened, figuring she'd be grateful. Ora Lee wasn't grateful: she turned on Murray then, her eye on the day job. Seven P.M. to 7 A.M.,

I was there for her nightly shift. I never saw anything, didn't hear Marmee complain, but Marmee began to show bruises. William came by with a jar of honey and a jar of jam for Marmee's birthday; Ora Lee pointed out the bruises. "She beat the baby, too, chase her with a newspaper," I heard her telling William. William hired Ora Lee's cousin Alberta to do day cleaning at the house, now that there was a child living there, and Murray was pleased. "Finally, the man see the load I got here," she said. "That good-for-nothing Ora Lee never wash a sheet, never sweep a floor, eat everything I cook. William know that, why he don't fire her, I don't know. She say she a professional sitter, all she do is *sit*. They don't train you in no school just to sit, sit on your ass, you learn that when you six months old." I pointed out to her that maybe Alberta wasn't a good sign, that she was Ora Lee's cousin. "That skinny wench better not mess with me," she said, excited.

Parker didn't find me at Marmee's, but he did find me at work. "How's Stephen?" I said when he walked into the office. Charlotte was in the middle of a huge sheaf of papers; she put it down, grabbed her purse, and moved toward the door.

"Hi," he said. I cocked my head at him. He looked at Charlotte, hoping the timing would be right, that she'd leave and he could tell me he hadn't seen Stephen, though just the day before Charlotte had seen them together at Old Bayou Village; this time a Wal Mart was coming in. It took a photographic genius to do anything with Wal Mart, she'd said: Parker had scaled the outsized gazebo in the parking lot and shot it at an angle, so you could see the mock Acadian architecture of the rest of the center, the pitched roofs with fake dormers, echoed in the Wal Mart, with an overgrown pitched roof that looked, Charlotte had said, as if a crazed Cajun Brobdingnagian lived there. Stephen had had a hissy fit: "You're absolutely going to kill yourself," he'd said, and he'd covered his eyes, as if instant death wasn't what was supposed to happen. Arthur even had had little live oak trees

planted along the bayou-side boardwalks, expecting Old
Bayou Village would still be viable in a hundred years, when
the trees amounted to anything. They'll be gorgeous, Charlotte had said, and their roots'll rip up every pathway and
portico. She'd laughed, a great cackling laugh, still loving
Arthur, I could tell.

"Stephen's just fine," Parker said, looking at Charlotte.
Charlotte gave him a satisfied smile and walked out.

"She wants me to see you; funny she'd stand there until
you told the truth," I said.

"People like Charlotte want all the facts out in the open;
it's a disease with them."

"Lay off Charlotte."

"I say the woman's a stickler for the truth, and you act
like I've called her a sociopath."

"It was your tone," I said.

"Sorry."

"Quit apologizing," I said. Bad enough that I knew he
wanted me, no matter what I thought the reason was. I
wanted him to be difficult. The Hubig's pie rack dreams, the
fantasy of standing before him in nothing but a London Fog;
I hadn't forgotten. Somebody lurking nearby, Parker not
wanting me, there had to be something like that, not I'm
sorry, here's a present, let me buy you, let me do whatever
you want.

Parker shrugged. The old double-bind, you can't win for
losing: there he was, mired in it. I wanted to switch places.
If I had a choice, I wanted to be on the unrequited side.
Daydreams are no fun when you picture yourself lying there,
loved from all sides, not giving a damn about your lovers.
Where's the tension?

"I could take you to court," he said.

"That's a great ploy, Parker. Honor says she hates me,
then thinks that'll make me take her to K&B."

"She doesn't have an attorney."

"Neither do I." I could picture William, defending my
right to continue humiliating my family in New Orleans,

raising a child everyone was sure was going to be a lesbian with no father. Letty would have beaten William up, the way she claimed she'd done when they were small. William had had legs and arms like Knotknee in the comics, but he couldn't run, just snap a bone when it'd get Letty in trouble.

"Well, you better think about it," Parker said.

"That's all I think about." I wasn't going to say that I thought about it so much that I'd moved out of my house; maybe he still came by at odd hours and thought he was missing me by minutes. But I lay awake at night, hearing Marmee rattling doorknobs, Ora Lee sleeping on the job, then Ora Lee hearing the racket and finally coming after her, her tone gentle near my door, more ferocious when she got Marmee farther away. "You get back into that bed, you hear me?" "You stop it," Marmee screamed, but I didn't know what the offense was. Marmee was like Honor: frustration could be more painful than a stunning blow. I thought Marmee should do herself a favor and die in her sleep, and I'd quit feeling protective of her long ago.

"Please go to lunch with me," Parker said. I shook my head no.

"I am too thoroughly furious with you," I said. "I don't want to be, but what the hell am I supposed to do?"

"Just stop."

"Get out."

"You think about it," he said. I looked at him as he left, wanting his face to dissolve into something ugly. When I was younger and a boy hurt my feelings, he went through a metamorphosis, so that the aquiline nose that I thought was so fine suddenly looked sharp and mean, the dark eyes that seemed so intelligent suddenly weren't appealing because they weren't green, the hair on his chest that I craved touching was coarse and repulsive. I could hate a face on Tuesday that I couldn't get enough of on Monday. Parker's face wasn't changing, the lines were still beautiful, the green of his eyes unmatched except by Honor's; and his body, I remembered his body. "Goddamn you," I hollered after him, and my luck was that Sister Roberta was out of the building that morning. Charlotte told me that everyone, all the way down to Exit Control, had heard me and laughed.

William fired Murray on New Year's Eve; knowing William it had more to do with the beginning and end of the fiscal year than with anything personal. He was at the house at quarter to seven in the morning, and Ora Lee let him in, grinning like a fool; I could see that she was missing her upper left canine. Honor went tearing down the steps in her nightgown, expecting a disaster; it was as if a disaster was going to break at that house one day, we just had to stick around and wait for it. "Get her upstairs, and *keep* her upstairs," he said. "Fine with me," I said, tucking Honor under my arm like a piggie, having to turn sideways on the landing to let Marmee pass on her way down. "Time to go back upstairs, Miss Cecile," Ora Lee said, taking her gently by the arm. Marmee jerked away from her. "Nigger bitch," she said. Marmee could read and count and tell colors, Marmee who'd stood in front of Frantz School with a placard so little black girls could learn reading and counting and telling colors. All the censors were gone, replaced by a late-flowing honesty that sometimes I coveted. Ora Lee coaxed, "C'mon, be a good girl." "Not with *you*," Marmee said. Ora Lee was taking furtive little side glances at William to see whether he noticed that she couldn't control Marmee. But William wasn't paying attention; he was running a finger over a copper lustre pitcher on the hall table, and I could see the line in the dust from halfway up the steps. "That man that been wanting to see you, he waiting for you, up in your room," Ora Lee whispered, and Marmee turned around, taking the steps at a fast clip, like a two-year-old, leading only with her left foot.

I deposited Honor on the top landing, put my finger to my lips, and sat down next to her, two kids at a New Year's Eve party.

It was over in five minutes. "I want your house key back, you'll get your check in the mail Friday," William said.

"Hey, no gold watch?" I hollered down the stairs. Murray stood there thunderstruck.

"I told you to get upstairs," William said.

"I'm using Letty's legal part of the house, it just shifts from day to day," I said.

"Go on, baby," Murray said.

"No," I said, "I want to hear this."

"Murray has to have her key," Honor shrilled. I told her to hush. "You hush," she said.

"Those bruises on my aunt, we can't have that anymore, I'm sorry," William said.

"What you want me to do about it?"

"I think you know."

"I don't know *nothing*. That woman need to see a doctor, might be some blood disease."

"She's seen a doctor, the pattern's from body blows."

"You saying I did that?"

"I think you know I'm right."

"You tell me, I work here forty years, you never see a scratch on that woman, now all of a sudden you got them two hussies working in this house, she come up all battered and blue, you blame me? I'll take this to the Labor Board."

"She didn't do it, Ora Lee did it, I'm positive," I called down the steps.

"Look," William said, tired, probably figuring he was going to a party tonight and he was up before daylight and he was going to feel rotten for the bowl games tomorrow. "Aunt Cecile makes me nuts in five minutes, I don't blame you for hurting her, it's just got to stop."

"It'll stop all right, you get them two whores out of this house, it'll stop all right."

"Calm down, Murray."

"Calm down? You accusing me of a *crime*."

"I'll put you on pension."

"Yeah?" Murray looked interested. Just that fast. No punishment for a crime she didn't commit, but also no work, a monthly check; accuse her of anything, that's okay.

William pulled a business-size envelope out of his jacket pocket and unfolded a packet of papers. He handed it to Murray. She tried to look intelligent studying it, though Murray couldn't do a 1040EZ; I'd done her taxes for her every year since I got my first job. She'd never filed before that, just let Marmee send in her Social Security payments. "What this mean?" she said to William.

"It means that with this and Social Security you'll get ten dollars more a week than your take-home, and you don't have to get up in the morning to do it." He looked pleased, the lord high executor of the affairs of New Orleans's great liberal lady of the fifties. Call Murray names for forty years and never let her see her own kids grow up, then give her enough to live out her life on, provided she never leaves her house; that was about what it amounted to, not even enough margin for cable TV. But the fine points of math were not something Murray knew how to bother with. William had probably practiced on clients just like Murray.

Murray took the envelope, reached into her pocket for sixty cents bus fare, and was out the door.

Honor went tearing down after her, and I followed. " 'Bye, Murray," she screamed. Murray stopped, bent down on one knee, gave her a hug. Honor planted a half dozen sloppy kisses on her cheek, hitting the same spot, like a little woodpecker.

"I call you," she told me.

A week later, my vacation almost over, I phoned her. "Can I bring Honor to your house?" I asked.

"Aw, no, baby," she said. I could hear Indira in the background. "I'm retired."

CHAPTER 19

The queer thing about living in the city you grew up in is that you don't have to grow up. Unless you become disconnected, move to a part of town your relatives have never heard of, make friends your mother wouldn't let in through the front door twenty years ago. In New Orleans that can be easy, because New Orleans is a patchwork of wards, villages cast in stone, little depending on your color. There were overlays; salt-and-pepper neighborhoods didn't matter. If you lived uptown and you were white, that was one thing, if you lived uptown and were black that was something else entirely. I could have moved to Treme or Gentilly, but I hadn't. I'd stayed uptown, building a gossamer filament of support in Murray, as if she were a hundred-pound fishing line. She'd held for three years, and then I had no more refuge. Living in Marmee's house with Alberta and Ora Lee was different from living with Tikki; this time the need to run away was serious, with hazards more real than cigarette smoke and thoughtlessness.

I stayed in that house until the day after I called Murray, watching the tolerance for me chip and chunk away. "Darbeee," Ora Lee called up the stairs, Ora Lee now moved up to the day shift, where she sat so professionally, leaving the cleaning for Alberta, who slept away the night shift. I came to the head of the stairs. "Darbeee, you come get these dishes out the zink." My salad plate, Honor's bread plate, two cut-glass tumblers, that was mine, and then a greasy skillet, a burned pot, and a pile of dinner plates, not mine. I put my dishes in the dishwasher, left the rest, went back upstairs. "Darbeee," she called again, "You got to help out around here, we shorthanded."

Marmee had no new bruises, and William was pleased. Marmee was blowing up with edema, from TV dinners and canned corn beef hash fried up in butter, but William didn't know to look for that; he was a lawyer. They were trying to kill her off as surely as Murray had been, sodium being to Marmee what potassium cyanide was to Rasputin; you'd think you were getting somewhere, but after a while it seemed you'd need a gun and an ice floe in the Neva River to blow her off the natural earth. They had a peculiar credo, destroy whatever sustains you, but they didn't see past their inborn hostility, and they took more pleasure in watching Marmee die slowly than in the paycheck. There was always another paycheck somewhere, look how easily they'd wheedled into this one, but a chance to blow up an old white Jew lady until she burst didn't come along every day. Trouble was, Ora Lee would thaw chicken for eight hours, put it back in the fridge, leave it for me to get salmonella. Oysters, mayonnaise, cream: they'd be sitting on the counter when she thought I wasn't looking, and when I wasn't careful I'd puke my guts up all night. Ora Lee took home the safe stuff, the liquor, the hard-frozen pork loin. "I done heard what you told Mr. William," she said to me one morning. "Didn't do you no good." I called Charlotte, loaded up my car, and started to leave. As I walked to the door, Marmee came out of the kitchen. I'd seen too much of her lately to notice what she really looked like. I took her in freeze-frame, a very old woman who, without her money, would be walking up and down Magazine Street with a Winn-Dixie shopping cart full of shiny fragments she'd found in the gutter, Barq's root beer cans and two-liter Coke screw-on caps and foil wrappers from Wendy's. She'd be hit by a car, taken to Charity Hospital, no identification. I thought about losing her on the side of the road, an abandoned dog, a swifter death than a jigger of salt a day. Murray was gone, though Marmee hadn't known Murray's name in almost two years. I looked familiar, Honor looked familiar, Marmee's mother and Marmee, Marmee and Letty, maybe even Letty and me: she remembered something when she looked at the two of us. We had suitcases; even dogs grieve when you take down the suitcases. I kissed her good-bye, and she ran her hand gently, sensuously down my arm. I shivered with revulsion, but let her do it. She bent over to kiss Honor, the kiss was so delicate as to be sexual, and Honor recoiled, already letting the taboos out. I felt tears coming; that often meant I wasn't going to see the person again. Sometimes I thought I had prognosticatory powers, but then common sense kicked in. I was sad to leave the ones who couldn't protect themselves. It was the same fear I tamped down each morning when I left Honor at nursery school, knowing she was going to climb the pipes and barrels on the play yard, knowing she was going to ride in Isaiah's cab with no shock absorbers, no seat belts, and probably no ball joints.

"I've never asked for this before," I whispered to Charlotte over Honor's head.

"I know," she said, pleased.

"Two hours," I told her. "I can take care of it all in two hours."

"I want to come with you!" Honor screamed after me as I went down the walk. Charlotte was holding her hand, and Honor broke away.

"You can't," I said, detaching her from my skirt, finger by finger, each popping back as fast as I could pry it loose. Arthur walked out the front door. "We'll play War, how about it?" he said.

"For money?" Honor said.

"For money." She ran back.

"You know about Stephen?" he called after me. I saw Charlotte give him an elbow to the ribs, light but not playful.

"Yes," I said, assuming I knew what he meant.

I opened my front door, threw in the suitcases, the toy bag, my purse, caught the musty smell, no garbage, no rot, nothing dead under the house, and walked out. Across Tchoupitoulas Street, the Audi was there; I knew it would be. Not for any logical reason, just that for once something had to fall into place. Up the elevator: it went to three, the door opened, and the gate swung free.

Parker made his living space work by pretending that there was an invisible eight-foot ceiling, everything down to that scale. Low partitions, close-to-floor furniture. Futon, low-slung hammock, pillows, diminutive appliances. That was why the bed looked so out of place. I walked into his sleeping corner, and there was the hospital bed, higher than even a normal bed, making Parker's things look like so many toys strewn around a spoiled child's room.

They were both in there, Parker sitting on the floor cross-legged, Stephen on the side of the bed, legs dangling, same pose as on TV. He was thirty pounds thinner, cadaverous, but the eyes were there, opaque and mean when he saw me. Parker's back was to me. "How'd you get in here?" Stephen said.

"Nothing's locked," I said.

"I left it open for John," Parker said.

"I want to talk to you," I told him.

"You need to get out of here," Stephen said.

"Hey, this is my place," Parker said.

"You watch it, Parker," he said.

Parker beckoned me to follow him in the direction of the elevator. There was nowhere to sit. "I have to wait for John," he explained. "John?" "The hospice worker." "Ah, the angel of death." "Sort of."

"I'm moving back into my house," I said. Parker shoved his hands into his pockets.

Stephen came up on us. His pajamas had wide navy and white vertical stripes; all he needed was a matching cap to look like someone in a 1944 newsreel. He was bent with pain, struggling to breathe. "You couldn't wait until I was dead," he said.

"True," I said, and Parker snickered.

"You trying to justify your existence again?" He was taking shallow breaths, but I supposed that self-preservation isn't a big issue at such times. On a death sentence, I'd have gone to the Himalayas; so what if I couldn't breathe? I looked at him, not understanding. "Fag hag, know what that means? Means you're not all there. Baby's a nice front, but you're not fooling anybody, don't kid yourself."

"Fag hags run around gay men. I ran around a straight guy who turned gay so you'd let him take pictures of shopping centers at sixty dollars an hour. Hell, I'd go to bed with Richard Nixon if I could get sixty dollars an hour."

"That's not the way it works," Stephen said. Parker was making a small arc on the floor with the toe of his sock, over and over, mesmerized by the motion, maybe waiting to see if a sliver from the rough-hewn boards would snag the sock, go through and hurt his foot.

"Proximity, that's what does it, you can't tell me every man who goes to prison is gay when he goes in."

"The advertising business isn't prison," Parker said softly.

I laughed, thinking of Charlotte, married to a man trapped by kitsch, by bad taste and hype and plastic. She didn't even want visiting privileges, went to supermarket openings only to make Arthur look married and solid, part of the hype.

"I've moved back into the neighborhood," I said. "I only came to tell you I want freedom of movement. I don't want to hide when the doorbell rings, I don't want to scan the block when I drive up. You have to leave me alone. And you have to stay out of sight; you're good at that when you want to be. I can't take looking at you, and I'm fucking sick of running away."

Stephen looked at Parker. Parker shrugged his shoulders, gave him a conspiratorial smile. Stephen had a power over him. Guilt, I imagined, the kind you can't go to confession about because it isn't a sin to sneak off and try to love your child, even if you're sneaking around behind someone who's half-dead. I couldn't blame Parker for that, planning in advance not to have bad dreams. My father gave me thirty dollars more than I asked for the last time I saw him, and the dreams still came, the unfinished business.

"You deluded bitch," Stephen said. He looked around; he couldn't stay standing much longer. I thought maybe I could wait him out. He shuffled over to a folding chair that sat next to the elevator, dragged it back, sat down. "That baby isn't even Parker's."

I looked at Parker; he wasn't looking at anyone. His sock had finally caught a snag, and he was wiggling his foot back and forth, concentrating; the challenge was to undo it without bending over.

"Oh, I get it," I said. I walked over to Stephen, delighted that he was so fragile. I grabbed the lapels of his pajamas, held them loosely; that was all I needed to do. "Now hear this," I said. "You are angry at the *wrong* person."

He couldn't take that in. His lips drew into a tight, Sisters of the Holy Comforter line; maybe that came of loving your own kind too much. He was silent for a while. "I don't want that hideous little bastard of yours getting my money," he spat out.

"That's it, pick on a kid you never met, that's goddamn low." My tone was even, I was winning, I felt a shimmer of pleasure. "What money?" I said.

Stephen let out a sour guffaw that wheezed through two octaves. Parker took a step backwards. "She knows what money," Parker said. "You go back to bed."

"Right," Stephen said. He folded his arms across his chest, and I could see through the light fabric that he was all bone. "I leave you my money, you give it to that kid, and I'll come back and rattle your furniture all night," he said to Parker.

"Futons don't rattle," I said.

"Shut the fuck up," Stephen said.

"Don't talk to her like that." Parker's eyes were wet. I couldn't look; I knew what that did to green eyes.

"I don't need your help," I said softly.

Stephen was whispering, but the acoustics of the place did him no good. He was struggling too hard to breathe; every puff of air over his vocal chords came right out to me. "You said she was after you."

"She was."

"You two deserve each other," I said and walked over to the elevator, pushed the button. It wasn't waiting on three, but coming down or up from another floor. The door opened, and a huge man walked out, tall, three hundred pounds, a beard covering no chin. Being fat was a sign of health: I'd noticed lots of chubs in the Quarter, advertising with their fast-grown beer guts that they were disease-free: fat was excellent for the sex life. I cried in the elevator, quiet feelgood tears.

Two days later, Stephen threw a blood clot and died, right there in the warehouse on Tchoupitoulas Street, I learned from Charlotte, phoning her when I saw the obituary in the *Times-Picayune*. I learned to read the obituaries from my father; it was an exercise of sorts. Part of it was a sense of getting away with another day of borrowed time, part of it was fear of going to look for someone one day and not knowing that person had been dead for two years. After a while, my father told me, you got confused, assuming that people were dead when they weren't, just because it was about time. He did that mostly with movie stars, knowing more of them than of other people. The format of the obituary page changed, the pecking order all confused; anybody and nobody got a write-up. Relatives of the publisher and kings of Carnival and kids who drowned got photos; some got an eight-point blurb, others got only what they paid the funeral home to put in. Stephen got an eight-point blurb, no photo. Fair enough, I didn't begrudge him that. It occurred to me that at the rate I was going, I'd be lucky to get what the funeral home put in. I didn't have life insurance; Letty would have to pick up the tab. No one would write up a library cataloguer, unless I drowned.

Sunday night I phoned Letty and told her I had to come over. I had no resources. I'd put everything on Murray, who smoked two packs a day and never got sick enough to stay home from work, even when Honor started bringing home those virulent germs that can't get into tiny bloodstreams and do much damage, but will float out into the air and half-kill an adult. Two men lived next door to me on my left; they were on social security and put away a gallon of cheap sweet wine a day. The neighbor on my right was old enough to be retired, too, but she had a job, five jobs, cleaning people's houses for twenty-five dollars cash, no reporting to the IRS; everyone agreed to it. I thought I might go in to work, ask around the library: anyone have a daughter sitting home, watching her own kids, want extra cash? All I wanted was for Letty to keep Honor for a single day.

Eddie hid behind the newspaper, never turning the page. Honor was bolder: she dumped a duffelful of Barbies onto the rug in Letty's living room and proceeded to do a verbal fugue with us, her Barbie dialogue one step behind ours. "I have exercise class at nine, couldn't do it until after ten, ten-thirty. I need a shower," Letty said. Honor's Barbie did a high kick, then another, and another; "I must get my exercise," she said, falsetto. "Oh, wait," Letty said, "I forgot. That portable telephone, Eddie, you know that portable telephone?" Eddie didn't answer. This was rhetorical talk; he didn't need to. "Anyway, it picks up every passing car phone, it *rings* every time a car phone goes by, I guess, drives me nuts. You have to bring it in within three days, or tough luck." Honor put her Barbie into her pink Corvette. "Oh, it is so lovely to take a phone *everywhere*," Barbie sang out.

"You could take her with you," I said.

"You ever try to take a child in the phone store?" Letty said. "They run wild, you have to wait about an hour, *I* had to wait about an hour, and I was paying good money. Not just renting, not just bringing in a bashed-up phone; I was buying one of their precious AT&T phones. I am not going to put up with that, bad enough I have to sit there and wait for an hour; at least I could read a book."

"I've been in the phone store, I read a book to Honor, she was fine," I said.

"Reading to children is boring," Letty said. Eddie rustled the newspaper; he still hadn't turned a page.

"Why do you hate me, Letty?" Honor said.

"See what you've done with this child?" Letty said. "If I hated you, why would I want to have you over tomorrow?" she said to Honor, then she turned to me. "I can go to the phone store after aerobics. I'm sure I'll be back by noon." To Honor, "Want to come over for lunch, how about it?"

"Letty, I have a job."

"You take that job so seriously. It doesn't pay you anything."

Eddie put down the paper. "Let her alone, how about it?" he said to Letty. He offered to take Honor to the store with him for the day. I went over and kissed him, told him no thanks, and picked up my purse to walk out. Honor was in the middle of a Barbie drama. "Not now!" she said.

"Now," I said.

"No." She folded her arms across her little chest, stuck out her lower lip. I began stuffing Barbie paraphernalia into the duffel bag. "Stop it, you're messing everything up." She smacked my hand. I slung the duffel onto my shoulder, picked her up around her middle, her back to me. She couldn't bend her way out, it was a trick that had taken me too long to learn. "I hate you, Darby!" she screamed as I carried her out.

Charlotte said, Bring her, not a moment's hesitation. It was the only option I hadn't considered, probably because the issue at hand was keeping out of trouble with Sister. All I could think of was making sure Honor and I were in two different places.

I repacked the duffel with great respect, not rumpling the clothes, giving the fool Barbie breathing room, not nicking the sports car with one of Barbie's tiny baubles. It occurred to me that Honor had never seen a nun before. When I was three, they were everywhere in great numbers, none in mufti, though you can almost always still recognize one, the plainness, the haircut, the GI glasses. For a Jewish child in New Orleans, the sisters in full regalia were as mysterious and dangerous as snakes; you didn't get to sit in a schoolroom or catechism class and hear their voices, smell their breath, get any notion that they were earthbound. My father's eye doctor, a Jewish eye doctor on Prytania Street, had many sisters as clients, some deal with the archdiocese, no doubt. I can get it for you wholesale, he probably said to the archbishop: there was a bit of the Jewish merchant in every Jewish professional. I was in the waiting room; one sister went into the bathroom. I listened at the door, heard her tinkle, stood rapt in amazement. I hated to think what Honor might do.

"Hi," she said to each of the library ladies, and they said, "Fine." Hi in New Orleans means How are you? to blacks, say hi, and they say fine. Probably that's a way to get to the origin of words, but there aren't too many places like New Orleans. I marched her straight to Sister's office; I certainly wasn't going to try to keep her under my desk all day; I knew what she'd do. "Sister, this is Honor," I said when she looked up.

Honor extended her hand. "I'm pleased to meet you, I've heard so much about you," she said to Sister Roberta. I let out a whoop in spite of myself, and Sister looked at Honor sympathetically.

"I have no sitter as of today. I have only two choices, keep her here or go home. We're backed up from the holidays, so I'd suggest that we make it possible for me to stay here," I said, and they both looked at me queerly.

"Would you like to stay with me?" Sister said to Honor. Have her soul, I thought, take her to the chapel, put holy water on her head, do what you want, you can't make something else out of a spoiled little Jewish girl. Honor could take catechism, she could make her first communion, she could be confirmed and immerse herself in every sacrament known to man, but she was still going to be just like Letty, only she'd confess every week or so instead of once a year on Yom Kippur. "She's yours," I said to Sister.

"Only for today. You find some alternate plan before tomorrow," she said, and I thought about the backlog on my desk and the dried-up trail of options I had. Newcomb reopened next week, but that was only three hours in the morning, more of an aggravation than a boon; kids went there because their mothers had nothing else to do besides sit in the car-pool bay and drive a half dozen kids in forty-five-dollar outfits home to their maids while the other mothers were out shopping. Honor and I shopped on Saturdays, not for recreation, stood in line at every checkout, her patience wearing thin fast so that she had to be bought off. All the kids at her school had to be bought off for something; it was just that I could least afford it. Sister set off with Honor; maybe Honor was going to get to see the convent kitchen, maybe the bedrooms, the laundry room where all the secrets lay, except those buried under the narcissus. The terrible part was that Honor's instincts were so fine: she'd know how much I wanted to hear, and she'd tell me that she forgot.

The library was in keeping with the medieval theme of the school, the harking back to church power over learning. Marble staircases with statues of half-dead Jesus waiting at the landings, low-slung archways, leaded glass transoms, so very cold except in summer, when the heat was sealed in tight, windows locked because Gert Town was across the canal. I went from office to office all morning, talking to women I barely knew, even after eight years. I need a baby-sitter, you know anybody? I didn't want them to be insulted, didn't want them to think that I had to have a black mammy for my kid to beat up on. I was trying to be casual, and it was a mistake, because they saw no urgency, but rather an easy way out of helping. Charlotte, my final stop, had the only suggestion. Parker. I wanted to slap her. "He's got the flexibility," she said, still hanging on to the notion that a family of three was right, that she and Arthur were two, and Honor and I were two, and we could be fixed where they couldn't. "Forget it," I said, no point arguing; I'd wind up hurting her feelings.

At noon I skulked down to Sister's office, sure that by now Honor had asked her some question like, Do you have a penis or not, you talk like a girl but you have hair like a boy? They weren't there. I went out to Sister's secretary.

They've gone to the day-care center. What day-care center? The day-care center on Audubon Street, right by the school. She pointed in the direction of Gert Town. Shit, I said and tore out the front door.

At noon Gert Town was like a border town; even when it wasn't hot out, dogs were under houses, skinny cats were lying loose in patches of sunlight, no one was on the streets. I ran down Audubon Street until I reached the school and began looking. The day-care center was in a shotgun house. Like mine it was sandwiched in between two other shotguns; you could hear the neighbors puke at night if your windows were open. It could have been a crack house, that's how informal Gert Town real estate was. A building stays empty for a while, the dealers move in or the Sisters move in, the dealers leave empty vials and a stench of urine, the sisters browbeat high-school kids into slapping bright paint on the walls.

It was about to be lunchtime, and two dozen kids were hyped up with hunger, bellies emptied from breakfast and light on their feet. You couldn't miss Honor, her strawberry blond hair catching bits of fluorescent light, all the little girls standing around her fingering her hair. They had pink barrettes and yellow ribbons and blue rubber-band balls on their plaits, but nothing like this. To them Honor was Alice in Wonderland, and she was eating it up. She was used to being beautiful at Newcomb because even little white girls usually had hair shorter than hers and fell in love with her, but this was something new. She was so puffed up with her importance that she was forgetting to exhale.

Sister was in the kitchen; at least she hadn't just abandoned Honor to the surefire glory of being in a fine dress with fine hair with kids whose mothers were off at vo-tech school or making beds down at the Marriott. "I want her out of here," I said. Sister looked at me with disgust, as if she'd finally found a way to uncover a Jew's secret hatred of blacks. "The kid already thinks she's God's gift, I don't need her sitting here playing jungle goddess." Sister smiled smugly;

she'd caught me out, sure. "You know what I mean, you can't tell me that you don't get a lot of satisfaction walking through this neighborhood with your lily-white face, pretending you love everybody, then going back and hollering at Maintenance because they haven't fixed your air conditioner."

The second it was all out, I knew I'd gone too far. Sister's face went to all horizontal lines, like an oriental cartoon, everything parallel to the old wimple line. "It is time for us to have a talk," she said.

"I'm sorry," I said.

She looked at her watch. "My office, in an hour. I suggest you leave the child here."

It was the sort of moment when only knowledge of the law kicks in; everything else shuts down to make way for it. In 1892 Lizzie Borden killed her stepmother first, let all the blood coagulate, then hacked her father up, called the neighbors in when he still looked like a fresh-killed chicken, blood still spurting onto the walls. Massachusetts law would have given his estate to the stepmother's relatives if he'd died first. Lizzie and her sister Emma got it all; Emma probably killed them anyway. I read that in the 364.15s. With Sister Roberta, I knew the law, I sense even Honor knew it on some primal level; maybe that's where the fairness of law lies. Sister shooed Honor out. A little girl named Trellis was hanging on her arm. Trellis was half a head taller than Honor and wanted to own her. "Trellis, you take Honor to the lunch table." Trellis stood stock-still. "Now!" Sister boomed; Trellis grabbed Honor's arm and fled.

Sister Ignatius was also in the kitchen, slapping bologna onto white bread with globs of mayonnaise; she acted deaf, though she was taking it all in. Sister Ignatius was a drone nun, chosen by God to be menial, cook for others, dust for others, live with her low IQ, a gamma in the spiritual order. Sister Ignatius had street sense, though, could carry a rumor fast and efficiently if you planted it on her. That was how Brenda got caught in the till: Sister Ignatius was mopping the floor behind the desk, overheard Brenda tell a boy to pay his hundred-sixty-dollar fine in cash, saw her slip the five twenties into her purse. It was like putting a piece of tape over the hundreds column on a keypunched phone bill back in the seventies: hack off a digit for the records, no one will ever know. Sister Roberta knew in five minutes. Sister Ignatius would have word of my firing in *Oblate World* by tomorrow if I didn't get her a better story.

"For the record, I don't want to quit," I said. I wanted to quit, to be done with all the piety and icons in the name of repressed sexuality. But if it came to leaving, I wanted unemployment compensation. I knew the law. "Hear me, Sister?" I said, turning to Sister Ignatius. She didn't look up, but the knife slipped with a clunk into the almost-empty mayonnaise jar.

"I'd better take Honor with me," I said. I didn't want to come back here. I could imagine Sister Ignatius, Charon at the door, not letting me have her back without proof. Besides, Honor hated bologna; she knew about nitrites. She could foment revolt: This stuff will kill you, it'll give you cancer and you'll shrivel all up, she'd say, and the children in the day-care center would eat white bread and mayonnaise, with Sister Ignatius throwing out the bologna day after day, never figuring out that peanut butter might be a good idea. "Suit yourself," Sister Roberta said.

I left Honor perched on a high stool at the card catalogue table. She was dizzy with pleasure at the height, proud to be balancing there. I thought she might not move, being too scared to jump.

"You don't like this job, you've never liked this job," Sister Roberta said when I took the chair opposite her desk.

"That has nothing to do with it," I said.

"I know you moonlight, that's strictly against university policy."

"No, it's not." The faculty all would be starving to death if they had no outside sources of income. The most brilliant professor on the history faculty wrote questions for "Scholastic

Challenge" on Channel 26 to put his kids through school. It
was no secret; they flashed his face every Saturday afternoon.

"It is for nontenure track personnel."

"Oh."

"I'm trying to give you a graceful out." But not a grace-
filled one. Would she have to confess, putting me out on the
street with my half-orphan? University policy, church policy,
nowhere near as refined as the U.S. Constitution. No time
for subtleties. "You and I have an agreement, it dates back
three years."

"I haven't missed a day in three years."

"Not true. Six months into the agreement, you left this
campus without authorization."

"My kid was in the hospital!" More Sister Ignatius, I bet.

"You left the campus today."

"It was lunchtime."

"Miss Cooper, people reach contractual agreements, spoken or otherwise, to mutually constrain their behavior. I have
allowed you to continue here, you have received your pay in
a timely fashion, I have kept my part. To the letter. And you
have not. I'm giving you an opportunity to resign."

"I want to stay," I said softly. "I told you I was sorry."

"I'll have no choice but to terminate you." I felt the blood
rush to my head, the opposite of fainting. I was excited suddenly, Oh, please Br'er Fox, don't throw me in the briar patch.
Honor was standing in the doorway. She was trying to look
forlorn. For my money, it was a pretty poor job, one shoulder
slumped so the neck of her dress gaped a bit, mouth turned
down, toes pointing inward, but Sister bought it. Her uterus
was probably the size of a raisin, the estrogen in her body
had long since been sucked out, her bones hollow and her
spine folding in on itself, but she felt something for Honor.
Not even as a little heathen girl she might take to be chris-
tened, but as someone like herself, who got her stature by
funny constructs, of a delusion of being better than everyone
around herself. "You could have been honest with me," she
said to me. "For her sake, I'll say I had to lay you off."

I asked her to allow me one question; freedom's just another word for nothing left to lose. She shrugged, okay, curiosity getting the best of her, probably.

"You remember three years ago, someone told you my motherhood was no accident?" She nodded. "Who was it?"

"Some young man. Phoned, wouldn't give his name."

"He sound limp-wristed?"

"I don't think in those terms."

CHAPTER 20

*A*s superstitions go, my state-line ritual was not one of the best, as it required a certain amount of disruption to protect me against a forgotten threat. You had to put your hand out the window at the state line, or something bad was going to happen; I thought maybe that you wouldn't return to the state you were leaving. I learned the practice on college trips to Destin, all the girls reaching for the windows as we went into Mississippi, crossed into Alabama, ten minutes later, after the tunnel in Mobile, crossed into Florida. I taught it to Honor, who usually was asleep by the time we hit the Mississippi line going to Pass Christian: it meant opening the windows, letting the warm air out and the piney chill in, startling Honor into new behavior. We made the commute every week, and it didn't take long to notice her transformation. Crossing the state line made her into a rural Mississippi girl.

The Pass Christian house was across Highway 90 from the beach, with no phone since Marmee had quit going, a roof antenna but no television, just our wits to entertain us, my computer and Honor's Fisher Price plastic town to work at. Four days there, the beach cold and empty, three days in the city, dragging to Unemployment and Newcomb and rich people's houses to hand-list books. Newcomb ladies were peevish, that Honor was missing out on the continuity of the program, Tuesdays, Wednesdays, Thursdays, absent Fridays and Mondays, all the socialization undone. Never mind that they had perky college students wafting in and out, disappearing after they had their credits, failing to show when they had hangovers. The school had a waiting list, and Honor wasn't using her place. "Amanda says Honor is never in school," Amanda's mother said into my car window, one Wednesday at noon. "She's in school *now*," I said. "You know what I mean," Amanda's mother said. She had a blond-pageboy sort of haircut that hung loose and casual, an excellent haircut, even an excellent coloring job. Junior League haircut. "My friend Pixie is waiting list, had to put her little boy in the afternoon class, it hardly seems fair."

"Look," I said, "I spent four years at this godforsaken college, having my growth stunted and my head emptied out. They *owe* me a place, even if I *never* bring my kid in." She backed away from the window. I had a candy-apple red paint job on the Karmann Ghia. Some people took it for a valuable classic, their mistake, go back to their new Peugeot station wagons and think because we had kids in the same school we all spent our afternoons stocking the shelves in the Thrift Shop, so the poor people could wear our unpilled hand-me-downs.

The house in Pass Christian was a raised cottage modeled after Beauvoir, Jefferson Davis's home up the beach, a tenth its size but still as neoclassically perfect as the original. My father had chided Marmee for living in a mock Confederate shrine, and she had said, "Everyone's got one virtue; this man happened to have had good taste." When I was about five, she'd screened in the porch that wrapped around the house, backing up the screen with glass when city crime and air conditioning came into her life shortly thereafter. She had a bed of azaleas in rich dirt on each side of the front center staircase, but from there to the two-hundred-foot picket fence the front lawn was dotted with patches of sandy scrub. Honor had taken over the gazebo and had built her own world in the damp, cold sand, crude tunnels and turrets, peopled by the little Fisher Price figures, with their plastic helmets of hair all that was visible sometimes. "The niggers are going to kill them, I buried them in the sand," she said. "Who told you the word *niggers*?" I said. "Amanda did. We bury the mommies and babies in the sand at school. Amanda says the niggers are the monsters. Where're the niggers, they have

niggers in Mississippi? I know they have them in New Orleans, Amanda said they walk by her house." I told her *nigger*
was a bad word. "Like *stupid*?" Worse, I told her. "And don't
use a word when you have no earthly idea what it means."
She nodded solemnly; I was all she had in Mississippi. She
wore corduroy overalls, moisture seeping through where she
sat on the sand, her cotton eyelet panties sporting two ovals
of beach dirt when she undressed. I let her free. Marmee's
two acres were fenced all around; I gave her a whistle. Mid-
morning I blew one loud blast; she blew back, let me know
she hadn't left the property, run out into the highway or the
Gulf. Lunchtime I blew twice, and she came in for homemade
vegetable soup and crackers. "Murray gave me grilled cheese,
very buttery, every day," Honor said the first time, looking
at the soup, not a lover of multiple textures. "Tough shit," I
said. "*Shit* is a bad word," Honor said. "It doesn't hurt anybody's feelings," I said. "You hurt *my* feelings," Honor said.
"Sorry," I told her.

We walked the beach at dusk, comparing footprints, picking up shell fragments. Honor took the bits of shell and
sometimes iridescent plastic that we found and stashed them
in a sandwich bag; she made tiny plates and cups for her
Fisher Price weebly people, filled the shallow bowls with sand,
"You eat your soup!" she said. I bought her a sea biscuit and
a bag of tinted shells at a roadside stand, a-dollar-fifty-nine
total, and they became the weeblies' neighbors. I slid open
the glass door on the porch, and I could hear her from the
gazebo, as I was taking my handwritten notes on rich people's
book collections and giving them the precision and order that
a computer would accept. Sunday afternoon of the first week,
Honor came in before the afternoon whistle check, threw her
skinny arms around my neck, dripping dry sand down inside
the back of my shirt, planted a happy warm kiss on my neck.
I pulled her onto my lap, typed with two fingers on my right
hand, her head nestled into my neck until she was too bored,
and she squirmed down between my knees, crawled out from

under the desk, and ran back out the door, giving me two toots of her whistle.

The sickness of being in New Orleans came back on her fast each time, like an allergy so bad that one whiff puts you in anaphylactic shock. Crossing the Pearl River at the state line, she fumed about her overalls; it was only going up into the upper thirties across the Gulf South, and she couldn't wear a dress, I told her. She screamed, unhooked her seat belt and threw herself across the tiny backseat. I couldn't see out the rearview window with the flailing around; if we had an accident she'd be killed, and she was setting us up for one. "Tell you what," I said, and she didn't stop screaming. "I'll make a deal with you!" I hollered, and the noise stopped; she'd give me a chance. "We pull up in front of school, I'll get a dress out of the trunk, you take it in and I'll change you." "No, no, no, no, no!" She was bouncing up and down on the hard little backseat, her backside too bony for it to feel very good; the pain made her scream louder. "We'll do it in the car, then," I said. "Now?" "No, not now, I'm driving for Chrissakes." "Pull over." "This is a fucking interstate highway, Honor." "*Fucking*'s a bad word." "Shut the fuck up." I said. At that time of day, the trucks were making the final leg of their run into New Orleans, cigarettes and apples for Lucille's store, and the traffic was fierce for a Karmann Ghia; we were buffeted across the highway, caught in every current of air. Honor began sobbing loudly. The welcome station was coming up. "I'll stop!" I shouted. "Okay," she sniffled.

The phone call came that night around seven-thirty. We were long past the winter solstice, but it was dark out, a new moon. "Do you have Mother's key?" Letty said; not hello, she never said hello, thought it wasn't creative enough. I told her yes. "You need to go let Alberta in." I told her I had a small child, remember? "William doesn't answer, you're the only one I know of with a key." She's your mother, I said, and Letty said, "Not really, anymore," and I recalled that

she'd seen my father's mother the same way, locked in Theresienstadt just as Marmee was stuck in the fatty deposits in
her head like a mouse in a glue trap. When they were out
of touch, Letty considered them dead.

Honor was in her nightgown: footed pajamas were for
the beach, where the cold won out over vanity every time.
Her hair was fresh from a shampoo, her pores all open. I put
socks and boots on her, a sweater and a car coat, my wool
scarf around her head. "I look stupid," she said, tugging at
the scarf, loosening the knot. "You'll be glad to look stupid
when you get outside," I said, throwing on a jacket.

The house was dark when we drove up, and Alberta was
sitting on the front steps, ready to bolt. I walked over first
to the side of the house, and Honor skibbled across the dry,
short-cropped lawn, liking the night freedom; she'd never
had it before in the city.

"I don't like this at all, maybe we should call the police,"
I said.

"I'm not walking to no Time Saver even one more time,"
Alberta declared.

I stood at the front door. It was silent inside. I began to
tremble. I turned the key in the lock. The burglar alarm beep
announced someone had walked in, but the steady buzzer
didn't go off, forty-five seconds to turn me off or I summon
the police. I didn't think about it, but if the burglar alarm
wasn't armed, then Ora Lee hadn't taken Marmee on a field
trip. I flipped on the hall light, saw nothing, searched the
downstairs, Honor trailing me. Alberta remained on the front
steps until I gave her an all-clear. The television was in the
kitchen: of all the things—the Rouault, the Lowestoft—it
would be the TV that anyone would take. I reported back
to Alberta, so far so good, nothing downstairs. She stepped
into the lit foyer, but left the door open.

I found Marmee on the landing: two steps up: a landing;
three steps up: another landing; there she was. I knew nothing
about such things, but I could tell her neck was broken. I let

out a sob; I'd been grieving for her for years, and now it was over. An anticipated death, I thought the sadness ended instantly, all done in advance.

"She's broken!" Honor screamed. She reached out tentatively, to touch her, and I jerked her arm away. "She's dead," I whispered, and Honor advanced on her again, curiosity winning out. We'd seen a dead fish on the beach two days ago, and she'd gone closer until the smell had hit her, but Marmee didn't smell bad. Honor tried to jiggle her chin, her surefire method for rousing the dead; Marmee moved as a piece, and I pulled Honor away gently. "Please take this child," I said to Alberta. "No, thank you," she said and pulled the front door shut, retreating into the living room, now that she knew what part of the house to stay away from. She looked at her watch: she expected to be paid for this time.

I took Honor's hand and went into the back hallway. Still a dial phone for the servants. Fingernails had scraped the dirt off in a circle under the dial; it was darker the closer to the O, the path less traveled. I dialed the police, not nine-one-one, no point in that. The number was eight-two-one, two-two-two-two, chosen originally, I realized, because it was fast to dial, two-two-two-two, chop-chop-chop-chop. "My grandmother's dead," I said to the operator, and burst into tears. This hour of the night, she got all the calls for the dead, the bad calls, the ones that didn't happen in hospitals, where death came with certitude, and when it didn't, they cut you up like a toss-away frog, protecting themselves from the lawyers. She took the particulars; rigor mortis had set in, I told her, feeling quite competent, and she hung up. From experience she knew that minds settled after the police were called, order came, people remembered the family, Mr. Sontheimer if you were quietly self-assured, Mr. Bultman if you were assimilated or Unitarian or pretentious: those were the two Jewish options.

I thought about what I would say to Letty. I remembered how she told me about my father, Your daddy died. She would hold it against me if I didn't get it right, anger would be her first order of business, and I'd catch it with snippy remarks.

She didn't answer on the first ring, as I would have if my mother had a fifty-fifty chance of being found dead; at least those were the odds that I'd gone over with. Two more rings, one more and the answering machine would pick up. I'd have to hang up on it, leave a message at the sound of the tone, beep, your mother's dead. I smiled for a second, a private joke with myself. Honor was watching my face. She put a hand on her hip and shook her head from side to side in disgust; she watched too much television. Letty picked up with the machine, hollering over the message, "I'm here, I'm here." The message continued, I can't come to the phone right now. "Okay," I said loudly. We waited for the beep, whatever we said would be recorded for as long as we talked. "Turn that thing off," I said. "I can erase it in a minute, don't worry about it." "Oh, boy," I said. "Letty, sit down," she was going to have this on tape, she could play it back for people if she wanted. Sit down, that's what she'd said, calling from Caracas. I waited a few seconds, Letty had three phones downstairs, countless chairs, it wouldn't take her long. "I'm sorry, Letty, Marmee died."

She broke into instant sobs, no shutdown for Letty. "She's not Marmee, she's my mother, my mother died, Eddie, Mother died." Sounds became muffled, the TV sound went off. Eddie took the phone after a moment. "You okay?" he said. This was going on tape, good; at least Eddie was doing things right, though Letty wouldn't see it that way. "It's awful, she has a broken neck, I know it." "A broken neck," he echoed to Letty, and she came back on the phone. "You didn't tell me a broken neck," she said, her voice soft, sniffly, wanting me to feel I'd made a gaffe. I told her I wasn't sure, it just looked that way to me. "Well, don't go saying stuff you don't know yet."

I told her I was sorry; it was now on tape. "I can't come over there," Letty said, as if I'd asked. "It would be just too horrible." I told her I understood, on tape; I couldn't say, Great, and your granddaughter will have nightmares and multiple personalities and psychotic tendencies, but you can't take it. I'll keep you posted, I said. I figured the police would have to have their say first. In my neighborhood, I learned you were supposed to call the police; at least that's what happened when the man two houses down away from Tchoupitoulas died. He was old, he simply didn't wake up one morning, his wife called the police, and they called an ambulance. He went out in a rubber bag on top of a stretcher, and I was surprised how small he looked in that bag. The last time I'd seen him he'd had a proud paunch, but he was very flat inside that bag, as if all his body fluids had melted into a pool.

The police took their sweet time, no rush on a dead grandmother; the ambulance came when they did. They asked a million questions, and Alberta and Honor were dancing around impatiently, each in her own way, wanting to be let go. Alberta fidgeted, walked from room to room moving ashtrays and cigarette boxes and lamps fractions of inches, Honor did cherry twirls in the living room until she was dizzy, fell down, did some more, each time coming perilously closer to the copper lustre that sat on a low shelf. "Alberta there is Ora Lee's cousin, and Ora Lee's the one responsible," I'd said straight off, in case Alberta had any notion of going home and telling Ora Lee to get out of town. "This is either criminal negligence or homicide," the officer said to me, "Where's this Ora Lee?" to Alberta. I realized that I didn't know Ora Lee's last name. We were even; she didn't know mine, Alberta didn't know mine, Alberta only found Letty because she was married to Eddie Marino, and that was a big deal. Alberta went for her purse, rummaged for an imaginary slip of paper, "I got her number back home, you could take me back home," she said. "She's your goddamn cousin, have them take you to *her* house, you've got to know your goddamn cousin's address," I said. The coroner's men were unpretzeling Marmee in the front. I could hear them mumbling angrily, feeling sorry for her; they had to do that to stay human.

I took Honor on my lap in Marmee's chair in the kitchen. Honor wanted to see what the men were doing. In a minute, I told her. A minute'll be too late, she said, not easily fooled. An officer was on the phone, so I couldn't call William. William was my goddamn cousin, whom I'd never phoned, but whose phone number I knew.

But it was Letty who got to him first: her phone had a redial option, and she'd pushed that redial button for as long as it took William to come home from whatever civic duty was occupying him that night. William practically lived at the Jewish Community Center, filling up his life. He was already sobbing when he walked into Marmee's house; the ambulance lights were still rotating silently, throwing red-blue-red-blue onto the neighbors' houses until they were all on their individual lawns. It wasn't the sort of neighborhood where everyone congregated and whispered right out in front of the house where the ambulance was; that was too tacky. They'd see what they could see, read about it in the paper tomorrow if it was bad enough, otherwise get the story from their housekeepers by the next nightfall.

"I'll call the D.A. and make sure that woman spends the rest of her life behind bars," he said. He was Letty's cousin, all right, never mind the Kubler-Ross stages of grieving, denial first: they both got angry first, at something as distant as a dip in the Dow-Jones, as immediate as Marmee's death on what should have been Murray's shift. He took one look at Honor. "Get that kid out of here," he said, not for Honor's benefit, but because she was too metabolically revved up to have around. I shrugged and started to put on her coat and scarf. "You told me I could watch," she said, angry, fighting the scarf off. "Be cold, see if I care," I said, and dragged her out the front door.

The medical examiner had to pluck Marmee's innards, or the funeral could have been on Mardi Gras day. A cortege to Metairie through all the blocked traffic: it would have been ridiculous. Jews are supposed to bury their dead within twenty-four hours. "Hey, she'd appreciate getting sent off on Ash Wednesday," Letty said. Letty had cried that once, when I'd told her, and now she had caught Eddie's contagion: make a fool of yourself at sad times. It had taken me a long time to forgive Eddie for talking about my father having killed himself with a vegetable bag from Winn-Dixie; it became a bigger joke the longer my father had been dead. After Honor was born, I told him it wasn't funny, and he hadn't mentioned it since.

I took Honor up Tchoupitoulas Street to Henry Clay, where the truck parade lines up. After Zulu and Rex have passed, the trucks roll on their route; any bunch of people who can decide on the same costume can ride a truck. They have to sit until almost noon on Tchoupitoulas, drinking beer and pitching Popeye's fried-chicken bones into the street; for throws it was better than two weeks of stingy parades all in one. Honor was dressed as a fairy godmother, blue satin gown and bejeweled organza wings, with a thick white sweater underneath, not detracting from her sense of herself at all. We walked the parade line: we rolled past them instead of their rolling past us, first the river side of forty trucks, cut in front of the first, trace back along the lake side, no one knew we'd already begged from their clubmates. Honor had a satin drawstring bag to match her dress, and it was filled halfway through our walk, but she wanted more. I began putting the overflow of beads around her neck, then started stuffing throws into a plastic garbage bag I'd brought along; just in case it rained, I could cut a head hole in it and cover Honor. The more she accumulated, the more she wanted. She got a taste of high-grade giveaways: a lady on a truck liked her costume and handed her a red-and-green-feathered spear, the most coveted catch of Mardi Gras. Now beads and plastic squirting frogs weren't good enough. She had to have the ball cap with the Fiddle Faddle bear on the brim, the long-stemmed plastic rose, the crotchless panties that everyone dangled to the crowds but never threw unless there was a

promise of getting laid afterwards. Honor would jump up
and down next to a truck, bang on the papier-mâché deco-
rations, "Throw me a flower, please!" It was getting later in
the morning, everyone already had pissed a bucket of beer
into the Port-O-Let, and Honor looked pretty cute with her
petulance. The garbage bag filled, and I carried Honor and
twenty pounds of useless junk six blocks back to the house.
I'd make it all disappear handful by handful; she'd never
notice.

William was waiting on my front steps. He had his face
painted, black circles around his eyes, warpaint stripes across
his cheeks; he was wearing chinos and an oxford-cloth shirt,
couldn't throw himself totally into the Carnival spirit, never
could, no matter that he was supposed to be grieving over
his aunt, who surely left him a bundle.

"I saw you coming," he said. "I was only going to leave
this in your mailbox." He was brandishing a manila envelope,
business size.

"I'd have never seen it," I said. Mardi Gras was a postal
holiday; I wouldn't have looked inside my mailbox until at
least tomorrow. Sometimes I didn't look for days. It was a
big rural box, nailed to the side of the house, and it never
held anything of interest. I subscribed to *The Atlantic*, but
what was in there could keep for a year, no problem.

He handed me the envelope. I told him thanks and fished
my house key out of my pocket. A five-dollar bill fell out.
You didn't carry a purse on Mardi Gras, no matter who you
were. I stuffed the bill back into my pocket, hoping I'd remember before it and my driver's license went through the
wash.

"They catch Ora Lee?"

"Got her in Central Lockup."

"You're kidding."

"It's her fault, no matter how you look at it. Criminal
Code, Section Thirty-two, death of a helpless person caused
by gross neglect of one charged with his custody and care:
that's the least she'll get, up to five years. Says Cecile fell, she

panicked. We'll see. I hope they get her on a murder charge, let her rot."

"I thought you liked her."

"My mistake."

"Gross neglect of a helpless person, you're in trouble," I said.

"Cut the crap, Darby." I shrugged, thinking of Murray, who was going to run a full-color spectrum of feelings over this one. I opened the door a crack, my back to him, an invitation to leave. "You aren't going to let me see what's in the envelope?" William said.

"I don't know what it is."

"Cecile wrote you a letter, said to give it to you when she died. I've had it for twenty years."

I tried to be Lizzie Borden, anticipate the law. It seemed to me that Marmee couldn't take anything away, she could only give me something, even if it was only advice. William couldn't argue with me if he saw the letter as he'd delivered it. I shrugged, waved over my shoulder for him to follow me in, opened the door the rest of the way. Honor sat down on the steps with her chock-full satin bag, not moving. "What's the matter with you?" William said. "I'm too tired." He offered to carry her bag for her, picked it up; she wouldn't let go. He dropped it as if he had acid on his fingers. "Just leave her," I said, starting to close the door. "No!" she screamed, not moving. I closed the door a bit more. "I want you to carry me!" I shook my head no, closed the door another inch. She trudged up the steps, falling dramatically, like a cartoon man in the desert, her bag dragging behind, threads snagging on the cement.

"Nice kid," William said, "reminds me of my sweet cousin Letty."

"Reminds me of my sweet mother Letty," I said.

I gave William a hot cup of coffee: I'm no Letty, I was saying. Honor dumped her bag of goodies on the floor, started making piles by categories, part of reading readiness, no doubt: Newcomb got them all prepped for expensive private schools. Honor was going to have to take the WPPSI in the fall if I didn't do something radical soon, show off her cleverness on mazes and analogies so I'd have the privilege of paying six thousand dollars a year for her to stay with her friends. William studied his coffee, sloshed it around to cool it, careful not to spill. I read the letter.

It was Marmee's old bold handwriting, aqua ink, from a cartridge pen, the kind I liked to chew on in school until the corner of my mouth was stained.

October 29, 1961

Dearest Darby,

I suppose this is the oddest letter I will ever write. In a way I'm writing it to a stranger, at least I hope that I am. I expect to live quite a long time, and you won't be reading this until I have passed away. You're eleven now, maybe you'll be a grown woman before I'm gone. It is good that I'm writing this now, though, when I see what life might have in store for you.

Today your grandfather and I went down to Cousin William's office to draft our wills. I'm making a special provision for you, and I want to tell you why I'm doing it. (Forgive me if my writing seems stilted, I'm picturing a beautiful little girl as I write, and I can't quite picture you grown. Though I'm sure I'd recognize you if I didn't see you for twenty years. You are one of a kind, you know.)

If your grandfather predeceases me (there, now I'm talking to you like an adult!), I will have use of his entire estate until I pass away. I have made a similar provision for him. Whichever way it goes—and I think he will go first, the way he drinks, to tell you the truth—you will be given a home at my death. We have two houses, two very different houses, and it will be your choice where you want to live. (Of course, if your grandfather is still living, you will have to wait until he passes away.) That's all in my will. But I have a reason for doing this, and I don't want you second-guessing me, or, rather, I don't want William, Letty, and your father second-guessing me. In case they ask, you can tell them.

Darby, dearest, don't ever forget this: I am from Chicago. I was the third generation of my family there, and it's in my blood. New Orleans is not. I'm sure you see me as a New Orleans lady (I'm talking to the eleven-year-old Darby now, forgive me), but I don't think I am one on the inside. It's just that the mores here get to a person after a while, honest. Maybe now that you are reading this you are a New Orleans lady yourself, I see that as very possible. As I look at you at eleven, as I watched you on our trip, I saw you could go many ways. If you stay here, you are going to have to become more ladylike, that's why I worked on you so mercilessly on our European tour. I'm sure you thought I was evil incarnate, but you needed to learn how to act right. Letty never has quite picked up on it, but she's a pretty girl, and this business of marrying your father was the only bit of originality she ever tried to show. I know how much you love your father, and I'm not detracting from him, but he's not a successful man, and you can't live in New Orleans happily unless you're successful. Or wealthy. But if he can't do it on his own, I'm not doing it for him. Part of the New Orleans ethic, I suppose, is that it's all right to live off your own family's money, but if you marry for it, you are going to have a lot of people talking badly about you.

I have the city house and the beach house, and you may choose. I can't tell right now which will be of more value ten, twenty, or thirty years down the road. Right now the city house is assessed higher, but that could change. There is only so much beachfront property in the world. (On the other hand, a hurricane may come in the next decade or so, and then you'll have only a pile of sand, and the decision will be easy.) Anyhow, value doesn't really matter, does it? If you have grown up to be the

sort of lady who wants to hold her head up in polite
society, then the city house is about the best you can have,
the boulevard will never go down in value. Or you may
already have a fine home, and then the Pass Christian
house will be a nice little extra. But something tells me
that you are high-spirited, that you may want something
different, something besides sitting in New Orleans and
hanging on your mother's skirts the way Letty has her
entire life. Then you may want the beach house. I've often
wished I'd lived over there year-round, but I'm not a lot
braver than dear Letty, to tell you the truth. Who knows?
After all this, you may have left the South altogether, or
maybe the country. (I'm writing to the future, will you
be on the moon?!) The house you choose is yours to
dispose of, but I hope you'll stay in the spirit of this gift,
that you'll use the money the way the house would want
you to. Does that make sense? I hope so, since I won't
be there to explain.

Darby, I want you to be happy. And I want your
children to be happy, if you're not too high-spirited to
have them! This is my gift to you, my little stranger in
the future. I love you, oh, so much.

Marmee

I imagined Marmee in 1961, younger than Letty was now.
It didn't take long, to become nothing at all. Marmee on the
landing: the 1961 Marmee would have killed herself, rather
than come to that indignity. I began to cry, the tears for my
father finally coming, my father portaged off a ship in a bag,
with all the passengers who'd eaten ham with him the night
before standing in the corridor, staring and glad it wasn't
they. They both had their say. I could see my father, dying
with his head in a Winn-Dixie bag, realizing in that sad final
minute that it was a joke Eddie Marino was going to appreciate. Marmee wrote a letter; you could send messages after
you were dead, but that didn't keep you from having unfinished business. I felt so sorry for both of them, Marmee on

the landing, a grotesque. I couldn't stop crying, and William and Honor sat and watched me in embarrassed silence. I knew William wasn't going to leave until he saw the letter, so I handed it over to him without looking, put my head in my lap, and let the imaginings come, the single frame of film, Marmee on the landing, my father in William's office, handing me two twenty-dollar bills. I could hear Honor, taking care of the business at hand again, now sorting her carnival beads into piles according to color, pulling the best of each, the faux pearls from the whites, the string of blue plastic fish, the green china beads, fat garnetlike red balls on a string, each good enough to wear around her fairy godmother neck.

"She was such a bitch," William said, slamming the paper down on the sofa. "I assume you want her real house."

"I don't know," I said into my lap. "I'm not thinking about it." I didn't challenge him on what was a real house; I knew. There was no letter giving William a house, a fancy uptown house maybe, that would get his ex-wife or someone just as young and beautiful to want to live out her life with him.

"Like fun you're not. I don't think she can do this, this is highly irregular, I'm going to check the statutes, you can't do a will like a Chinese menu, for God's sake."

"Get out," I said.

"Yeah, get out," Honor said, enjoying herself immensely.

EPILOGUE

I spent two weeks inside my own head, playing out sure dialogues, eliminating the people I might talk to. I want the regular house, then I can go to Trinity, that's where Amanda's going, she said so, her sister goes there. For Honor, just turned four years old, I'd have to stay in the city. I really do depend on you, I'd miss you terribly. Letty's reason for living, to write poems and flaunt them at me, when I was such a machine of a person, to half-bake frozen pies, send them home with me and Honor so she could stay so healthy and outlive us both. Charlotte called every week with a dinner invitation. In the shopping center business there was a never-ending stream of entrepreneurial types: He's franchisee for all of southeastern Louisiana, you'd never have to worry a day in your life. Franchisees for all of southeastern Louisiana usually opened offices somewhere in Metairie, bought low-to-the-ground cars for driving to Houma and Hammond to look at their operations, put their wives in uptown houses with Buick station wagons. I'd already have the uptown house, furnished so tastefully, once all the pee stains were exorcised from the rugs. I played the dialogues, kept it to myself, no point in arguments when I knew what I wanted.

I walked into Marino's; Eddie was at his desk signing checks, the end of the month. "Hey, Darby, you doing okay?" he said. I shook my head no. He looked at his watch. "You want lunch, how about I buy you lunch?" I nodded.

It was only eleven-thirty, and Domilise's was almost empty, its patrons school kids and clock punchers who got forty-five minutes at noon. Drippy roast-beef po-boys, Eddie could manage one with no napkins, maybe because he had large hands. "You want me to make a decision for you?" he said first, before I could even tell him what was going on. I nodded, gravy and mayonnaise dribbling down my chin.

"I'm going to tell you what I told Linda. Trouble is, maybe I'm too late; I had Linda in hand when she was eighteen. I said, you get the hell out of this city. Go away to school, find yourself a boy from anyplace but here, that's what your education's for. So she goes to LSU, makes lousy grades, doesn't learn much of anything except that she sure don't look Italian, marries this nice dumb boy, and gets the hell out of here. I got my money's worth out of LSU, as good as if she'd gone to Vassar."

"What about Letty?" I said. He cocked his head; what did I mean? "I know she wouldn't want me to go."

"All the more reason," he said, smiling even though he had a mouthful of sandwich. It wasn't repulsive at all; he had yellow rabbit teeth, and I thought he looked sort of cute. He closed his mouth, chewed hard, swallowed. "Leave Letty to me. She's different from you, half the time I don't think you see that. Hey, I give Letty everything she wants. You want a diamond watch, Letty? Fine, here's a check. You think you need the kitchen repainted, it's only been a year and a half, sure, call the painter. Letty's fine, you just have to spoil Letty, don't worry. You can send your kid back to Newcomb for college, they can bury you in Metairie Cemetery, but for now I'd get the hell out."

I stood up, put my arms around Eddie's neck, gave him a kiss on the cheek, close-shaven and loose, old-man skin, grandfather skin. My father would have been that old, though he'd taken such poor care of himself that he'd probably have been dead by then anyway. Eddie told me to run along, he'd pick up the check. I still owed my father forty dollars. Parting when a debt still hung was scary, but I thought I might gamble, see what happened.

When I was in Sunday school I had a teacher in fifth grade who skipped all the biblical stuff and worked on reality. That was probably the prescribed curriculum for fifth-grade Jewish kids. "I drove through Mississippi," the Sunday-school teacher said. "Stopped in a little town, thought I'd buy myself a soft drink. Know what the sign said on the door?" He wrote on the chalkboard, NO JEWS, DOGS, OR NIGERS ALLOWED. "They couldn't even spell! You ever have to be in Mississippi, make sure you're going straight through."

The only friend I'd made in Pass Christian was a black woman, Chelsea, an M.D., who took care of Honor one Monday morning when she was screaming with an earache. Her daughter was four, too, more fairy-princess arrogant than even Honor could hope to be. I figured a lot had changed in Mississippi, and nothing had changed in New Orleans. I'd buy heavy insurance on the beach house, and in a hurricane I'd evacuate to a shelter like everyone else.